AN IRISH KISS

With an anguished groan, Foster slowly reached for her, pulling her closer, and her heart soared. She was so close she could smell the scent of him, manly and warm. She tilted her face toward his.

Then he placed his hands on either side of her face. In a hoarse voice, he whispered, "I have wanted to do this since the moment I first saw you."

Lowering his head, he tenderly placed his lips upon hers.

Sighing, she closed her eyes and gave in to his kiss.

His lips were warm, soft, and inviting . . . inviting her to take more from him. His hands slid from her face to her neck and then down her shoulders and along her back, drawing her into his embrace.

Mara's arms found their way around him, reaching up and clasping his neck as their kiss deepened. A wondrous thing it was, this kiss. It was a deliciously wicked and incredibly intimate kiss. Never imagining a kiss could be like this . . . this mad, overwhelming, all-consuming rush of desire that flooded her whole being.

On and on it went. Nothing else in the world seemed to matter. It was as if they had both been starving, and kissing each other was their sustenance. She never wanted it to stop . . .

The IRISH HEIRESS

KAITLIN O'RILEY

ZEBRA BOOKS
KENSINGTON PUBLISHING CORP.
www.kensingtonbooks.com

ZEBRA BOOKS are published by

Kensington Publishing Corp.
119 West 40th Street
New York, NY 10018

All Kensington titles, imprints, and distributed lines are available at special quantity discounts for bulk purchases for sales promotion, premiums, fund-raising, educational, or institutional use.

Special book excerpts or customized printings can also be created to fit specific needs. For details, write or phone the office of the Kensington Sales Manager: Attn.: Sales Department. Kensington Publishing Corp., 119 West 40th Street, New York, NY 10018. Phone: 1-800-221-2647.

Zebra and the Z logo Reg. U.S. Pat. & TM Off.

First Printing: August 2019
ISBN-13: 978-1-4201-4465-9
ISBN-10: 1-4201-4465-0

ISBN-13: 978-1-4201-4466-6 (eBook)
ISBN-10: 1-4201-4466-9 (eBook)

10 9 8 7 6 5 4 3 2 1

Printed in the United States of America

To my beautiful sisters,
Jane, Maureen, Janet & Jennifer.
I don't know what I would do without you in my life

Acknowledgments

Once again I need to say how very thankful and grateful I am for my family and friends on the east and west coasts who make my life better in every way: Riley Anderson, Jane Milmore, Shelley Jensen, Maureen Milmore, Janet Wheeler, Scott Wheeler, Jennifer Malins, Greg Malins, Yvonne Deane, Kim McCafferty, Cela Lim, Lynn Abbott, Gretchen Kempf, Jenny Goodenough, Adrienne Barbeau, Billy Van Zandt, and all my sweet nephews. I especially thank Christopher Robinson for believing in me even when I don't, oh and for our pajama days . . . yet.

I also wish to thank my amazing agent, Jane Dystel, and my wonderful editor, John Scognamiglio, for their constant support and encouragement.

Note to Riley
Try it, you'll like it.

1

Premonitions

September 1894

It was happening again.

When it occurred in a public place, Lady Mara Reeves tended to panic at the very thought of it happening to her. As it was just now . . .

There really was no way to stop it once it started. At least not a way that she was aware of as yet. No, Mara's only recourse was to find a quiet corner and hope this particular episode passed quickly. It hadn't happened to her in quite a while, but she recognized the prickly signs immediately. And they were inordinately strong this time, as if making up for their long absence with a vengeance.

It reminded her once again how different she was from everyone else.

Casting a silent prayer that no one would notice her, with hurried steps Mara retreated to a small alcove along the massive hallway, as she suddenly grew very dizzy, almost faint. Her elegant champagne-pink silk ball gown grew restrictive around her chest. She reached out to a marble pillar for support, the cool white stone sending chills right through her long white gloves to her heated flesh.

Then, just as she knew it would, that peculiarly familiar tingling sensation crept over her skin ever so slowly, awakening each and every nerve in her body. Her heart raced and she grew warm and yet she shivered. The hair on the back of her neck stood on end and she clenched her teeth. Pressing her fingers to her temples, Mara closed her eyes and held her breath. The lively music from the ballroom receded into a dark cloud of silence. Sharp pinpricks of awareness lit up inside of her, flashing sparks of light from within.

And then it happened . . . Misty wisps of images began to take shape in her mind.

Fire. Glints of flames. Blinding bursts of light. Shimmering walls of golden orange and brilliant yellow. Breathtaking, scorching heat. Trapped in the burning building, blazing embers and smoky ash filling the air, Mara didn't know where to go. Gut-wrenching, tormented screams echoed against the rush of flames. Her own panicked, terrified cries reverberated around her. Scalding tears, knowing it was her fault, knowing it was too late. Blinding heat and black smoke and swirling flames, the vicious sting of fear and the horrific smell of imminent death.

Her death. She was going to die in this raging inferno.

Then nothing. A short breath of blessedly cool air. She gasped.

A man. Frantically calling to her, his hand outstretched, reaching for her, a look of love, mixed with anguish and horror, awash on his handsome face. His eyes, oh, his eyes! Deep green and filled with abject longing and desire, they implored her to come with him, to believe him. And she wished to be with him with a certainty that belied all else. She held out her hand to him, trusting him implicitly, the terror that engulfed her dissipating at the touch of his fingers. Flooded with relief and elation, buoyed with happiness and hope, Mara clung to him, his strong arms embracing her.

He pulled her tightly to his broad chest and she was safe, secure, loved. In spite of their dangerous surroundings and the acrid smell of smoke thick around them, she could breathe easily within his sheltering embrace. A profound peace enveloped her. Never had she felt such an ebullient happiness and tranquility. This man loved her deeply and she loved him. She looked into the greenest eyes she had ever seen. The desire to be with him overwhelmed her. She was his and he was hers. The certainty, the rightness of it, was all-consuming.

She belonged to him. They belonged together.

And just like that, the intense images evaporated, as if Mara had simply awakened from an incredible and vivid dream.

Yet Mara had not been sleeping. She had been very much awake.

Shaken by what she'd just seen, she remained motionless, fighting the urge to cry. The loss of the exquisite connection with that man and the inexplicable sense of warmth, happiness, and pure love brought tears to her eyes.

Mara trembled, as if she were shivering from a cold wind.

Whenever she had one of her strange premonitions, it was always about someone else, never about herself. It had been that way her whole life. Sometimes she could foresee the future, getting a glimpse into what was going to happen to the people she loved. Sometimes she saw good things, other times she saw things she did not wish to know. But they always presaged the actual events themselves. And she had never been wrong. When she saw something in her visions, it always came to pass.

Ever since she was a little girl, she had kept these premonitions, these feelings or intuitions or signs or whatever they were called, to herself. Locked deep inside. She'd mentioned them to her father once when she was about seven years old, and from the panicked and worried expression in his paternal eyes, she learned not to mention them to him ever again. Another time, she had half-heartedly confided in Sara about them, but her cousin seemed baffled by her revelation.

However, this time her premonition was completely different from any of the others she had ever had.

This time the vision was about . . . *her*. *Mara* was the center of it all.

Mara was the girl in the flames.

Fire had haunted her whole life. Was it any wonder that a vision that involved her included flames and smoke? Fire fascinated her and terrified her. There was no mistaking what she had seen and felt just now, even if she could not discern what it meant in any real context. Was she in danger now? When would this come to pass? Tonight? Tomorrow? A year from now?

The only thing she was certain of was that it *would* happen.

"Mara . . . ? Mara, are you unwell?"

In a daze, she blinked up at a familiar face.

Her cousin, Phillip Sinclair, placed a steadying hand on her arm. His voice full of concern, he repeated her name. "Mara?"

Bracing herself, trying to refocus her mind, Mara finally responded with an automaticity that surprised her. "I'm perfectly fine, thank you."

"Well, you don't look perfectly fine at all." Phillip shook his head, his boyishly handsome features lined with skepticism. "You look ghastly and about ready to faint. Let's go sit in the drawing room for a moment, so you can rest. You're lucky I happened to come along when I did."

Nodding in wordless agreement, Mara followed Phillip away from the grand ballroom, where the sounds of lively music from the orchestra and the exuberant rise and fall of laughter and voices muddled together. All the guests were enjoying a wonderful evening of dancing and dining to celebrate Uncle Jeffrey's birthday. Meanwhile an icy-cold knot tightened in the pit of Mara's stomach.

What had just happened to her?

It was unlike anything she had experienced before. Of all the visions, *the seeings*, she'd had in her life, this one had been drastically different. Still trembling, she took a gulp of air and walked unsteadily beside her protective cousin, holding tight to his arm, grateful for his calming presence, for it anchored her in reality.

As they moved down the marble-floored corridor and passed by her aunt and uncle's other guests, Mara looked up and into the face of the man she had just seen in her vision. She gasped.

Eyes of the deepest forest green, fringed with dark lashes and framed with dark brows, arched in matched surprise as they met her own. These eyes gazed into her very soul, until Mara felt as if she were drowning in them, consumed by them. The man did not look away from her, nor did he flinch from their locked gaze. Strange feelings washed over her.

Instant recognition. A sense of knowing and belonging. A feeling of wonder. A blossoming of something exquisitely wonderful. Mara could not breathe. There was a connection so strong, she could only stop abruptly in place and stare back at him, utterly speechless. Frightened by the power of it, by the sheer beauty of it, she was motionless.

It was him.

She knew it was *him*. Not only that, she knew his name.

Mara sensed Phillip's confusion as he stood beside her, wondering what had caused her to suddenly become still. She heard Phillip's voice greeting the man from her vision. "Good evening, Lord Sterling."

The man's green eyes never left Mara's, although he addressed her cousin. "Waverly, isn't it?"

"Yes, I believe we met at the races last spring," Phillip continued amiably, "May I introduce you to my cousin? This is Lady Mara Reeves. Mara, this is Foster Sheridan, Lord Sterling."

Utterly transfixed by him, Mara remained immobile and incapable of forming words, while he and her cousin exchanged pleasantries.

It was then Mara took in his whole face. The masculine features of Foster Sheridan, the Earl of Sterling. She *had* seen him before! Oh, yes, she had . . . It was a few months earlier, and she had been distracted and worried about her cousin Sara that evening, and did not speak to him. But Mara had watched this attractive man from afar during Lady Cabot's ball that night. Thinking him quite handsome, she had even asked Lord Bridgeton about him that night, to learn his name.

That had been all there was to it. They had not spoken or even exchanged glances and she had not seen him again. She hadn't given him more than an idle thought since that summer night.

Until her vision.

Until now.

And here he was before her, saying what a pleasure it was to meet her, the rich tone of his voice sending excited shivers throughout her body. Mara heard mumbled words escape from her own lips but hadn't a clue what she'd actually said, for she was momentarily mesmerized by the magnificence of his smile. His attractive face lit up from within and his eyes danced with merriment, with enchanting crinkles at the corners. Warmth emanated from this man and enveloped her like a luxurious velvet blanket. She clenched her fingers, fighting the urge to reach out and touch him. To actually caress his smooth-shaven cheek, to run her fingers along his strong, chiseled jaw, to brush them across his full, inviting lips.

Lord Sterling. Foster Sheridan.

It was *him*.

He was the man in the premonition that had just shaken her to the core. The images in which she felt such indescribable happiness and peace. With him. With this man who left her feeling completely unlike her usual self. With this man she had never really crossed paths with before. Yet she knew, with an unwavering certainty in her soul, that their futures were irrevocably entwined.

So lost in her little reverie of wanting to touch this man, to *know* him, she was only vaguely aware of her cousin bidding him farewell. *No! No! Not yet! It's too soon!* Mara wanted to cry out with the loss of him, yet she could not think of anything to say to prolong their encounter.

Lord Sterling gave her a gentlemanly bow. "Lady Mara, it's quite early yet, but I must admit that meeting you has most definitely been the highlight of my evening."

She merely nodded and smiled, for she couldn't form coherent sentences at a time when her little world was suddenly turned upside down. Before she knew it Phillip was guiding her along the marble hallway again, as if nothing extraordinary had just happened. She fought the overwhelming desire to run back, back to Lord Sterling and his remarkable eyes. And that exquisite feeling she had while standing near him.

However, Mara managed to steal a quick glance over her shoulder. Lord Sterling simply stood there watching her walking away, looking as bewildered as she felt. And the longing in his eyes echoed the feelings that flooded her being.

She wanted to be with him.

Phillip led her to a private drawing room that belonged to Aunt Yvette. Once she was seated upon a blue damask divan, Phillip asked, "Mara, you are not at all yourself. Can I get you anything? A glass of water? A cup of tea? Some champagne, perhaps?"

When she found her voice, she answered, "Tea, please. Thank you." A cup of tea might take him longer. She simply needed to be left alone for a bit to collect her thoughts and calm down.

"You rest here. I'll bring you some tea." He paused hesitantly, his look questioning. "Would you like me to fetch your mother or father? Would you prefer to go home instead?"

"Oh, no. I'm quite all right, Phillip. Truly. Please don't worry my parents. They are enjoying Uncle Jeffrey's birthday party. I'm just light-headed because I haven't eaten much of anything today. I suppose I'm just hungry." She gave him a half-hearted grin. "It's all my own fault."

It was a fib about not eating, for she'd had quite a hearty lunch, but it was all Mara could think of to explain her dizziness. She surely couldn't tell him the truth. *Oh, Phillip, I just had the most life-altering premonition, which left me dizzy and breathless and then we ran smack into the man I am certain will change my life!* Her cousin was sweet and understanding, but she could never reveal her true feelings to him that way!

"I shall bring you a plate as well then, you goose. There is a mountain of food at the buffet. I shall return straight-away." He patted her hand comfortingly.

"Thank you, that would be wonderful. I'm sure I'll be fine as soon as I eat something."

He gave her another concerned look before he left the room.

After the door to the drawing room closed, Mara was alone in blessed quiet and solitude. For a time anyway. Phillip was a sweetheart to worry over her so, but she simply needed to be alone. With a sigh, relief flooded her but she felt uncomfortably warm. Slowly she removed the long white gloves that covered her arms up to her elbows. She detested wearing gloves! They were too constricting. She lay back against the soft cushions on the divan, closed her eyes, and took a deep breath.

In truth she was more exhilarated than anything else by what had just happened to her. And a tiny bit frightened too.

That premonition! That man! It was indescribable.

But there was great sadness too, in that vision she'd had. There was gripping fear and blazing flames.

Fire.

Mara knew firsthand the deadly ravages of fire. Fire plagued her life and terrified her like nothing else. It was a fire that had killed her mother one night when Mara was just a little girl, and Mara had been unable to save her.

But what did it all mean? The fire particularly worried her. Was she in some kind of danger? Her premonition evoked two distinctly different feelings, deathly fear and utter peace and love. And there was something else too . . . Something she couldn't quite name.

The sudden click of the drawing room door caught her attention. Was Phillip back already? That was ridiculously fast! Disappointed by his quick return, she reluctantly opened her eyes.

And saw *him*.

Lord Sterling stood at the foot of the divan, gazing at her in wonder.

A long, silent moment passed between them.

Good heavens, but he was the most gorgeous man she had ever seen. Tall and well built, with an air of quiet strength around him. Dark brown hair, the color of rich chocolate, was slicked back from his classically handsome face. A streamlined nose, straight white teeth, and those eyes! Those eyes!

Finally he uttered, "I beg your pardon, Lady Mara . . . I didn't mean to intrude . . . It's just that I-I—" His deep voice faltered for an instant and he shrugged, as if completely baffled by his own actions. "I must confess. I just had to see you again."

She could barely breathe. He *had* to see her. He'd had to see *her*!

"I'm glad you came to see me." Yes, her own words. She could actually speak in front of him!

He smiled at her then, and her heart seemed to melt inside her chest. She found herself grinning back, helplessly.

"There *was* something just then in the corridor between us . . . There is something about you . . . I don't know." He seemed almost startled by his own thoughts, his handsome face a mask of bemused confusion.

Once again, they stared at each other silently for a few moments.

"May I?" He gestured to the divan.

Instinctively Mara sat up slightly and scooted her stylishly slippered feet over, adjusting the skirt of her champagne-pink silk gown to make room for him to sit at the foot of the divan. Yet he sat even closer to her than she'd expected. It was a highly improper act, decidedly scandalous, in fact, for a gentleman she barely knew to act so familiarly with her. If anyone entered the drawing room and found them this way together, her reputation would be quite ruined.

But for once in her life, Mara didn't care. And neither did Lord Sterling, apparently. The risk seemed trivial. Things like etiquette and proper deportment did not matter at a time like this.

And what time was that, exactly?

Mara was sure she didn't know. Yet it felt momentous. Special. Magical. Thrilled by his unexpected appearance and the prospect of speaking with him privately, she could barely contain herself.

Had he felt what she had when they met?

Judging from his expression and his presence beside her on the divan, he must have felt the same magnetic pull to her as she had with him. If she felt it, good heavens, how could he have not?

"Who are you?" he murmured, more to himself than to her.

"I'm myself." She felt a bit foolish answering that way, but what else was she to say? He wasn't simply asking to know her name. And she couldn't tell him the actual truth. That she was the woman who would change his life.

He nodded, yet seemed unclear. With a gesture to the divan and her appearance of malaise, he asked, "Are you unwell?"

"No, no, I'm quite all right." She waved her hand airily. "I just had a bit of a dizzy spell. My cousin is very over-protective of me and insisted that I rest. It's nothing though. I am fine. I probably didn't eat enough today." It was so odd, her sudden rush of words. Mara did not feel as shy or self-conscious with Lord Sterling as she did with other gentlemen. They usually made her feel nervous and silly and as if everything she said was foolish.

Men were typically drawn in by her attractive appearance and then, after a moment or two, they seemed bored or completely uninterested in her and drifted away. She supposed it was all her fault. She was not a natural coquette or a social butterfly, like her cousin Sara Fleming, who had gentlemen constantly vying for her attention. Lady Mara Reeves had never been mistaken for the belle of the ball.

"You have the trace of an accent," he noted, eyeing her closely. "Is it Irish?"

"Yes, I was raised in Ireland. My father is the Earl of Cashelmore. Our home is there, but we spend a good part of the year here in London."

"I've never been to Ireland."

"Oh, it's beautiful." She smiled at him. "You shall just have to come visit me there." Goodness! Had she just flirted with him? Invited him to stay at her home? What on earth had come over her?

His eyes lit up. "I cannot imagine anything more wonderful than going somewhere with you, Lady Mara Reeves."

"Then let's go somewhere together." The words flew far too easily from her lips. Somewhat aghast at her brazenness, she almost put her hand over her mouth. This was not her usual self talking!

"I would like nothing more than to take you away somewhere." He shook his head reluctantly. "I feel as if I've suddenly been bewitched. By you. And such a beautiful witch you are." Lord Sterling reached over, and as if it were the most natural occurrence in the world, he picked up her hand and held it in his.

Mara caught her breath in suspense. His hand was warm and it fit hers perfectly. The touch of his skin sent shivers of delight washing over her. There was such a sense of belonging. Belonging to him. Belonging *together*.

"You are the most exquisitely beautiful woman I have

ever seen." He brought her hand to his lips and placed the softest of kisses upon the top of her fingers.

All the manners she had been trained to employ, all the deportment lessons that had been drilled into her, and all the endless hours of instructions and rules about proper behavior with gentlemen that had been given to her over the years, completely evaporated into meaningless fluff. Which only reinforced her belief that something extraordinary was happening to her. Happening with this man. To them both. All the conventional rules of courtship would not apply to them. Of that she was quite certain. *This*, whatever this was between them, would be vastly different from anything she had been prepared to expect.

Thrilled by his words, his touch, and his sweet kiss, happiness surged through her entire being. He thought she was beautiful! Little Mara with her colorless hair and too wide eyes who always felt invisible in a room full of people . . . Yet to him, to *him*, she was beautiful. Her heart fluttered and soared.

Lord Sterling gently lowered her hand to rest with his on his lap, their fingers intertwined. For as unusual as it was, it seemed to be the most natural thing for him to do.

"I don't know what it is about you, Mara . . ."

Even the intimate use of her first name should have shocked her. But it did not. It only drew them closer together. "You felt it too then?"

"I'm not altogether sure." He shook his head slightly, looking baffled. "I've never felt quite like this."

Neither had she, and it thrilled her to know that no one else had ever made him feel this way. "I saw you once before," she confessed.

"You did?" His face lit with pleasure. "Whenever it was, I know I did not see you. I certainly would have remembered you."

Elated that her confession pleased him, she continued.

"Yes, I saw you, but you didn't see me. It was a few months ago, at Lady Cabot's ball."

His brows furrowed slightly. "I can barely recall that evening."

"Well, I recall it quite well and I definitely saw you there. I'm so pleased to see you here tonight at my uncle's party."

"The Duke of Rathmore is your uncle?" he asked, a note of surprise in his voice.

With a nod, she added, "And I'm very happy you came in here to see me."

"I am too." A brief sigh escaped him. "Although I should not be here with you like this, Mara." Yet he did not let go of her hand.

"I don't mind," she said softly. "I'm not worried or scandalized or frightened by you, if that's what you are thinking."

A shadow darkened his expression. "Yes, your reputation is one thing. But I should not be here, taking such liberties with you, saying these things to you, my beautiful little Mara."

At his words, she knew she was his. *His* Mara. She belonged completely to him. There was not a doubt in her mind. They were linked together, bound together by something outside of themselves. Fated. And they had finally found each other. Brimming with a blissful sense of purpose and rightness that belied anything she had ever known or been taught, she beamed at him. Her heart, her destiny lay with this man. She knew it.

And he knew it too.

Her world careened around her, while rushing feelings of love and desire wreaked havoc with her usually reserved self. How could she feel this way, so strongly, so suddenly, and so perfectly? The need to kiss him was overwhelming.

Mara had never kissed anyone before. Ever. On pure

instinct she slowly leaned forward to kiss him. She closed her eyes, hoping he would take the hint and kiss her too . . .

"No."

The harshness of the word shattered the intimate moment between them. *No?* Her eyes flew open in surprise. She stared at the lips that she had been wantonly leaning toward. Had they just uttered the word *no*? No to a kiss? Surely he'd known that she wanted to kiss him. What had she done wrong? Did he think her too brazen?

Before she could utter a word in response, Lord Sterling abruptly stood up and stepped away from the damask divan, where she still lay. "You are much too beautiful and deserve someone far better than I. I should not have come in here, Lady Mara. Please forgive me. Really, I must leave now."

Startled by the abrupt change in mood, Mara was about to protest, but the stricken look on his face stopped her cold. What had happened? What had changed? Everything had been wonderful, even magical.

And then it wasn't.

Hot tears pricked behind her eyes. She blinked rapidly to keep them from spilling down her face.

"Good night, Lady Mara."

And just as suddenly as he appeared in her life that evening, Lord Sterling was gone.

2

Realizations

L ater that same evening, Foster Sheridan, the Earl of
Sterling, filled with a sense of dread, trudged up the
steps of his London townhouse. It was going to be ugly, but
there was no avoiding it. Which was a shame because it had
been such an extraordinary evening otherwise, and he hated
to have it ruined.

Who would have thought he'd meet someone as special
as Lady Mara Reeves at the Duke of Rathmore's birthday
party? He hadn't even wanted to attend in the first place,
but it was an escape from Rose, truth be told. But now he
felt invigorated. He felt alive again, when he'd been dead
inside for more years than he cared to admit. Who could
have predicted that a lovely, ethereal slip of a girl could
have an effect on him this way? Could make him feel happy
and hopeful and glad to be living? It had happened so
suddenly and inexplicably that he could almost believe it
hadn't happened at all.

The evening began ordinarily enough. Foster had made
his way around the Duke of Rathmore's lavish and dazzling
ballroom, stopping to speak with friends while managing

to avoid any dancing. He had gone outside for a bit of air and was on his way to the buffet, simply walking along the corridor, minding his own business, when he managed to catch the eyes of a strikingly pretty blonde.

And her eyes, so soft and yet so mesmerizing . . . He could not look away. He'd never seen such eyes. They were almost gray, a misty green perhaps, fringed by thick lashes. Her wide, luminous eyes had stared at him in wonder, as if she'd seen him before. As if she had *known* him . . .

The encounter had been uncanny and left him shaken. This lovely, bewitching little creature had stirred something within him, something he couldn't name. Even though he knew he shouldn't, Foster simply had to follow her into that drawing room, especially after he saw her cousin leave. The sound of her voice, the look in her eyes, everything about her drew him in and caused a burst of feelings to ignite in his heart as he sat there talking to her.

She had been about to kiss him too, which he innately sensed was not something she did with ease. At least he'd had the good sense to stop her from doing that. A kiss between them would only have caused more problems than he already had in his life.

Not that he hadn't wanted to kiss her.

Good God, how he had wanted to kiss those sweet lips! But that pretty miss was not one to be trifled with. She was the daughter of an earl. The niece of a duke. After a kiss with her, they'd both want more. She would expect a marriage proposal from him. And that was not something he could give her.

No. It was best left alone.

Still, there had been something almost magnetic between them.

Shaking his head in amazement, Foster handed his coat to his butler, Preston, and made his way to his study. It was time to face the inevitable. The harangue began as soon as the door shut behind him. As expected, she'd been waiting for him in his usually quiet refuge. He barely had time to catch his breath before she started.

"I'm only in town for a day. One day. One single night. And you couldn't be bothered to spend any time with me at all, could you, Foster? You couldn't even pretend? Just for an evening?" She scowled at him, her displeasure with his behavior quite evident.

He slowly loosened his cravat, as a deep weariness crept into his bones. A heavy sigh of resignation escaped him. It stung that she'd assessed the truth of the situation correctly. He *hadn't* wanted to spend any time with her. But they had been long past the point of pretending with each other.

"I asked you earlier if you wanted to attend the Duke of Rathmore's ball with me. You refused me. *As always*."

She bristled at his barbed remark, her face drawn in a sour pout. "You could have given me some warning. Even if I could have brought something with me, I no longer have anything appropriate to wear to such a grand event. How could I possibly attend?"

Foster moved to the sideboard of his study and poured himself a glass of scotch from the crystal decanter. She exhausted him. And broke his heart. And piqued his anger as well. Yes, he'd asked her to join him out of courtesy, knowing full well that she would refuse him with some flimsy excuse, as she had always done in the past. He would have been completely stunned if she had accepted his invitation.

Foster downed some of the amber liquid and faced her. "You have a wardrobe full of costly gowns. I've seen the bills from your overpriced dressmaker, so I'm quite certain you had something suitable to wear to the ball. And if you had given me some warning that you were coming to London, instead of arriving unannounced on my doorstep this morning, I could have let you know about the ball a little sooner, Rose." He took another long sip of scotch.

Her unexpected arrival that afternoon had thrown his usually calm and orderly household into a tizzy. Preston had been frantic, as had his housekeeper, Mrs. McCafferty. They hadn't known how to accommodate her. Foster was not aware that Rose was traveling or even in London. If he had known, more than likely he would have arranged to be out of town to avoid seeing her, as he usually did. As it was, Christ, how long had it been since he had actually seen her? Three years? Four? He could barely remember. Their last meeting had been acrimonious at best, and since then they'd maintained their relationship only through a few terse letters concerning financial matters.

Their awkward greeting that morning had been frosty and brief. He'd been more shocked by her appearance than her actual presence in his house. Rose had grown disturbingly thin, her pale face drawn and gaunt, her rail-like body spindly, with only sharp angles protruding. The dark gray dress she wore did not flatter her complexion either. She looked as if she were ill or in mourning.

Then again, he supposed Rose had been mourning one thing or another for her entire miserable life.

After a few curt exchanges about their health and the weather in London and his half-hearted invitation to the ball, he'd left her to her own devices for the evening and gone off to the ball without her.

"I've not a ball gown *with me*, Foster. And even if I did, well, you didn't truly wish for me to go with you, and I wasn't about to force myself upon you," she said with a little huff of annoyance. "But you certainly weren't gentleman enough to stay home with me either."

He couldn't help but roll his eyes at her remark. "Please, don't put on that false air of injury. You didn't come all the way to London just to see me."

"That's beside the point." She scowled at him, folding her arms across her chest in consternation. "You should have chosen to stay with me over going to a ball. It's the very least you could have done."

Foster stared at her in disbelief and confusion. Why was she suddenly making demands on him? When had she turned so ugly? Had she always been this way or had the distance and years apart done this to her?

He supposed that Rose had been almost pretty once, years ago, before her own bitterness and sourness had ruined her, before the scowl lines and frowns had marked her face permanently, causing her to look much older than her twenty-eight years. Her thick brown hair, once lustrous and shiny, now was held severely back from her face in a tight knot, giving her features a somber and pinched look. There was not an ounce of softness about the woman.

"Don't fret, Foster, I shall be out of your way first thing in the morning. You can go back to whatever it is you do with your time and all your women. You do not need to worry about me." Her brittle words did nothing to mask the accusatory undertone.

Ignoring her remark about his women, he said, "I do worry about you, Rose."

Oddly enough, he did. There certainly was no love lost between them, but Foster did worry over her from time to time when he managed to think of her at all. Rose cultivated jealousy, spite, and misery around her as devotedly as a gardener tended his prized orchids. Foster pitied her, actually. The poor woman never learned how to enjoy life because she was too preoccupied with being afraid of living.

"Don't make me laugh." She presented him with a withering gaze. "You would do a jig on my coffin tomorrow if I died tonight."

"No." Slowly he shook his head, appalled by her words. He would never rejoice in her death. "No, I would not. In spite of what you may think of me."

"It's not what I think, Foster." Her cold blue eyes pierced his. "It's what I *know*."

The venom in her words took him aback. Again, he sighed. It was pointless talking with her. Rose believed what she wanted to believe and there was no changing her mind. And she always believed the worst of people. There was nothing he had ever been able to say to convince her otherwise. Especially where Foster himself was concerned. She believed him to be the most wretched of all men.

"You're being rather dramatic this evening, Rose, don't you think?"

"I'm being honest," she retorted without missing a beat. "But I'll be on my way first thing in the morning."

"Back to Yorkshire?"

"Yes. Of course back to Yorkshire. Where else would I be going?"

She had a point there. He couldn't imagine Rose venturing anywhere besides London and their estate in Yorkshire, near where she grew up. She was nothing if not a homebody, and traveling and going abroad was not something she aspired to do. Her dislike and fear of meeting people and having new experiences kept her trapped in her own narrow little world where she felt comfortable and superior to those around her.

He ignored her sarcasm. "Have you concluded whatever business brought you to London in the first place?"

Foster had no idea why she'd come to town, and she had not volunteered the information when she arrived that afternoon. Not that he was all that interested, but she hadn't come to London in years, so whatever brought her here had to have been important.

"Yes," she said briskly. "Not that you would care what I do while I'm in town."

"You're quite right. It's immaterial to me what you do or where you go. Is that what you want me to say, Rose?" His words came out harsher than he'd intended, but she had provoked him. He had been trying to be decent with her, but as always, she made that impossible. The woman never gave an inch.

"I'd expect you to at least have an interest as to why I'm here."

"Why would I?" he remarked. "We set the precedent for that years ago, at your request. We don't get involved in each other's lives."

Rose Sheridan laughed then. A brittle, mocking laugh. "No, we don't get involved in each other's lives, do we, Foster? You are correct on that score. I suppose I don't care what you do any more than you care what I do. But I thought you'd at least put up a pretense for the one day I'm in town. I'd expected you to at least show a little respect to your wife."

Wife. The reference made him shudder. Rose had never been a true wife to him.

"I have always been respectful of you, if nothing else." He took another drink of scotch and then set the glass down, so hard it almost shattered. What the hell did she want from him? He'd given her everything she wanted. Everything she had demanded.

"Please," she scoffed in derision, her icy blue eyes hard. "Don't add more lies to your list of husbandly virtues."

Foster stared at the woman he had married ten years earlier, hardly recognizing the girl she had been. At eighteen years old, Rose Davenport had been somewhat attractive then, with soft skin and blue eyes. At least she'd had youth on her side then, to offset her morose and rancorous nature.

He had not loved her when they wed, and he certainly did not love her now. He could barely muster the memory of the slightest bit of fondness for her, for Rose was not the type of woman who invited affection of any kind.

"What is it you want from me now? After all these years? Is there something in particular you want or need? Lord knows I've given you everything I can. And we are long past pretenses."

"This is our marriage." She spat the words at him.

"What we have is *not* a marriage." His words hung over the two of them.

Of course it wasn't. A marriage was supposed to be a union of two people who made a life and a home and a family *together*. Theirs had never been a union at all. From the very start, it had been nothing short of a dreadful mistake.

"Yet, this was what you asked for, remember?" he continued. "What you begged for . . . For me to leave you alone. So I did. I gave you exactly what you demanded of me. So just what in the hell do you want from me now?"

Really, what more did she expect from him? He'd left her to her own life. He'd forgone everything that had mattered to him. He'd given up all hope of the prospect of a happy home or children to continue his family name. His only cousin was all set to take over the earldom, for Foster would never have legal heirs of his own.

"What do you want, Rose? A divorce? After all these years, is that it?" He flung the words at her scornfully, adding a cruel taunt. "Don't tell me you have finally taken a lover?"

In an instant Rose moved toward him and in one swift motion struck him hard across the face. She made a motion to strike again. On instinct, Foster grabbed her bony wrist and held it tight, preventing her from hitting again.

"That's enough," he ground out between clenched teeth, angrier with her than he could ever recall being before. As he held her arm, suspended tensely between them, he fought the overwhelming urge to hit her back.

She didn't usually inspire this kind of fury in him, even when she'd become violent with him in the past. Usually he felt a benign disinterest in her, as if she were a distant relative he barely knew and rarely saw, but was obligated to support. Which was a pretty accurate summation of the current status of their matrimonial affairs.

The unspeakable topic of a divorce had come up very early on after the wedding, during that first miserable year together. He'd even suggested an annulment. But Rose had been adamantly against it. They were married, and married forever as far as she was concerned.

As the years fell away and Foster saw less and less of her, he'd resigned himself to the disastrous state of his so-called marriage and got on with his life without her. She lived on the estate in Yorkshire and he lived in the town-house in London. It was not an unusual arrangement as far as some society marriages went, oddly enough. He could easily name two other men he knew who were in similar circumstances with their wives.

But they had at least been able to have children.

And now . . . Now he just wanted Rose out of his sight. He thrust her arm away with a little more force than necessary.

"Don't ever say that word to me again," she threatened, but she took a step back from him as she said it.

"Why the hell not?" he spat out. "We don't have a real marriage. We don't even like each other, so what is the point of carrying on this blasted charade anymore? Why not get a divorce? We're not fooling anyone. We have no life together. We have no children."

God, it pained him to say it aloud. What he was missing. What he would never have. Usually he managed to keep those agonizing thoughts at bay.

Seeing her again only reinforced what he already knew deep in his soul. Rose would never change. She would never want the things he wanted. Her selfishness had ruined his life. And it was too late to rectify it.

Her blue eyes glittered with malice. "Because we are married, like it or not. You married *me*. I am your wife, Foster, and you are my husband and that's all there is to it. I am your wife until the day I die." She spun around and stalked from the room, slamming the door behind her.

It was Rose's signature exit. A slamming door.

Foster picked up his glass and poured more scotch into it. He downed it in one shot. Then he sank into the deep leather chair near the fireplace. More than a little shocked by their almost violent altercation, he was surprised that he'd brought up the prospect of divorce when he'd resigned himself to his married fate years ago.

He'd made a decent enough life for himself in London over the years. He fulfilled his obligations and maintained the earldom. And of course, he had kept himself entertained with lovely women and good friends. But more importantly he pursued a business he'd started which invested in modern innovations. Foster considered himself a forward-looking man and it was an exciting time with so many wonderful new inventions. He loved obtaining the newest and most modern conveniences and was even about to have electric lights installed in his townhouse. All these new devices, like the telephone, were the way of the future.

Yet what about his own future? Suddenly this life seemed hollow and lonely and he had the urge to be free of Rose. To be free to live a real life.

He sighed heavily.

He was legally tied to Rose and being with her was hellish.

That truth stung even more so tonight because he'd just gotten a glimpse of heaven on earth . . . in the form of Lady Mara Reeves.

3

Variations

"Do you mean to say that you don't wish to go to Ireland with us next week?" Declan Reeves, the Earl of Cashelmore, stared at his only daughter in confusion. "I don't understand, darlin'."

"I'd just rather stay in London for a little while longer, Papa." Mara attempted to sound nonchalant, but she heard her voice quaver.

She simply couldn't leave London. Not now. Not after meeting Lord Sterling last night. Not after what had happened to her. She just could not go, but she couldn't explain the real reason to her parents without sounding like a simpleton. They would believe her to be utterly crazy.

She feared they already knew that she was.

Her whole life had changed last night and it was absolutely impossible to tell them that. She had met a man who turned her world upside down by being the center of her premonition, and she had to stay to figure out why. She had to see him again. That feeling! That feeling in her premonition was indescribable. Powerful. All-consuming. She had to find out what it meant! Leaving now was completely out of the question.

But being allowed to stay was another matter altogether.

Their family spent every summer in Ireland and she had always loved going. Mara was born in Ireland and felt at home there in a way that was almost magical. She loved the green hills, the rocky gray walls, the misty rain and all. But she could not possibly go there now.

"Well, I still want to go!" Her younger brother chimed in. At seventeen Thomas Reeves's boyish spirit loved any kind of adventure, and sailing to Ireland was one of his favorite things to do. At the moment he was piling a second helping of scrambled eggs, sausage, and toast onto his breakfast plate with gusto. Eating was one of her brother's other favorite pastimes.

"I don't understand, Mara . . ." Paulette looked across the table at her with growing concern. "We've had these plans for the last month. I have things to attend to at the Dublin bookshop, in addition to the house. Your father has his duties at Cashelmore Manor to manage as well. We postponed our trip when Aunt Juliette arrived, and then with Sara's wedding and Jeffrey's party and everything else, we've really put off going as long as we can. We've missed the entire summer as it is."

Mara avoided her mother's eyes. Paulette could always read Mara better than anyone, and she did not want to have to explain what happened to her last night. Yet she did not want to arouse any suspicion either. They were certain to refuse her request if they knew the reason she wanted to stay. And oh, how she wanted to stay! She simply had to remain in London.

"You can all still go without me," Mara offered casually. "I'm twenty-two years old, almost twenty-three now. That seems reasonably old enough to remain here in London on my own."

The breakfast table grew silent as her father set down the letters he'd been idly scanning. Mara noted the brief glance exchanged between her parents. Even Thomas stopped eating and sat up straighter, the conversation having suddenly become more interesting to him than eating. Mara held her breath as her family stared at her with varying looks of confusion and surprise.

"You're not going to let Mara stay here alone, are you?" Thomas finally asked, his blue eyes wide.

"No, we're not," Declan answered most emphatically. "Honestly, Mara, what is this nonsense all about? We've always gone home together."

With all of their eyes upon her, Mara lost her nerve. "I just . . . I just don't feel like going is all . . ." she offered up feebly. She stared down at the uneaten eggs on her plate. With the knot in her stomach, the thought of food made her feel queasy.

It had been a lost cause from the start. She should have known that her parents would never let her stay in London by herself. At least she had tried, which is more than she would have usually done. She could never explain to them why she needed to stay in London so desperately. Mara could barely explain it to herself. But there was no hope now. With a sigh of resignation, she slowly picked up her fork and began to push the eggs around on the plate, more for the need of something to do rather than from any desire to eat.

Well, there it was.

In less than a week she would be sailing to Ireland. Away from Lord Sterling. A heavy blanket of disappointment filled her chest. Just what she thought would happen with

Lord Sterling if she stayed, she was not sure. But now she would never find out, would she?

The awkward quiet that had fallen over the breakfast table was interrupted by Paulette's soft voice. "I think perhaps Mara has a point. Maybe we should discuss this a little more, Declan."

Mara froze, her heart suddenly surging with renewed hope, and stared up at her mother with a grateful smile. That was one of the reasons Mara loved Paulette so much and called her Mother. Paulette *understood* Mara and she always had, from the very first day they had met in the bookshop.

Paulette Hamilton had married Mara's father when Mara was only five years old, and she was the only mother Mara had ever really known. Paulette had changed their lives for the better and Mara loved her all the more for it. Beautiful Paulette, with her enchanting bookstore and her large and wonderful family, had transformed Mara's world and brought her out of the silence and darkness that had enveloped her since her own mother had tragically died.

"You cannot be serious, Paulette!" Declan exclaimed in surprise, his gaze now fixed upon his wife.

"I think we should at least consider it before we make a decision. She is an adult after all." Paulette stood her ground.

Mara cheered for joy in her heart. Oh, Paulette was simply magnificent! Her mother could be quite determined when she thought she was right.

"I am not leaving my young, unmarried daughter alone in London!" Declan protested heatedly. His brows drew together in disapproval, giving his usually handsome face a dark scowl.

"I agree with Papa," Thomas interjected excitedly. "Mara should come to Ireland with us."

"You may be excused, Thomas," Paulette said briskly. "Leave us to discuss this with your sister."

"But I'm not done with my breakfast!" he cried, food always foremost on his mind. His wide blue eyes filled with confusion. "Besides, I'm part of this family too, aren't I? We always make decisions together."

"Not this time, Thomas," Paulette said in the manner that meant the conversation was at an end. "You can take your plate with you. Go finish your breakfast in the garden. It's a lovely morning, sweetheart."

With a last-ditch look at their father, who offered no help, Thomas gave up. He knew better than to cross their mother when she used that tone. Amid quite a bit of grumbling, her brother took his breakfast and left the dining room, but not without a parting comment about how unfair it was to be ousted from the discussion.

As Mara set down her fork, her hand trembled slightly. Was it possible? Were they actually considering allowing her to stay? All last night she'd lain in bed thinking of how she would broach the topic with them. She certainly couldn't sleep after all that had happened with Lord Sterling. It had been a dreamlike and extraordinary meeting and she wasn't about to leave the country after such an event.

"I don't know what you're thinking, Paulette," Declan began, looking quite annoyed by the whole incident. "You must be daft if you think I'm going to allow Mara—"

"Declan," Paulette interrupted her husband calmly. "I think we should *listen* to her. She's trying to tell us something." She paused for effect and gave him a knowing look, adding softly, "When has Mara ever asked us for anything?"

Mara watched the change come over her father. He turned to face her, and his entire expression softened as he looked at her. They had always had a very special bond between them and she was not unaware of the tender spot he had for her. She knew it was because he feared losing her again, as he had when she was a little girl after the great fire.

Although she hated to trouble them, her parents were already worried about her. A twenty-two-year-old daughter who did not have a husband or the prospect of one would give any parents cause for concern, if not outright panic. After a few seasons had gone by without an offer of marriage or even a romantic interest on Mara's part, her marital status had been quite the delicate topic of discussion in her family. A young girl was supposed to marry, and set up a home of her own with a husband, not become a dreaded spinster and therefore a drain upon her family.

What is wrong with Lady Mara? Doesn't she want to get married? Those two questions followed her around at every social event, those she was asked directly by well-intentioned acquaintances and those overheard as whispers behind her back.

Oh, Mara had seen the anxious and troubled looks on the faces of her father and mother, had noted the confused expressions of her aunts and uncles, and had caught a few pitying glances from so-called friends. Yet she never meant to cause worry or alarm for the people she loved.

It wasn't that Mara didn't wish to marry or have a family of her own one day. It was just that Mara had always known that she would never marry. She *couldn't* marry. Not after what had happened with her own mother. No, she feared too much how that would turn out, so she deftly steered clear of any romantic entanglements that could possibly lead to marriage.

With her subtle ways, Mara could dissuade any interested suitor who was drawn to her quiet manner. It only took a few times, and then after a while the word got out that the Earl of Cashelmore's daughter was a hard sell and destined to be on the shelf, and the gentlemen stayed away from her. And as Mara declined invitations, she received fewer invitations, and her reputation as reclusive, shy, and a bit odd continued to grow, to the great astonishment of her family.

As each social season passed, Mara became less involved. In fact, she wouldn't have even participated in this past season at all, if Sara and Aunt Juliette had not arrived from New York unexpectedly. Mara had merely gone along with attending balls and parties because she promised her cousin she'd go with her. Last night she'd only been at the ball because it was Uncle Jeffrey's birthday celebration.

Her father, Mara knew, worried about her more than anyone. Although she hated to cause him any trouble or pain, she could not marry simply to please him.

"What is it, Mara, darlin'?" her father asked, the sweetness back in his voice. "Why don't you want to come to Ireland with us?"

"It's hard to describe . . . It's just a strong feeling I have, Papa." She attempted to explain as best she could. "Something in my heart tells me I need to be in London for a little while longer. I'll come join you eventually, I promise. Could I please stay? At least a little longer? Just a few weeks?"

Her father's brows drew together, his expression full of worry and concern. "Is it one of those . . . odd feelings? Like the ones you mentioned having long ago?"

Reluctantly, Mara nodded her head. So he remembered her telling him of the premonitions she'd had? He'd been so aghast that she'd never mentioned them again. Mara feared that the feelings, those premonitions, meant that she had some sort of terrible mental illness.

Paulette sighed in sympathy. "Although I don't entirely understand your reasoning, I do respect your desire to remain in London. And if some part of you believes strongly that you should stay, then I understand that too. I would stay here with you if I could, Mara, you know that, it's just that leaving you all alone places your father and me in an awkward position—"

"But I wouldn't really be alone at all!" Mara exclaimed, suddenly seeing a solution and wondering why she hadn't thought of it sooner. "I have Aunt Colette and Uncle Lucien and Phillip and Simon. I could stay with Aunt Lisette and Uncle Quinton. Or with Aunt Yvette and Uncle Jeffrey. Not to mention all the cousins. I wouldn't be alone in London at all."

"The sweet lass has a point." Declan gave her a wry smile. "We do have quite a lot of relatives here in town."

Paulette looked surprised that she had completely forgotten about her entire family. She was the fourth of the five Hamilton sisters who were remarkably close with each other. With a little laugh, she said, "Why, yes, that's true. I suppose you could stay with any one of them."

"Of course I could." Mara would have preferred to stay in her own home, but she wasn't about to push her luck any further. Staying in London with one of Paulette's sisters was not at all a bad trade. Mara loved each and every one of her aunts and would be hard-pressed to choose which one of them to stay with.

"Is there something you're not telling us, Mara?" Paulette eyed her closely.

"Good heavens, no!" Mara gave a nervous smile. "What is there that I wouldn't tell you? You know how I am. If anything were wrong I would tell you, I promise."

Her parents exchanged another secretive look.

Mara always envied that easy, wordless communication between the two of them. Was it simply something that happened to all couples who were married for a long time, that they could have a whole conversation with each other without speaking a single word? Or was it a special bond between two people in love? Whatever it was, she always wished to belong to someone that way, to someone who understood her so completely that words were unnecessary.

"Are you sure this is what you want, darlin'? For us to go to Ireland without you? I'd rather not leave you behind," her father questioned, still hoping she would change her mind.

"Yes, I am quite sure." Mara's heart beat faster just knowing that they were about to say yes. She wouldn't have to leave London after all! There was now a chance that she would run into Lord Sterling again. Anything was possible! Mara felt as though she could float right off her chair.

"We're not leaving for a few days yet, so you can always change your mind, you know," Paulette said kindly. "And meanwhile, I'll check with my sisters to see which of them you can stay with for the next month or so. We were planning to come back to London just before Christmas anyway, but if at any time you want to come join us, you know you can."

"So it's settled then?" Mara questioned, almost holding her breath. "I can stay in London?"

After a suspenseful pause, her parents nodded their heads.

"To be clear, I'm not happy about this, but I can't fight you *and* your mother. Two beautiful ladies is my limit," Declan said reluctantly, his handsome face drawn in concern. "I've never made you do anything you didn't wish to, darlin', and I'm not about to start now."

"Oh, thank you, Papa!" Mara jumped from her seat and rushed to his side. She placed a kiss on her father's cheek. "It means so much to me."

Then Mara went to Paulette and hugged her. "Thank you so much for understanding."

Paulette hugged her back tightly, whispering, "I'm not so sure I do understand, Mara, but it seems quite important to you."

"It is." Mara sighed with relief, as she returned to her seat at the table. She'd never felt this way before. She was grateful to not have to go away with her family, yet excited to stay and to discover the meaning of her premonition.

An unfamiliar exuberance bubbled within her. For the first time in her life Mara was standing up for herself and doing something on her own. She rather liked this new feeling of independence.

4

Invitations

"We'll have a grand time together this evening!" Simon Sinclair declared with enthusiasm. He smiled at Mara with glee as they rode through the park in the open carriage. It was a gorgeous September afternoon and Green Park was filled with fashionable people in fancy carriages, taking in the scenery.

Mara was now safely ensconced in a lovely guestroom at Devon House, her aunt Colette's massive townhome in Mayfair. Her parents and brother, Thomas, had sailed for Ireland the day before, and Mara was more convinced than ever that she had made the right decision by remaining in London. She'd also carefully chosen to stay with Colette. Aunt Lisette and Aunt Yvette had younger children, but by staying at Devon House, Mara was sure to be escorted around by her cousins Phillip and Simon, and therefore giving herself a better chance of running into Lord Sterling somewhere. At the very least she would be able to find out more about him from her cousins.

Now that she had managed to remain in London, she needed to figure out how to find Lord Sterling. She knew next to nothing about him, and she couldn't very well ask her cousins to take her to call on him. The best plan she could think of was to attend as many dinners, musicales, parties, and balls that she could with the hopes of meeting him at one. In the meantime she would endeavor to quietly gather any information about Lord Sterling through those she met.

It was well-known that attending social events was not her favorite pastime, and she wondered if her sudden interest in parties would raise the eyebrows of her aunts and uncles. But Mara had no choice but to venture out and about if she hoped to ever see Lord Sterling again.

The feelings in her premonition had been too powerful and too wonderful to ever ignore or forget. She simply had to pursue him, if only to find out what it all meant. And why things had ended so abruptly between them that night. So she would endeavor to find out all she could about him and hope that they crossed paths again. And she had a feeling they would.

"Yes, we'll have a lovely time this evening," Mara agreed with Simon, brightening her smile.

"I'm glad you're getting out a bit, Mara," Aunt Colette said.

Colette Sinclair, Marchioness of Stancliff, seated beside her in the carriage, was an elegantly dressed, undeniably pretty woman with lovely blue eyes. With the exception of her coffee-colored hair, Aunt Colette looked and sounded remarkably like Paulette, which gave Mara a wonderful sense of comfort with her parents away. If her aunt had been shocked by her decision not to go to Ireland, she didn't show it, and for that Mara was most grateful.

"But don't let my boys pressure you to attend something you don't wish to, either," Aunt Colette continued. "You have the freedom to do whatever you like and, of course, Lucien and I are perfectly delighted to have you staying with us at Devon House. You know I'm always happy to have your help at the bookshop. And having their pretty cousin here, keeps Simon and Phillip on their best behavior," she added with a wink.

"Thank you, Aunt Colette. I shall do my best to keep the boys in line. And I adore helping at the store," Mara replied.

Mara never minded working at the family's bookstores, in London and in Dublin. In fact she loved Hamilton's Book Shoppe. If it weren't for that particular London shop, her father never would have met and married Paulette Hamilton. Since she was four years old, the bookshop had been an echanted place for Mara and she had a special fondness for the children's section.

"We don't need to be kept in line, so much as to be kept occupied," Phillip said, but the look on his face contradicted his words. At twenty-three, the charming and handsome heir to his father's marquisate, Phillip Sinclair was one of the most eligible young men in London. He looked just like his father, Lucien Sinclair, with his dark hair and dimples. Popular and well liked, the Sinclair brothers were always in demand at parties and enjoyed a busy social calendar. "We'll make sure Cousin Mara has fun, won't we, Simon?"

"Of course we will," Simon chimed in. Younger than Mara, the boyishly attractive Simon resembled the Hamilton side of the family, with his lighter hair and blue eyes. "We always love escorting Mara around."

"We're glad you decided not to go to Ireland," Phillip said. "You'll have a better time here with us."

Mara wished she could ask Phillip straight out what he knew about Lord Sterling. He'd been with her the night she met the man and it would certainly be easier. But she was too afraid to mention it. Ever since they were all children, he and Simon had been like brothers to her. They treated her more as a little sister than a cousin, and she instinctively knew she could not confide in them about her interest in Lord Sterling. Phillip and Simon would undoubtedly become even more overprotective and more than likely tease her unmercifully about it. *Cousin Mara has finally been love struck!* She couldn't abide that.

No, what she needed to do was to chat casually to a stranger and gather information about Lord Sterling that way, without arousing her cousins' suspicions.

"We're all happy you're staying in London with us, Mara," Aunt Colette began. "I admit I'm more and more intrigued by your idea for a new bookshop. Ever since you mentioned it to me, I can't stop thinking about it."

"What are your thoughts, Aunt Colette?"

"Well, I've discussed it with Lucien, and he's a little skeptical. We already have the largest selection of children's books in London at Hamilton's, and he doesn't see the need for a separate store for children. But I can't help but believe it's something not only that we could do, but something we *should* do. There's never been such a place! A special shop devoted solely to children's books! It is quite an innovative concept! And perhaps tomorrow you can come with me to the shop and we can discuss your suggestion in more detail."

The idea for a children's bookstore had always been something that Mara had thought about. Hamilton's Book Shoppe had a lovely children's section, with miniature tables and chairs, which had seemed a charming and enchanted place to her when she was a child. But an entire store, devoted only to books for children, with inviting spaces for them to read and look through books, had been a favorite daydream of hers. Oddly enough, she had never shared her idea of a children's bookshop before, not even with her mother.

Yet on the spur of the moment only the day before, Mara suddenly told her aunt about her vision. Aunt Colette, being the oldest of the Hamilton sisters and the one most vested in the family business next to Paulette, did not scoff at her idea. In fact, she was intrigued by it.

"Of course, Aunt Colette. I should love to come to the shop with you tomorrow," Mara said happily. All the Hamilton girls worked in the shop at one point or another. Her mother, Paulette, had even opened another Hamilton's Book Shoppe in Dublin.

"I am actually excited to have a new project we can all work on together," Colette continued excitedly.

As the carriage made its way back to Devon House, Mara fell silent. It would be good to have the bookshop as a distraction. Her thoughts were too preoccupied with Lord Sterling and her premonition.

"Good afternoon," Parkins, the Devon House butler, greeted them as they returned home.

"It's such a lovely afternoon, let's have tea outside, shall we? We don't have many days left before the weather turns colder. Don't you agree?" Aunt Colette asked them.

"That sounds wonderful," Mara answered, thinking some refreshment would be welcome after their drive.

"These just arrived, my lady." Parkins held a silver tray holding some letters to Aunt Colette. "Lady Mara, there is a letter here for you also."

"Thank you, Parkins," Aunt Colette said before giving instructions to the butler to set up tea out on the veranda.

Mara took her letter from the silver tray and glanced at the unfamiliar writing with puzzlement. It looked quite masculine. And it was not her father's nor her brother's writing. Bold, clean strokes neatly spelled out her name. *Lady Mara Reeves.* Suddenly that peculiar tingling crept along her spine. Goose bumps appeared on her arms and her mouth went dry.

The letter was from *him*. She knew it.

"I shall join you all in just a moment," Mara mumbled,

her heart pounding wildly in her chest. "Won't you excuse me, Aunt Colette . . ."

She fairly flew up the grand staircase to her room. After shutting the door behind her, she threw her parasol and gloves on the blue toile-covered divan, and took a deep breath. Still trembling with excitement, she sat upon the bed, letter in hand.

It was from Lord Sterling.

She didn't even need to read it to know it was from him. Her heart skittered in her chest. Here she was, wracking her brain trying to devise a way to find him, and he found her! Why had he written to her? And more interestingly to her way of thinking, how had he determined that she was at her aunt's house? For the letter was clearly addressed to her at Devon House, not her family's townhouse. So not only had Lord Sterling discovered where she lived, but also that she was staying with her aunt and uncle. Whom had he spoken to about her? And why would he not simply call upon her or send his card?

A letter was not the expected manner with which a gentleman expressed his interest in a lady. Then again, the way the two of them had acted when they met had not been expected either.

A thrill of excitement welled within her and with bated breath she unfolded the sheet of thick, monogrammed paper upon which Lord Sterling wrote to her. His address on Brook Street was inscribed at the top as well.

My Dearest Lady Mara,

Please forgive the great liberty I have taken in writing to you. Although, somehow I feel you will not mind my doing so.

I must confess I have not been able to stop thinking of you since the night we met. The circumstances were most unusual and I have been

*captivated by thoughts of you ever since. Not
knowing when I would see you again, I felt
compelled to seek you out. However, I cannot call
upon you in the customary manner.*

*Would you do me the great honor of meeting with
me? If you could arrange to be walking in Green
Park tomorrow morning at half past nine, I will be
waiting for you near the start of the Queen's Walk.*

Yours,
Foster

Mara practically stopped breathing. *He wants to see me!
Tomorrow morning!* Hardly able to contain her excitement,
her absolute joy that he'd written to her, she squealed. Then
she reread the letter three more times. She even memorized
it. She didn't know which pleased her more, that he said he
was captivated by her, or that he hadn't been able to stop
thinking of her, or that he'd signed his name simply, *Foster*.

Foster Sheridan, Earl of Sterling.

It was a good name.

She sighed, longing for her cousin Sara's presence and
advice. Sara had always been her closest confidante. Now
that Mara thought about it, Sara Fleming had been her only
confidante, even though Sara lived in New York! It suddenly
struck Mara as inconvenient that she had no other close
friends. She'd always wished for a sister, and Sara had
come close to filling that role. But more often than not,
Mara spent most of her time alone or with her family, which
normally did not bother her. She was a private person and
content to keep things to herself. But now, when she had
the most exciting news of her life, she had no one to share
it with who would understand.

Oh, she had so many questions for Lord Sterling. How
had he found her? Why did he wish to see her? And most

importantly, why could he not call upon her in the customary manner?

Mara glanced at the letter again, rereading it, gently running her fingers across the words he'd written. He *had* been thinking about her as much as she'd been thinking about him.

Tomorrow. She would see the man she had been longing for at the park tomorrow morning! For there was not a doubt in her mind that she would meet him there.

5

Suggestions

He was utterly crazy. Certifiably insane. What was he thinking to write to her? What on earth did he hope to gain by it? There was no way this could end well.

Foster Sheridan, Earl of Sterling, paced back and forth in front of the entrance to the park the next morning. The crisp September air told him that they had seen the last of the warm days of summer. Autumn had officially arrived. The leaves on the trees glinted in the clear morning sunlight. It was early yet. Or rather, *he* was early. It was only half past eight. He was an hour early, but he could not contain himself. He was too eager to see her and feared that they might miss each other. Idiot that he was, he would willingly walk the length of the Queen's Walk back and forth all day waiting for her, if she wasn't there on time.

For a mature man of thirty, he was behaving like a callow schoolboy. He was actually nervous! Nervous about meeting a beautiful woman. Glancing around, he noted there were no people about this early, which had been his goal. He wanted to avoid meeting up with anyone either of them knew.

He simply needed to see her again. To see if she was real. He feared he imagined all that had happened between them the night of the Duke of Rathmore's ball. There had been something so magnetic about her. About them together. It defied description.

Yet Foster was not free to call on her. He was not free to do anything with her. He shouldn't have sent her the letter. He should never have dared to ask her to meet him. But he simply had to see her one more time.

He was a fool! A great fool! He would apologize to her. He would ask her forgiveness at his audacity and be on his way. He would do the proper thing and just walk away, never to see her again.

Lady Mara Reeves deserved far better than someone like him.

He continued pacing, wondering if she would be late. It occurred to him, not for the first time, that he knew next to nothing about her. Over the last week, he had discovered her whereabouts. It left him wondering why was she staying in London with her aunt and uncle? Lady Mara Reeves was a complete mystery to him. Yet a bewitching mystery he felt compelled to unravel.

And suddenly there she was . . . the beautiful object of his thoughts.

Lady Mara Reeves was walking straight toward him, her stride elegant, graceful, and purposeful.

She looked like an angel, with the morning sun glistening on the pretty bonnet framing her fair hair, giving the effect of a halo. She wore an attractive fitted gown of apple green that showed off her perfectly shaped figure. Her sweet face beamed at him while a delighted smile touched her pink lips. She was happy to see him.

And she was almost an hour early!

"Mara . . ." Her name escaped his mouth on a raspy whisper. He was so elated to see her, he could barely speak.

"Foster," she responded a little breathlessly as she came to a stop in front of him.

Goodness, but she was a tiny thing! He could easily lift her in his arms with no trouble at all. He'd forgotten how petite she was, how delicate. She was utterly lovely.

"You're here early." He marveled at the fact that they both had arrived an hour ahead of the scheduled meeting time.

"So are you." She smiled up at him, her misty gray eyes soft and luminous, framed by thick lashes. "But I simply couldn't wait any longer to see you and I had a funny feeling you'd be here too."

The earnestness in her voice, her whole manner, was almost his undoing. There was not a shred of artifice about her. This beautiful, ethereal little creature was happy simply to see him and was so eager to do so that she couldn't wait. He grinned helplessly.

"I'm glad you came," he said, longing to pull her into his arms. He yearned to touch her, to know that she was real and here with him. But he knew better. "I wasn't sure if you would."

"I'm so happy and relieved that you wrote to me." She gazed up at him, peering from beneath the brim of her jade-colored bonnet, her eyes appearing greener than he recalled them being. Hadn't they been gray? She added softly, "I didn't know when I would see you again."

Foster's heart slammed into the wall of his chest with a force that almost knocked him over. This beautiful woman, this wisp of a girl, touched something deep inside of him. Something he had long believed to be dead and gone. Under the warmth of her sweet gaze, that deadened, cold place in his heart hesitantly began thawing, like the unfurling of a tender new leaf in the spring snow. Astonished by this unique feeling, a sense of panic enveloped him as well.

"I don't know why I sent that letter. I only knew that somehow, some way, I had to see you again, Mara." The words fell from his lips of their own volition. Yet he spoke only the truth. He had no choice but to see her again. No matter how wrong it was to the rest of the world, to Foster it seemed the only right course to take in his life.

"However did you manage to find me?"

"I discreetly asked a few friends who know the Duke of Rathmore," he explained. "What was not as easy to ascertain was the reason you are staying with the Marquis of Stancliff and his family at Devon House . . ."

A shy look came over Mara's angelic face. "My family has gone to our home in Ireland until Christmas. There was no prospect of seeing you again if I went with them, so I decided to remain here in London with my aunt and uncle."

A deep silence grew between them as the meaning of her words sank in. The heavy thud of his heart against his chest echoed in his ears. He could not believe what she was implying. "Then you stayed . . ."

He paused in confusion, for he had to be mistaken. She couldn't possibly be suggesting that she left her family on the off chance of their seeing each other again. "You stayed in London simply to see me?"

"Yes." Her voice was soft. "I had been trying to figure out a way to find you, when your letter arrived."

Her response took his breath away. It was astounding. He repeated what he could not quite believe. "You stayed here for me?"

"Well, if I went to Ireland, who knows when we would have seen one another again?" she continued, oddly matter-of-fact in her explanation of something so extraordinary.

"Then all things considered," he said, "I must admit that I'm very pleased you chose to remain here in London."

"You are pleased then?" she asked hesitantly.

He nodded, his heart beating erratically. "Very pleased."

Again those luminous gray-green eyes of hers, that almost seemed to see through him, lit up at his words. The look she gave him did something to him. If they had not been standing in the middle of a public garden, he would have pulled her into his arms and kissed her thoroughly then and there. And how he longed to do just that! Foster fought against every natural instinct in his being to not reach out and simply touch the softness of her cheek.

Then her expression grew quite solemn and her delicate eyebrows drew together. "That night we met . . . It was rather remarkable. I can't explain it fully, but I felt as if I knew you, yet that's impossible, for I know nothing about you."

"I will tell you whatever you wish to know."

"I have so many questions for you, I'm not sure where to begin."

She was adorably earnest in her manner. He'd never known anyone quite like her. "You are most enchanting, Mara."

"Thank you." Flustered by his compliment, her cheeks turned slightly pink. "Should we go somewhere we can talk privately?"

"Go somewhere?" he echoed.

"We can't very well stand here much longer or someone will notice us together. Although people already gossip about me, I'm sure being seen alone with you is not anything that would help my reputation. Brighton, my lady's maid, is waiting for me back by the carriage, but I'd rather we speak privately, don't you agree?"

His mind spun with the ramifications. What could he say to her? He wanted more than anything in the world to be alone with her. He longed to talk to her, to learn everything there was to know about this lovely woman. He was inexplicably drawn to her.

Yet he had to refuse her. It was the proper thing to do. The right course of action. He should not spend another moment in her presence. He should inform her that he was not free. Not free at all. He never should have written to her. Never should have invited her to meet him there. It was all wrong. He should escort her back to her carriage and send her home right away.

"My carriage is just over there," he heard himself say to her. Going against everything he knew that was just and proper, he continued his descent. "Can you come for a ride with me?"

A delighted smile lit her face again. "I would love to!"

And just like that, Foster whisked her off to the seclusion of his enclosed carriage, hating himself every step of the way. She sat across from him, staring at him expectantly, and rather adoringly, and it tore at his heart. As the carriage lurched into motion, he made a silent promise that they would just go for a quick ride around the park while he told her that he was not free to call upon her, and then he would send her home. Yes, that's exactly what he would do.

Mara said softly, with a shy smile, "I was hoping we could do this."

"Pardon me?" he asked.

"I was hoping we could be alone to talk. There's so much I want to know about you."

His heart flipped over and he felt like a complete cad. She was so happy and excited to be with him. It was all terribly wrong. He *was* a complete cad.

"Oh, Mara, you've no idea about anything."

"But surely, you felt it too?" she asked. "Please tell me

that I didn't imagine how it felt the night we met. How it feels between us now. That it isn't just me."

"No. No, it isn't just you."

He couldn't explain it to himself, let alone to her, but yes, he had felt something incredible the night he first saw her. There was no denying it. There was an inexplicable link between them, but he should not have mentioned it to her! "I don't know what in heaven's name to call it," he confessed. "But yes, I felt it too."

She smiled with relief. "It was a magical sort of connection, wasn't it? A sense of knowing each other. That's what I felt. So strongly! I feel I know you, and I have never felt that way with anyone before in my life, Foster."

He loved the sound of his name on her lips. He loved how Mara looked at him when she spoke. How her misty gray-green eyes lit with excitement and her expression became animated. God, but she was lovely. Framed by flaxen hair, her features were delicate and fair. Her smooth skin looked so soft, he longed to run his fingers along her cheek. The ethereal quality about her drew him in like nothing else. Her beauty was somewhat otherworldly, as if she couldn't possibly belong to the ordinariness of living on this earthly plane.

"Have you ever felt anything like that night?"

"No. I can honestly say that I have not."

Not in all his life had he felt such an overwhelming connection to another person. As an only child, Foster had had a solitary childhood, mostly cared for by a string of nannies until he was sent off to boarding school. Then, as an obedient son, he married as his parents wished when he was twenty years old, to a woman who didn't love him and never would. He'd had a few discreet mistresses over the years, but he'd not felt anything but passing affection for them.

No, what he already felt for Mara, a woman he barely

knew, far surpassed anything he'd ever felt for anyone in his life.

"Well, what do you think it means?" She stared at him.

He laughed then. "I'm sure I haven't a clue, sweet Mara. What do you think it means?"

After a slight pause, she ventured, "Well, I have a notion that those feelings we have for each other mean that we are destined to be together."

Destined to be together.

If only he could be with this beautiful, enchanting woman! The light and energy that surrounded her drew his soul to hers, in spite of his brain screaming at him to run away. No good could come of this. No good at all.

Reluctantly, he shook his head, his stomach tied in knots. He forced himself to tell her the truth. "No. We are not destined to be together."

"Why?" Mara looked confused. "Do you think it means something else?"

"I know it does." He took a deep breath. He wanted more than anything in the world to say something completely different to her than what he was about to. He could not put it off any longer. It would only add to her pain.

Their pain.

"Mara, I wish I could tell you that our destiny is to be together, because I wish that we could be. I wish it more than you could possibly imagine. But there is something I need to tell you about me . . ."

She looked at him expectantly, her delicate brows furrowed. "Yes? What is it?"

"I am married."

All the color drained from her sweet face at his words. Her eyes grew round in surprise, like great pools of gray. Deflated, she remained speechless for a moment as their meaning sunk in.

Foster wished he could take the words back. Even more than that, he wished he weren't married. His stomach churned.

The carriage swayed from side to side. The sound of the horses' hooves clopping over the cobblestones seemed much louder than it had even a moment ago. Almost unbearably loud.

Suddenly Mara sat up straight. "Of course!"

"What is it?" he asked, surprised by her reaction to his news.

"You are married. That's why you didn't let me kiss you that night!"

Her train of thought confused him. "Well, yes . . . but I wanted to kiss you."

"I knew it!" She seemed oddly relieved.

"Knew what?"

"I have never kissed a man before and I thought I had done something wrong, or something to offend you that night and that was why you didn't kiss me and left so abruptly. But *you* wanted that kiss too. You were simply being a gentleman. It wasn't me at all."

"But it *is* you, Mara. Don't you see? I am not free to kiss you. I am not free to court you. I am not able to call upon you. I cannot do anything with you." He paused, his heart heavy. "I am a married man."

"But you *wanted* to kiss me, did you not?" She stared at him artlessly.

"Of course I did!" He almost shouted the words. His frustration was greater than he could bear. "I am not dead. Of course I wanted to kiss you that night, just as I want to kiss you this very moment. You're the most beautiful woman I have ever known." He heaved a sigh and closed his eyes. "And I cannot have you."

"Of course you can have me."

Foster's eyes flew open. Had the girl lost her mind completely? She seemed so calm. Oddly so. He had expected tears from her. He'd expected anger. Maybe even a slap across the face. Which he undoubtedly deserved. He'd expected that she'd be hurt when he told her that he was married. He had not anticipated this assuredness that he could still have her. What on earth was she thinking?

"Mara, you don't know what you are saying."

She gave him an appraising look. "You are not happy in your marriage, are you?"

"No." Again, he sighed heavily. "I am not at all happy in my marriage. I have never been happy in my marriage. She and I live hundreds of miles apart because we make each other miserable." Not one single day of his married life had he been happy with Rose. Not one. Not even close. Nor had she been happy with him. "But it doesn't matter whether I am happy or not. I am married, Mara, and I cannot ever be with you." The truth of that statement cut him deeply. "We shouldn't even be together now."

"Do you want to be with me, Foster?" she asked, apparently ignoring all he had just said.

"I hardly know you."

"That doesn't answer my question." Her eyes bored into him.

"What does it matter?" He clenched and unclenched his hands. "It's an impossible situation."

"It does matter to me. Very much so. This is my life. And I *know* we are destined to be together. It doesn't matter how. Or when. Don't you feel that between us?" she asked, almost pleaded.

It was pointless. All of it. The two of them being alone in his carriage, having this conversation. The things Mara was suggesting. The feelings that were flooding him. The burgeoning glimmer of hope that burned low within him, that his life might actually regain a sense of living. The hope of creating a family. With Mara. Of beautiful, gray-eyed, blond-haired babies. The prospect of a life full of love and happiness. It was terribly dangerous to even be thinking these things.

Because none of it could ever happen.

Leaning back, Foster opened the small window and instructed his driver to take them back to the park immediately. This was getting out of hand. Mara deserved a real life. A real future. She deserved a husband. She definitely deserved more than a half-life in the shadows with him, for that was all he could offer her.

The girl had not the slightest idea what she was suggesting they do, or how it would assuredly ruin her life.

"It's time to go," he said, feeling sick inside.

"You're taking me back already?" Tears welled in her eyes.

Now she cried? Now? Not when he told her he was *married*, but when he told her it was time they go home? She baffled him.

"Yes, I'm taking you back to your carriage. It's the only sane thing to do. One of us has to be the rational one. This is over, Mara. This is entirely my fault and I take full responsibility for all of it. I shouldn't have written to you or asked you to meet with me, and I hope you can forgive me. It never should have gone this far."

"But you don't really believe that!" she cried in protest. "And you cannot bring me back yet when we haven't finished talking."

"My sweet Mara, there is nothing left to talk about."

"There!" she declared triumphantly. "You called me *your* sweet Mara. You know I belong to you."

"You can't belong to me, in spite of my wishing it were so. I cannot have you and you cannot have me." He hated saying the words aloud. They were cold and harsh, and that made them all the more real. And heartbreakingly true. "I am a married man, Mara. I am already taken."

Mara took a deep breath and stated clearly, "But I am not."

They stared at each other for a long moment. Her words terrified him and for some reason, that tiny sliver of hope within him seemed to grow and take stronger hold in his heart. Mara was not deterred by his married state. In fact, she seemed quite unmoved by it. It stunned him. He did not know what she meant by that and did not dare to ask.

It was far, far too dangerous.

She stared at him, and for a moment he hesitated. With one kiss he could easily seduce her innocent ideals and begin a torrid affair with her.

Yet he could not. She deserved a proper marriage, with a loving husband, a beautiful home, and a happy family devoid of scandal and public scorn and humiliation.

The carriage came to a halt.

"We're back," he announced dully, his voice hoarse. "It's time for us to part, Mara."

Without another word, she left him, but not before she gave him a look of longing that would haunt him until the day he died.

As his carriage continued on through the park, he wished he could go after her. He wished she could be his. He wished they could have just driven away together. He wished things were different. His entire life was a mess.

Foster had never felt so alone.

6

Conversations

"I know, I know. I'm late! Forgive me. Vivienne has a bit of a cough, so I sat with her for a while." Yvette Hamilton Eddington, the Duchess of Rathmore, hurried into the room. She greeted her sisters warmly, then removed her gloves and adjusted the blond curls under her fashionable hat. As she took a seat in the elegant drawing room at Devon House, she asked, "So tell me, how are things?"

Colette offered Yvette a cup of black tea. Their weekly afternoon tea times together allowed the Hamilton sisters to keep each other updated on family matters. With one sister in New York and another in Ireland, there were just the three of them left in London.

Lisette, beaming with pride, said, "Well, Christopher and Charles are busy with their studies. But I think Christopher may follow in his father's footsteps and become an architect too." The middle Hamilton sister was married to Quinton Roxbury, an architect and politician, and they had twin sons and a daughter.

"Quinton must be thrilled with that!" Colette remarked.

"He is!" Lisette said. "Have either of you heard from Juliette?"

"The last letter I received from her simply said they arrived in New York safely and hopefully they would be back in London in time for Christmas. No details. No dates. She truly is the most dreadful letter writer," Yvette lamented.

Colette agreed with an emphatic nod of her head. "She always has been."

"So tell us, Colette, how are things with having Mara stay here?" Lisette asked.

"I suppose they are going along quite well, thank you," Colette told them. "She's been wonderful, but then Mara has never been any trouble. Even as a little girl, she was always like a little angel. You know I've always had a soft spot for her."

Lisette smiled. "You two have the love of the bookshops in common."

"Mara is quite special and I adore her," Colette added.

"I must say I was surprised that Paulette and Declan allowed her to stay behind. Have you determined her reason for remaining in London yet?" Yvette asked, her blue eyes curious as she spooned sugar into her tea. She was the youngest of the sisters, married to Jeffrey Eddington, the Duke of Rathmore, and the mother to three little daughters.

"No, not yet, but I think everyone is overreacting." Colette shook her head. "Mara has always been a quiet girl and not given to over-sharing. I believe it will take a little more time before the true reason comes to light. If there is anything at all."

"Well, it must be a man then! What else could it possibly be?" Yvette questioned with a raised brow.

Lisette Hamilton Roxbury laughed. "It's always about men with you, Yvette. There are a dozen perfectly reasonable explanations why Mara would want to remain in London with us."

"Name one." Yvette stared frankly at Lisette, who looked helplessly blank.

Colette laughed at her sisters. "Have you forgotten that our Yvette did the very same thing years ago? That's why she's suspicious of Mara's reasons for not going to Ireland. Remember that Yvette insisted on staying by herself in London instead of coming to New York with Lucien and me, for no real reason that we could see? All because she had set her cap for the wrong man?"

With a rueful smile and a careless wave of her hand, Yvette added, "It all turned out well in the end and you cannot deny it. I am happily married to Jeffrey *and* I'm a duchess."

"Are you saying Mara is scheming to be a duchess?" Lisette asked.

Yvette smiled knowingly. "No, not Mara. That is not her way. I'm simply stating the obvious. There is a man on the horizon, whether *we* know about him or not."

"I tend to agree with you, Yvette," Colette said with reluctance. "Even though Mara has not shown the slightest interest in anyone since she's been here, let alone for the last few seasons. Paulette and Declan are at their wits' end with worry over her."

"That's my point," Yvette ventured. "You know the old saying, still waters run deep? Well, Mara has about the stillest and calmest waters I've ever seen! There are things bubbling inside that pretty little heart of hers that none of us know about. She will surprise all of us one day. Mark my words."

Lisette looked thoughtful for a moment. "You may be right about that."

"Of course I am!" Yvette said pertly. "It's the only reason that makes any sense whatsoever. Even Jeffrey agreed with me."

"It would be nice if Sara and her new husband returned

from New York sooner." Lisette referred to their niece Sara, who'd recently married. Sara was closest to Mara and the two had been dearest friends since they were little girls. "If anyone had a chance of discovering what is in Mara's heart, it would be Sara."

Colette nodded her head in agreement. "I suppose I should keep a closer watch over her, but I don't see the need for it. Both Phillip and Simon said they know of no one who has shown a romantic interest in Mara or vice versa."

"Then it must be someone we don't know," Yvette offered pragmatically. "Someone unsuitable, perhaps?"

Colette rolled her eyes. "Isn't that always the way?"

"Yet, Mara is not flighty or reckless." Lisette gave a shake of her head. "Not in the least bit. She'd never involve herself with someone unsuitable."

Yvette said thoughtfully, "Perhaps I'll arrange to have Jeffrey speak with her. You know he can get her to confide in him."

The three Hamilton sisters nodded in agreement. Jeffrey Eddington would be the one who could wheedle a secret out of Mara if there was one.

"Well, at this point we know absolutely nothing. Not even if a man is the reason behind her desire to stay in London. In the meantime all we can do is wait and see." Colette picked up her teacup.

"Where is Mara now?" Yvette asked. "I was hoping to see her this afternoon."

"She is at the bookshop."

"Of course she is . . . I think I shall invite her over for tea later this week," Yvette murmured.

"Well, there's something else I want to talk to you both about . . ." Colette paused for dramatic effect. "Mara and I are working on an idea for a new bookshop."

"We already have two shops in London, not to mention

the one in Dublin," Yvette remarked. "Do we really need another one?"

"A new idea for a bookshop?" Lisette looked thoughtful. "What kind?"

"A children's bookshop," Colette announced excitedly.

"A children's bookshop?" Yvette echoed, looking puzzled. "Whoever heard of such a thing?"

"I don't believe that anyone has. But I think it's important for Hamilton's Book Shoppe to be on the cutting edge of progress," Colette continued. "It's such a daring and innovative idea, don't you think? I've written to Paulette to find out what she thinks. It was all Mara's idea too."

Yvette shook her head reluctantly. "We already have the largest selection of children's books in London. I doubt there are even enough children's books printed to fill a store devoted solely to children."

"But I think there are!" Colette countered. "And I think there will continue to be more written each year. Children's literature is a growing market. An untapped market, actually. I continuously have customers asking for more books that are expressly written for children."

Yvette, the sister who devoted the least amount of time to the family business, looked unconvinced. "It sounds rather risky. I can't imagine parents going out of their way to buy books at a special store."

"Oh, I can absolutely imagine it! I think a children's bookshop has definite possibilities. If we start with a very small space," Lisette added, slowly nodding her head. "A small shop . . . I think it could work."

"I've already begun to look at locations," Colette said, her eyes sparkling with excitement. She had always loved the challenge of beginning something new.

"We could even have Quinton design the shop if we

don't find anything suitable," Lisette added, with growing enthusiasm.

Colette grinned with approval. "I thought of that too!"

Yvette sipped her tea while waiting for a pause in their conversation. "I'm curious to know what Paulette thinks of this scheme."

"It's not a scheme, Yvette!" Lisette laughed.

Colette explained, "It's a novel approach to business and I've given it a great deal of thought this past week and I've talked it over with Lucien so many times that he asked me to give him a rest! But he does agree with me. And I know Paulette will see the advantages of this venture as well, especially because it was Mara's idea in the first place. Don't you see? We'll be giving customers something they don't yet realize they want. And I think parents would like a place they can bring their children to. We're only six years away from the start of a new century! The world is changing. Society is changing. And Hamilton's need to change too."

"I'm not entirely sure about that," Yvette said with a bit of skepticism.

Lisette tilted her head, her delicate features pensive. "That's not the reason Mara wanted to stay in London, is it? For the bookshops?"

"Hardly," Yvette said, finding it difficult to understand how anyone would put a business before anything romantic. "I think it's just a coincidence."

"In any case," Colette said, "I believe this children's bookshop is going to be a success . . . and when it is, we shall have Mara to thank for her idea!"

"Well, she seems to be the only granddaughter that has the same interest in the bookshops," Yvette remarked. "I don't see my three girls wanting anything to do with the business. They're too much like me."

"I suppose my Elizabeth might want to . . ." Lisette didn't sound too hopeful. "But it doesn't seem likely."

Colette sighed a bit sadly. "Yes, it makes me sad that our girls may not want to oversee the bookshops as we do. But we must continue to make sure they know about how Papa started the first store and how we lived above the shop and worked there. We were the ones who made it successful and expanded to three stores! Perhaps Elizabeth could come to the shops more often, Lisette. And Yvette, hopefully one of your girls will be interested when they are a little older. It's a shame that none of the boys seem inclined to the business either. But we have Mara to pick up the mantle . . . And I know she shall do it quite admirably."

Lisette raised her teacup. "To Mara then!"

Yvette and Colette lifted their cups as well to toast their niece, with the hope that Mara would carry on the tradition of their father's bookshop one day.

7

Declarations

That very same afternoon her aunts were having tea at Devon House, Mara rang the doorbell of a stately townhouse on Upper Brook Street. Her hand trembled and her heart raced as she waited for the door to open.

A tall butler with gray hair and a kind face greeted her. If he was scandalized to see an unchaperoned young lady on the doorstep, he hid his shock very well. "Good afternoon. How may I help you, miss?" he asked as calmly as if she had every right to be there.

She took a deep breath and blurted out, "I am Lady Mara Reeves and I would like to see Lord Sterling, if he is in." She paused before adding, "He is not expecting me."

With surprising composure, the butler swung the door wider and allowed her to step inside. "Please come this way, my lady."

Peering around the house, she quickly noted that there was nothing fussy or feminine about the place. It was sparsely decorated but not uninviting. In fact it appeared rather modern and attractive in a way she could not define. It was exactly what she would have expected. Not that

Mara knew what to expect when visiting a gentleman's home, but Foster's house seemed to suit him.

The butler ushered her into a study, which was filled with simple masculine furniture, dark wood, and rich colors. "I shall inform his lordship that you are here. I am Preston, my lady, should you require anything. Might I have something brought to you? Tea, perhaps?"

She hesitated, wondering if they should have tea. Would it lend some normalcy to what she was doing? She doubted it. Nothing could make this visit seem normal. "No, thank you, I think not."

With a nod, the butler left and closed the door.

Mara stood alone in the small study, which was done in shades of burgundy and forest green. Again she noted the simple and clean lines of the room and the feel of modernity about it. It was elegant, yet comfortable. Leather chairs and a sofa, beautiful wood furniture, and very few knick-knacks. Books lined the neatly arranged shelves. A few periodicals were scattered on a low table near the sofa. *Knowledge. The Hobby Horse. Amateur Photographer. The Fortnightly Review. The English Mechanic.* The titles indicated a man who was interested in a variety of subjects.

As she continued to glance around the room, she could smell the scent of Foster in there and inhaled deeply. With some trepidation she walked to a dark brown leather chair near the fireplace. Imagining that this was where Foster sat at night, perhaps enjoying a drink or reading one of his modern magazines, she ran her hands over the comfortably worn leather.

Then she caught a glimpse of herself in the mirror over the mantel. With her blond hair done up neatly beneath her green velvet hat that matched her smart plaid-trimmed green jacket with large bell sleeves and accentuated her cinched-in waist, she certainly didn't look the seductress. She looked pretty enough, she supposed, but as always, she appeared pale with too-wide grayish eyes. She looked frightened.

But then why wouldn't she be frightened?

Staring at her reflection, she wondered what on earth she was doing there in the first place. What kind of a lady was she? Why would she call upon a married man? Even though she knew he did not live with his wife. She had no business coming to his house so brazenly in the middle of the afternoon! What if someone had seen her? What if Foster became angry at her presence and sent her away?

Whatever had she been thinking to be so utterly reckless and bold? Acting in this manner was not like her at all! Quiet, shy little Mara always behaved properly. She would never conduct herself inappropriately or even dream of doing anything that hinted at scandalous. Visiting a married man at his home for questionable purposes was more like something her fearless cousin Sara would do, while Mara would be the worried one, trying to talk some sense into her.

While Mara had lain in bed last night, her mind wouldn't rest. She couldn't give up the idea of going to see him. To her way of thinking, she had nothing to lose and everything to gain by going to see him. She'd debated everything in her head over and over again. The cold manner in which they parted in the park the other morning was not what either of them wanted. She was certain of it.

At least she knew it wasn't what *she* wanted.

It all came back to that overwhelming sense of knowing that she and Foster *belonged together*. Her powerful premonition had touched something deep within her heart. It changed her. She did not know what the future held for the two of them, nor did she dwell on that fact for now. The premonition, and meeting Foster, signified a transformation in her life. It altered everything.

For once in her life, shy little Mara decided to take action instead of floating aimlessly along. First, she had remained in London without her parents. Next she spoke to her aunt about her idea for the children's bookshop. Then she'd met Foster Sheridan in the park.

Now she was taking another step forward on her own.

That morning, after giving very specific instructions to her lady's maid, Brighton, Mara went to work at Hamilton Sisters' Book Shoppe, as she usually did. Except instead of going to visit the original Hamilton's Book Shoppe as she said she was, she set out for Upper Brook Street. If Aunt Colette happened to stop in at one of the shops, she would assume Mara was at the other. But since it was Wednesday, and Mara knew that all her aunts were having tea together, it was unlikely that Aunt Colette would be venturing to either shop this afternoon. Mara wouldn't be missed until supper.

Or later, if Brighton followed her directions.

Here she was now. In Foster Sheridan's townhouse. Unchaperoned. Uninvited. What in heaven's name was she thinking to come here like this? Biting her lip, she had rationalized that she was simply calling on a friend. But she knew that was not true. What she wanted to suggest to him was scandalous.

But now . . . Now fear welled up from deep within her, and she suddenly felt as though she might be ill.

She had made a most dreadful mistake.

Panicking, Mara swung around and headed for the door. If she hurried, she might manage to exit the house before Foster even saw her. Yes, that's just what she would do. She would leave.

It was too late.

The door to the drawing room opened and Foster walked in, looking even more handsome than she remembered. Wearing a dark gray frock coat over a crisp white linen shirt and a claret waistcoat with a black silk tie, he looked quite dashing. His dark brown hair was combed back, accentuating his patrician features and the masculine line of his jaw. Naturally there was a hint of surprise in his green eyes, but a joyful smile lit his handsome face.

"Why, Mara, what a surprise to see you here!"

And just like that, her last-minute panic and doubts dissipated like morning mist in the sunlight. He was happy to see her! He wasn't cross with her in the least for being there. Mara hadn't made a mistake at all. Her initial instincts had been correct.

"Good afternoon." She smiled at him, her heart pounding wildly.

"Not that it isn't wonderful to see your beautiful face, but I must ask . . ." He paused and stared at her. "What brings you here? There is nothing wrong, I hope?"

"No. Nothing is wrong at all except that I needed to see you," she said. "And I wish to speak to you about something."

"I'm not going to tell you that you shouldn't be here unescorted, because you are certainly aware of that fact. But here you are, so please, do have a seat." He showed her to the brown leather wing-backed chair she had assumed was his, and when she was settled, he sat upon the sleek burgundy leather sofa across from her. His expression darkened. "I thought we resolved this the other morning. What more can we say, Mara?"

Mara took another deep breath before speaking. "Well . . . ever since we spoke in your carriage, I've been trying to understand our situation a little better and I require some answers. Might I ask you some questions about your marriage?"

His dark brown eyebrows furrowed with confusion. "My marriage?"

"Yes."

He gave a slow nod of his head. "I suppose so."

"Where is your wife?" she questioned. Mara needed to know why he said he did not live with his wife.

He answered evenly. "She lives on our estate in Yorkshire."

"She doesn't wish to live here with you?"

"No. We have not lived together since the first month we were married."

This was not completely unheard of, if not a little odd. Many husbands and wives lived apart and led separate lives. Foster's marital state of permanent separation also gave her another glimmer of hope. "Why do you not live together? I gather you do not love each other?"

Foster sighed with heavy resignation. "Ours was an arranged marriage, to please our parents and join our estates. I tried to love Rose in the beginning, I did. But Rose made loving her quite impossible."

Rose. Her name was Rose. Putting a name to his wife made her seem more real. Foster had a wife named Rose. Mara took a breath and asked the other question that made all the difference to her.

"And have you any children?"

"No." He laughed bitterly. "No, I have no children. Rose made having children quite an impossibility, since she would never allow me to touch her."

"Oh, my." Mara pondered the very personal implications of what Foster just revealed.

She was not unaware of the intimacies between men and women. Paulette had been quite forthcoming with her about those types of things and the two of them had had some very frank conversations over the years. Mara understood what happened in the marriage bed, or what didn't happen, in Foster's case, to create children. What he had just revealed to her was quite shocking.

She thought of all the loving and happy marriages she knew of, and her own family in particular. Her parents were still quite besotted with each other. They held hands, hugged each other, and Mara frequently caught them kissing. Aunt Colette and Uncle Lucien were happily married, as were Aunt Juliette and Uncle Harrison. And so were Aunt Lisette and Uncle Quinton, and of course Aunt Yvette and Uncle Jeffrey. And now her cousin Sara and the Earl of Bridgeton were wildly happy together.

She'd heard of unhappy marriages, certainly. However, for the most part, Mara had only ever witnessed husbands and wives who were quite contented with each other. None of them would ever consider living apart from each other.

Now Foster and his wife . . . Rose. Foster didn't have much of a marriage. It must be terrible to be tied to someone you did not love, let alone not even like. It made her sad to think of it. And also extremely puzzled. Who was this woman who could not love Foster Sheridan? What was there not to love about him? Or what was there to detest so greatly that she could not abide living in the same house with him? As far as Mara could tell, Foster was quite perfect.

"How long have you been married to her?" she asked.

"Ten years."

They'd been living apart for *ten years*? It boggled her mind to think of it. How did that happen in a marriage? How did it get to a point with his wife, with whom he was supposed to build a life, that they ended up apart?

"And in all that time you've never lived with her or kissed her or . . . or anything . . ." Mara's voice faded.

"In the beginning, yes." He began slowly, instinctively understanding what she was asking. "I shall be quite frank with you, Mara. Intimacy was never comfortable between us. Rose is not particularly easy to please or to be with. We were both young when we wed. I did make . . . attempts . . . at creating children with her. But she would cry and scream and carry on, so that I simply could not—"

He paused, staring at her with the saddest eyes she'd ever seen.

"I've never shared this with anyone."

Impulsively, Mara moved to sit beside him on the sofa, placing her hands in his. He accepted her gratefully. His hands were warm and instantly made her feel calmer. Whenever Foster touched her, she felt that inexplicable connection between them. She was now convinced that she made the correct decision in visiting him today.

"So for the past ten years you've not had a real marriage with her in the true sense at all, have you?" Mara asked.

He shook his head again. "No, we've never . . . It was simply easier to live apart. We have absolutely nothing in common. We share nothing together. Rose and I detest each other."

"Have you thought about . . . a divorce?" There. She'd finally said aloud the scandalous word that she had been wondering about. If they were so terribly unhappy, why would they remain together?

Once again a harsh and bitter laugh escaped him. "Have I thought about a divorce? Only every single day for the last ten years."

She gazed at him, seeing the years of hurt and disappointment reflected in his eyes. "Well, what prevents you from getting one? You seem to have grounds."

Foster sighed heavily. "That's a very good question. I'm not quite sure why I haven't pursued a divorce. There are many reasons. Pride. Convention. Aversion to scandal. Not caring enough anymore, I suppose."

Suddenly nervous again, Mara simply stared at him and then just blurted out the radical thought that had been spinning around her head since they met in the park three mornings ago. "Foster, I don't care that you are married."

He remained silent, but his eyes widened slightly at her words.

She continued to explain. "I have no wish to marry. Anyone. I never have."

Again he said not a word. His brows drew together in confusion.

"Don't you see, Foster? I have no designs on you. I am not interested in marriage . . . I simply want to be with you any way I can."

He shook his head in utter disbelief. "You don't know what you're saying, Mara."

"Yes. I do." She had given the matter of marriage a great deal of thought, for longer than she could remember. Mara knew she could never marry, would never marry. It was too dangerous to risk having children. Discovering that Foster was a married man actually made her situation easier. She'd thought of nothing else since she learned he was married.

"Mara, what you are implying isn't the life for a girl like you. You're the daughter of an earl, for God's sake."

But it's all she could have. It was the most she could risk. "I don't know quite how to explain it to you . . . But I'm not like other girls who wish for a husband, marriage, and a home with children. Especially children. So don't you see? It's a solution to both our problems."

With a skeptical glance, he said, "My darling girl. You barely know me. How can you wish for this . . . To be my mistress? Is that what you want to be? Because that is what you are intimating."

"It's not an ideal situation by any means." Her cheeks warmed.

It wasn't as if she'd dreamed of being a man's mistress her whole life. And to be completely honest with herself, suddenly hearing the word said out loud sent a slight shudder through her. But becoming his mistress would allow her to be with the man she loved without the expectation of marriage and children. And Mara knew without a doubt that she loved Foster Sheridan. With him she would be safe.

"You cannot become my mistress," Foster said emphatically.

"Are you saying you haven't had a mistress before?" She looked knowingly at him. "In all these years living apart from her, you've lived like a monk? I'm aware that I'm naïve, but I'm not stupid. You must have had a mistress."

"Whether I have had a mistress or not is beside the point, Mara." He rose from his seat, putting a little distance between them. "I cannot believe we are even having this conversation."

"So you have had a mistress." Mara idly wondered what the woman had been like. For that matter she wondered what his wife was like. An irrational pang of jealousy flickered through her at the thought of Foster kissing another woman. It was ridiculous, she knew, but still she couldn't help feeling that way.

Foster avoided her eyes. "Mara, you must go home now." His jaw clenched. "You are a lady. You are the daughter of an earl. You cannot become my mistress. Your father would undoubtedly kill me. Your reputation would be destroyed and your life would be forever ruined. You must leave here. Now."

Her heart began to race at the thought of leaving him. No. This was not how this afternoon was going to end. She refused to leave, not when she knew in her heart that the two of them were meant to be together.

"Will you kiss me first?"

"Mara, please don't do this." His hands balled into fists.

"I need to know what it feels like to kiss you. Please, Foster," she whispered, heat flaming her cheeks. "I've never been kissed by anyone before. Can I at least have one kiss from you to cherish before I go?"

He stared at her, his expression pained. "Mara . . ."

Inspired by the conviction of her heart, she rose from the sofa. "Kiss me once and then I shall leave if you still wish me to. I promise."

A taut silence grew between them. She trembled, not knowing what to do next, but she took an instinctive step closer to him. Her forward behavior was completely out of her usual character, but Mara did not waver.

Foster remained motionless as if he feared the slightest movement would weaken his resolve. "I'm afraid if I kiss you, I won't ever let you leave."

"Then let me stay with you."

An endless moment stretched between them. They both knew they were treading in very dangerous waters. With their eyes locked on each other, Mara held her breath, waiting for him to kiss her.

For a fleeting moment Mara wondered what on earth she was doing in this man's home . . . A man she barely knew. A married man, no less. Perhaps he was right after all. She should just go home. Standing there and practically begging him to kiss her was not only incredibly foolish, it was decidedly reckless. Idiotic. Shameful.

Even so, she wouldn't want to be anywhere else. She willed him to kiss her. And deep in her heart she knew that he would. It was simply how it was with them.

With an anguished groan, Foster slowly reached for her, pulling her closer, and her heart soared. She was so close she could smell the scent of him, manly and warm. She tilted her face toward his.

Then he placed his hands on either side of her face. In a hoarse voice, he whispered, "I have wanted to do this since the moment I first saw you."

Lowering his head, he tenderly placed his lips upon hers. Sighing, she closed her eyes and gave in to his kiss.

His lips were warm, soft, and inviting . . . inviting her to take more from him. His hands slid from her face to her neck and then down her shoulders and along her back, drawing her into his embrace.

Mara's arms found their way around him, reaching up and clasping his neck as their kiss deepened. A wondrous thing it was, this kiss. When his tongue entered her mouth she became weak all over. She sighed into his mouth, eager to melt into him. Oh, heavens! It was a deliciously wicked and incredibly intimate kiss. Never imagining a kiss could be like this . . . this mad, overwhelming, all-consuming rush of desire that flooded her whole being.

On and on it went. Nothing else in the world seemed to matter. It was as if they had both been starving, and kissing each other was their sustenance. She never wanted it to stop.

Her entire focus was on Foster. The feel of his hands on her body thrilled her. The taste of him on her tongue excited her. The masculine scent of him enveloped her. The sound of his heart pounding in his chest filled her ears. Or was that her own heartbeat she heard? Her pulse increased, as his hands slid back up and untied the laces on her velvet bonnet. In a swift motion her bonnet was off her head and lying on the floor. His fingers splayed into her blond hair as he deftly loosened the pins that had held her elegant coiffure in place. Her silvery blond tresses spilled around her shoulders and he gasped her name.

If she had ever dreamed about kissing a man, this would be her dream come true. They didn't need words or explanations. This kiss sealed their fate together and they both knew it. Whatever the consequences were, they would face them together. She felt it with a certainty, a clarity that buoyed her spirit and chased away any doubts over what they were getting themselves into. She was meant to be with this man. They were meant to be together.

With a sudden movement, Foster stopped kissing her

and cradled her face in his hands once more, staring at her intently. He whispered, "My God, Mara . . ."

She nodded her head. "I know."

"You need to leave now. Do you hear me, Mara?" His voice was raspy. She could hear the almost desperate plea in his words. "Turn away and walk out that door right now. This mustn't happen between us."

"It's already happened."

"No." He shook his head with decision, as if denying what she said was true. He seemed quite panicked. "No. It's not too late. Not yet."

"Oh, it is far, far too late. You see"—looking up at him, she smiled—"I'm in love with you."

8

Emotions

Foster could not breathe.

As he stared into the mysterious gray eyes of the beautiful creature in front of him, he could not breathe. She had quite literally taken his breath away with her sweetly whispered words.

I'm in love with you.

No one had ever said those words to him before. No one.

And here was this incredible woman he barely knew declaring her love for him after one kiss. Granted, as kisses go, it was by far the most splendid kiss he'd ever experienced. Not a doubt about that. So what was it about this particular woman? Why did she have this effect on him? What was it about her that made him yearn for something he could never have? Why did he long to spend the rest of his life with her by his side? What was this compelling connection he felt to her?

I'm in love with you.

How could she possibly love him? No one had ever loved him, for he was not lovable. He'd known that his whole life. His parents, self-absorbed with their own lives, had not loved him. His wife, cold and distant, had not loved him. None of the women he had sought comfort with over the years had loved him either. He'd heard talk of love, read stories of love, and seen love poems, but Foster had never truly experienced it. Although he had secretly longed for it all of his lonely life.

Yet again, Mara awakened something deep inside of him. It was hope.

Suddenly with Mara, there was a hope of escaping the miserable existence that was his current plight. Being shackled to an icy harridan with no feelings, who hated him, was the summation of his life. He'd failed at his marriage because he'd been unlovable.

I'm in love with you.

His heart flipped over in his chest. He'd never felt this way before. As he gazed into her fathomless gray-green eyes, he wondered idly if she were some sort of enchantress. He definitely felt bewitched by her. With her pale blond hair spilling around her shoulders, she looked more womanly and more beautiful than she had earlier. He wanted her, yes, but more than just physically. He wanted a life with her, as unattainable as that was. Everything about this, about her, was *impossible*.

But now . . . Now Mara gave him hope that anything was possible.

I'm in love with you.

He lowered his head and kissed her sweet lips again, completely losing himself and his heart in the process. He wanted to kiss her and never stop. But he did stop, because he had to.

"How can you possibly be in love with me?" he murmured in her ear, suddenly afraid to look at her. "You know nothing about me."

"I just know that I am. I've known it since the moment we first met."

He still couldn't face her. "This isn't right."

"I know it isn't right." Her voice was the softest whisper. "But I can't help it, because being with you feels right to me."

God help him, neither could he. As he held Mara closely in his arms, he noticed the darkening room. How had it grown to be so late? The sun had already begun to set and the drawing room filled with long shadows. In this half-light, in these dusky shadows, nothing seemed to matter but the two of them. Together.

The silence and dimness of the room enveloped them, cocooning them together. He continued to hold her, listening to her soft breath, caressing her silky hair, wishing with all his heart that things could be different between them.

They were on the precipice of falling into a situation that they could not easily extricate themselves from. He sensed her willingness, almost eagerness, to enter into it, and that terrified him. They would be crossing a line that would ruin her if anyone found out. He didn't give a damn about his own reputation, his own consequences. It did not matter. His life was ruined in any case. But Mara . . .

His precious Mara had her whole life ahead of her still.

There was no possible future for them if they embarked on this foolish course. The only outcome of an affair of this magnitude was ruin and scandal and heartbreak.

Yet as he held this beautiful woman close to his heart, he knew what she knew. They belonged together. He was hers and she was his, just as she said. He believed it too. Whatever it was that brought them together, whether it was called destiny, or fate . . . or a curse, he believed it.

"If we do this, Mara . . ."

She pulled away and looked up at him. "There is no *if*, Foster."

"There's so much more at risk for you."

"I know there is," she said evenly. "And I don't care."

He found himself lost in her eyes again, unable to deny her. He sighed softly. "Where does your family think you are right now?"

"That I'm still working at one of the bookshops."

"You work at a bookshop?" If she had said that she sprouted wings, Foster couldn't have been more astonished.

She laughed a little at his surprise. "Yes, it's my mother's family's business. I'll explain all about it at another time. But for now, no . . . my family is not expecting me home yet. And just in case, before I left today I instructed my lady's maid that if I wasn't home by half past six, to tell my aunt that I had a headache and would be staying in my room for supper. So I won't be missed at all this evening . . ."

"What are you saying?" Had the woman completely lost her senses? "You came here this afternoon with a plan in mind?"

"Well, I just wanted to be sure . . ." She hesitated, looking slightly embarrassed. "In case anything . . . did happen between us tonight . . . that I could . . . stay . . ."

"Mara."

She gave him an artless look. "Truly, as long as I'm home before breakfast, it'll be fine. No one will know I am gone or worry about me."

He cupped her face and kissed her, unable to do anything else. He knew where this was leading. He wanted it desperately and dreaded it simultaneously. Perhaps if they had more time? If they had supper first, maybe he could talk to her rationally and persuade her to end this before it went any further.

"Wait here a moment, Mara, please," he said, placing a kiss on top of her head. "I shall return quickly."

He walked to the door of the study, and he glanced back at her, standing there in the dim light, with her flaxen hair tousled around her shoulders. She smiled at him and his heart flipped over in his chest. How could someone so small and angelic have turned his world completely upside down with a single kiss?

Foster hurried to summon Preston, his butler, and gave him some specific instructions. Preston had been with him for years and knew how to be discreet. In fact, Foster's entire house staff was exceptionally loyal to him, but this was a very special matter. He could not have Mara's name bandied about. On that point he was quite clear.

As he made his way back to the study, he questioned his motives for this evening. His conscience battled with his heart, and not over any sense of loyalty to Rose or the hollow vows taken in a chapel ten years ago. As far as Foster was concerned, Rose was the one who ended their marriage and broke their vows on the very night of their wedding, when she'd turned him out of his own bed. And that had given him free license to do what he wished, even if that meant keeping a mistress or two or three or four over the years.

His conscience was pricking him as if with giant pitchforks.

His worry was solely for Mara.

Tonight would irrevocably change the course of her life. For as much as he wished for her to leave, for her to never see him again and go away and marry well and happily, he did not want her to. In a bafflingly short amount of time, she had come to be his. He didn't want her to be with anyone else. Foster wanted Mara to be with him. It was selfish and cruel of him, but he couldn't stop what was happening any more than he could stop a bullet discharged from a pistol.

He opened the door to the study, which was now almost completely in shadows, since his servants had not yet been in there to light the lamps. Mara's slight silhouette was outlined in front of the window. She turned as he entered and flew to his arms.

They kissed, and again he was astonished by the intensity of feeling between them.

"You're quite sure about this?" he asked her.

"Absolutely positive."

He half smiled at her. "I'm afraid that I'm not."

She stood on her tiptoes and placed a kiss on his cheek. "It will all be fine. I promise."

He wished he could believe that.

"I've arranged for us to have an early supper together. We can discuss all of this a bit more . . . and I hope that I can change your mind, Mara." He gave her a knowing look and gave a silent prayer that one of them would come to their senses and stop this entire hopeless matter.

"I won't change my mind," she answered calmly.

"Come with me then," he whispered, giving in to her. He took her small hand in his, loving how it perfectly fit within his, their fingers intertwined. He led her down the hallway to the dining room. The fire had been lit and the room had a warm glow from the silver candelabras reflecting off the polished wood of the long table, which was set for two.

Wondering how she could be so self-possessed, he helped her to her seat at the table. Her place had been set across from his seat at the head. After he sat down, she suddenly picked up her plate, utensils, and napkin and moved it all the length of the table to sit to the right of him.

"I don't wish to be way down there," she announced as she rearranged her place setting. "It's too far away from you."

Foster laughed, glad for what she had done. "I rather like the change and having you closer to me. But I suppose the distance would have been wiser."

Mara gave him a rueful smile. "None of this is wise, Foster."

Preston entered, looking a bit surprised to see that his table had been reset, but without a word he moved the candelabra from the center of the table closer to the edge where they sat, and adjusted their glassware.

"Thank you, Preston," Foster offered, grateful that he could trust his butler implicitly. No other servants except for Preston would be permitted to know that Lady Mara Reeves was even in the house. No one else had seen her, and Foster wanted to keep it that way.

"Yes, thank you," Mara piped up.

"It's my pleasure, my lady." He poured some red wine into their crystal glasses. "I shall be back momentarily with supper, my lord." With a slight bow, he left the dining room.

"What shall we drink to?" she asked, her smile excited.

Foster raised his glass to Mara's. "To meeting each other . . ."

She nodded and tipped her glass to his. "Yes, to meeting each other."

After they sipped their wine, Mara asked, "Did you have somewhere to be tonight? I feel foolish for not asking sooner. I arrived so unexpectedly on your doorstep. Have I altered your plans?"

If he had had plans for the night, he honestly couldn't remember what they were. Was it a supper party at Lady Abbott's? Or was he meeting with his friends at the club for some cards? Had he told his latest paramour that he would visit her later this evening? Was he attending an exhibit of the latest in photographic cameras? He was sure he had some such affair to attend. He usually filled his nights that way, but nothing else seemed to signify now. And he did not mind in the least.

"You have altered my plans considerably, Mara, but you are all that matters to me this evening."

She gave him a delighted smile. He took her hand in his and brought it to his lips, placing a soft kiss upon her fingers. She squeezed his hand in return. It was an intimate gesture and he felt thrilled to just have her seated beside him. Feeling like a love-struck schoolboy, he released her hand just as Preston returned, carrying a large silver tray.

"So please tell me about this bookshop you work in," he said when the butler had finished serving them a delicious fillet of beef and left the room. "I'm quite intrigued by the idea of you working."

"My mother's family has two stores in London," she began. "The original Hamilton's Book Shoppe and the Hamilton Sisters' Book Shoppe. We also opened another Hamilton's in Dublin."

"Why, I've visited each of those London shops!" Foster said in amazement. "Many times, actually. They're both wonderful places. I'm surprised I haven't seen you there before."

"I love that you've been there! Don't forget I spend half of the year in Ireland, so it's not surprising that we never saw each other at one of the London shops." Her gray-green eyes sparkled and reflected the candlelight. "Since I was a little girl I helped my mother, or I should say more accurately, my stepmother, in all the shops. I usually work in one shop or the other, about three days a week, depending. From assisting with customers, or arranging the bookshelves, to managing the employees, just about everything there is to do in a bookstore, I've done it. My favorite part of the store is the children's section though."

Mara's face grew beautifully animated as she spoke at

great length about the places and people she loved while telling the family history of the Hamilton sisters. Mesmerized by the warmth and beauty that emanated from her as she described her life, Foster hung on every word she said. He even managed to follow all the names of the different branches of the family and their children: the Sinclairs, Flemings, Roxburys, and Eddingtons. Foster had already met two of her uncles, the Duke of Rathmore and the Marquis of Stancliff, over the years, and the Sinclair brothers, but he had never realized how they were all connected by marriage to the five Hamilton sisters. Mara belonged to a large and very close family, something he had never had.

As they continued with their meal, he asked more questions about them.

"And your brother . . . Thomas, you said his name is? Does he help with the shops as well?"

Mara nodded enthusiastically as she explained. "Yes, Thomas works there from time to time, but not nearly as often as I do. My mother and her sisters think it's important for all of the Hamilton cousins to know how to manage the shops, but they especially want us girls to be prepared to oversee the business one day if we choose to. It's just not as necessary for the boys. Thomas will be the Earl of Cashelmore someday, and my cousin Phillip, who I was with the night we met, he'll inherit his father's marquisate. My aunts also prefer to have females managing the stores. They want to provide more opportunities for women to work and become independent."

"It's incredible and quite admirable of them, actually," Foster remarked. Mara spoke intelligently about her work and took pride in what she did, which was highly unusual. She was not a vapid society girl whose only interest was in pretty gowns, beaus, and marriage. "Your mother and her sisters have created a bookstore empire, so it seems!"

"Yes, I suppose they have." She beamed with pride. "And we may be expanding yet again with a new idea for a children's bookshop."

"By the look on your face, I can guess that a bookstore for children is your idea." He couldn't help feeling proud of her himself. She looked so happy with what she did.

She nodded modestly. "Aunt Colette and I are already looking into possible locations."

He paused a moment, a bit in awe of her. "You are a part of something quite impressive, Mara."

"It is rather exciting," she admitted a bit shyly.

Foster found himself admiring her and her family. "Tell me about Ireland."

If he thought Mara had been animated while talking about her family and the bookshops, it was nothing compared to the spark that was lit within her when she began to describe Ireland.

"It's a beautiful, magical place, full of troubles to be sure, but the countryside is truly magnificent," Mara said. "I suppose because I was born there I feel quite at home in the green hills, so at peace. There's a mystical quality to that island that draws me back whenever I'm away for too long."

"I'm honored that you stayed away from a place you love just on the chance of seeing me." It touched him that she had forgone time with her family in the land that she cherished, in order to be with him.

"It was a chance I was most willing to take and I'm very happy that I did," she said with a satisfied grin, and then brushed off her sacrifice with an airy wave of her hand. "I've spent most of my life in Ireland and will be returning there again very soon, so I haven't really missed anything at all by staying in London."

"Which place do you prefer? Living in London or Ireland?"

Mara was quick to respond. "Well, there is no comparison, since they are completely different places. London is a bustling, exciting city and my aunts, uncles, and cousins are all here. And the bookshops, of course. I love it here. But back in Ireland, we're out in the countryside where it is beautiful and calm and peaceful. I love to go for long walks along the rocky stream that runs near the main house or ride my horse across the green fields in the mist. And I can still have the advantages of city life and Hamilton's Book Shoppe there, because Cashelmore Manor, our home, is not that far from Dublin at all."

"I believe you extended an invitation for me to visit you there the night we met." He gave her a little wink and enjoyed watching her blush. "I shall have to take you up on that." And indeed he would love to see her in her natural setting.

"I do hope you will come," she countered. She paused a moment and looked at him apologetically. "But I feel as if I have been talking far too much."

"No, not at all." He could listen to her all night.

"I'm sure I have rambled on too long already. Preston is about to bring in our dessert. So please, Foster, tell me something about you now," she cajoled with a smile he found hard to resist.

"I'm sorry to disappoint you, but I've nothing half so exciting to share as you."

"My life is hardly what anyone would call exciting. Tell me about your family at least, and your childhood."

He sighed in acquiescence, for it seemed he could deny this woman nothing.

"I had the typical English upbringing for the son and heir to an earl. I've nothing unusual about my boyhood to regale you with. I was raised mostly by various stern and proper nannies on our family estate in Yorkshire until I left to attend Eton. I then went on to Cambridge. I was an average student by all accounts. I honored my parents by agreeing to the arranged marriage they orchestrated, and at twenty years old, I wed Rose Davenport, simply because it joined her family's estate with ours. Since then, both of my parents have passed away. I'm an only child, so I have no brothers or sisters to tell you about. I have a younger cousin on my father's side, who will inherit the earldom since I have no heirs of my own and I'm not very likely to at this point. I now manage the Sterling estate and live in London full-time, far away from the woman in Yorkshire who calls herself my wife." He sipped his wine.

He'd omitted the specifics about his neglectful and cold parents, his desperate and solitary childhood, and the sordid details of his dreadful marriage to Rose. Aside from that, he'd summed up his entire life story.

Yet Mara gazed at him quizzically. "I believe you've glossed over some rather important parts in that abbreviated version of your life. But I'll let that go for now." She paused before adding, "I saw some interesting magazines in your study."

He smiled, pleased that she had noticed. "You've hit upon my hobbies now."

"You seem to be curious about many things."

"I'm curious about everything." He nodded with enthusiasm. "We live during an exciting age and I like to keep up with the latest inventions and designs. There has been so much progress technologically and there are many incredible new innovations. I'm a member of various clubs that focus on these types of things and the most current developments. I've actually started a business, investing in the devices that I think will be the most useful and important in people's lives. I'm about to have my townhouse wired for electricity, which will change everything. However, the automobile is my newest passion."

"Oh my!" Mara's face was filled with awe. "That does sound exciting!"

"It is," Foster explained. "We're on the brink of a new century! Everything will be different. Everyone will have electric connections and telephones in their homes before long. It's the wave of the future."

"Do you truly think so?"

"It's already happening."

"So you're a modern man, then? A bit of a visionary," she remarked.

"I like to think of myself as one." He grinned at her, easily envisioning this woman in his future.

When they had finished a delicious trifle that his skilled cook had prepared, they made their way back to the study, which was now lit and had a fire burning to ward off the autumn chill.

He poured them each a brandy and he sat beside her on the leather sofa that faced the mantel, not daring to hope or think how this unusual evening would end.

"I recall you said something earlier about your stepmother. Paulette is not your real mother then?" he asked before taking a sip of his drink. He needed it to steady his nerves.

"Paulette has been my stepmother since I was five years old and has been a mother to me in every way, so I always call her mother. I love her as my mother, truly. She is the reason I have such a wonderful family and so many cousins and the bookshops. Paulette transformed what would have otherwise been a very depressing childhood into a very happy and loving one." Mara hesitated a moment before confiding, "But my real mother died."

Foster watched as her expression grew somber, almost haunted. Her eyes were so expressive and hid nothing. They fascinated him. Now they seemed full of darkness and perhaps a little fear as well.

"Did she die when you were born?" he asked gently. Many women died in childbirth. Sadly enough, it was not an uncommon occurrence.

"No, not when I was born." Mara shook her head slowly. "When I was four years old, my mother died in a fire."

"How terribly tragic!" The look on her face was something he'd never seen. Setting down his glass, he reached for her hand. It was as cold as ice. "I'm so very sorry."

"I was there when it happened." Her voice quavered a little. "I watched my mother burn to death."

"Good God, Mara . . ." He held her hand tighter, covering it with his other hand, hoping to infuse warmth into her.

"There at the end of the hallway outside her bedroom, with flames everywhere, I could see her, but I could not save her. She screamed and screamed and called my name over and over and I couldn't move. The flames consumed her."

Horrified by what she'd said, Foster could not imagine the wretched circumstances that led to an innocent child witnessing her mother's ghastly death, but he could so easily picture her as a sweet, wide-eyed, fair-haired little girl. However, the thought of a young Mara having to behold such a supremely gruesome sight wrenched at his heart.

"How did you manage to escape the fire yourself?" he asked.

"My father." Her voice still shook. "He saved me just in time. He carried me out of the burning house, but we could not save my mother."

"Oh, Mara. No child should have to go through something that horrific." He brought her hand to his lips and kissed her tenderly.

"I've never told that story to anyone before." She looked a bit surprised. "It seemed most everyone I knew was already aware of what happened to me when I was a child. No one ever talks about it with me."

"I'm honored that you'd confide in me." He didn't have the words to convey his sympathy and horror at what she had endured as a little girl. "Do you wish to talk about it now?"

"No. Not now. Not tonight." She gave him a weak smile. "I'm rather sorry I brought it up. I'd prefer to talk about something more pleasant with you. I certainly didn't wish to put a pall over our lovely evening together."

"You couldn't possibly ruin this night." He still held her hand in his.

They both grew quiet, lost in their thoughts of what this night together meant for them. The fire flickered in the hearth. The clock on the mantel chimed half past eight. He'd thought about it all through their early dinner, what they were about to do. He was hoping one of them would end this foolishness. But he couldn't bring himself to it.

"It's not too late, you know," he murmured low. "I can take you home right now. In fact, I'm absolutely sure I should take you home."

"I don't wish to go home," she whispered. "I want to stay here with you."

His heart skipped a beat. "God help me, but I want you to stay with me more than anything I've ever wanted in my life." He leaned closer and pulled her into his arms.

She was warm and soft and willing, and delightfully eager. He breathed in the sweet smell of her floral perfume, which was now seared into his memory. The delicate scent of lily of the valley would forever elicit Mara's image.

Feeling protective of her, touched by her confidence in him, and wanting to ease the pain and heartbreak she had endured as a child, he kissed her tenderly, his lips moving with gentle pressure over hers. But she was having none of his gentleness and kissed him back with a ferocity and fervor that surprised him. How this exceptional woman came crashing into his life, he would never understand, but he knew nothing would ever be the same for him. Or her. They were now jumping into these perilous waters together.

He could happily drown within her and never come up for air.

9

Passions

It was utter madness, but a madness of the most delicious kind.

In a swift movement Foster lifted her off the velvet sofa, into his strong arms, and carried her from the study. He held her as if she weighed next to nothing. With her heart pounding and her head spinning, she clung to him, her head resting against his chest as he made his way down the corridor and up the main staircase.

She knew exactly where he was carrying her and she did not mind in the least. She wanted nothing more than to be with him. When they reached his darkened bedroom, he laid her gently on the bed.

"Are you sure, Mara?" he whispered.

"Yes," she whispered back.

He stepped back from where she rested upon his bed, and lit one of the gas lamps, which cast a gilded light in the room. Mara sat up on the bed and swung her legs over the side. She removed her little plaid jacket and then began to unlace her boots. It seemed such an ordinary act to perform under such extraordinary conditions. Removing articles of clothing was something she did every day. Yet the reason behind doing so now was drastically different. And knowing that Foster watched her as she did so was quite thrilling.

Her second boot had just fallen to the floor when Foster called hoarsely, "Stop. I'll do the rest."

She glanced up and saw that he stood beside the foot of the bed, already having removed his own shoes. He'd lost his black jacket and cravat and was only in his breeches and white linen shirt. He stepped toward her.

Slowly she slid off the side of the huge four-poster bed and, without a word, presented him with her back. A quiver went through her as she felt him undo the buttons down the back of her green plaid dress. After a bit of finagling they managed to remove the dress from her body. With astonishingly deft fingers, Foster undid the laces of her corset, freeing her from the bonds of its relentless confinement. Then he ran his hands along her shoulder, down her back to her hips, caressing her softly through the thin fabric of her chemise.

Mara luxuriated in the feel of his hands on her body, sighing deeply. He lifted her hair from her shoulders and kissed the nape of her neck, which sent delighted shivers through her. She leaned into him, pressing her back against the length of his body and he wrapped his arms around her. Never had she felt so secure and protected as she did with his muscular arms holding her.

"Foster?" she whispered, grateful that he could not see her face.

"Yes?" He continued placing hot kisses along her neck.

"Do you know how . . . ?" She could barely say the words, but she knew she had to. "That is, I . . . I . . . don't wish to end up with child."

"Of course I know what to do. I will take care of it. But Mara, please," he pleaded, "we should stop before we can't go back. Tell me to take you home now."

She turned around in his arms and faced him, trying to see his eyes in the dim gaslight. She reached up and placed her arms about his neck. "I'm with you. I am home."

He stared at her in disbelief for a moment or two. "I don't deserve you, Mara Reeves." Then he lowered his head and kissed her.

This kiss claimed her as his. Marked her as his. His lips were hot and demanding and as their tongues intertwined, she rejoiced in his possessiveness of her. Reveled in the belonging to him, of their belonging to each other. The searing kiss made her only want to be closer to him.

Before she knew what was happening, Foster had lifted her back on the bed and covered her small body with his. It was then she thought she'd died and gone to heaven. The sheer force of his masculinity was centered above her and it was the most exquisite feeling to have a man so close to her. She clung to him, their mouths still hot on each other.

Mara could barely breathe, couldn't see anything but the expanse of Foster's broad chest covered in white linen. They kissed and kissed and kissed some more. He lifted himself off her and she felt his hand stroking her thigh and sliding toward the garter that held her stocking in place. Again, with skillful fingers he undid the garter and, so slowly she thought she might faint from the suspense, he painstakingly rolled the pale silk stocking down the length of her leg, placing feather-light kisses against her heated flesh as he went.

Mara gasped in delight and almost fainted from pleasure when he turned his attention to her other leg, caressing and kissing her as he slid that stocking down as well. The wonderfully exquisite sensations left her weak.

She felt about ready to jump out of her skin when he rose above her and lifted his linen shirt over his head, tossing it to the floor. He arched over her once more and she was presented with the tantalizing gift of his bare chest.

With an awed reverence, Mara splayed her fingers across his broad chest, discovering the smoothness, the hard planes, and the crispness of the hair that covered the muscular expanse of male flesh and bone, marveling at this masculine body which was so different from her own. She placed her lips against his skin, feeling the warmth of him flow through to her. He sighed as her lips brushed his skin, and that emboldened her to explore with her tongue. She didn't think she could ever get enough of tasting his skin with her tongue, feeling the muscles in his arms, smelling the virile scent of him, looking at his magnificent body, and hearing the deep sound of his voice as he whispered her name.

Foster groaned and grasped her hands in his, raising them over her head, and in a smooth motion he divested her of her chemise, leaving her completely naked beneath him. She should have been nervous or hesitant or guilty or terrified. Yet she felt none of those things. Oddly enough, the sheer power and strength that emanated from him only comforted her.

Mara felt only a sense of rightness. Of certainty. Of belonging. Of being exactly where she was supposed to be. With this man. As Foster rolled to the side and he rested on his shoulder, he looked down at her nakedness with admiration.

"Mara, you're so beautiful." He lowered his head and kissed her tenderly on the lips.

Awash in feelings she never knew existed, she wound one hand around his back and up his shoulders, along his neck and into his thick brown hair. Feeling its softness between her fingers, she stroked his hair.

"Tell me to stop before it's too late, please," he implored her yet again, resting his forehead against hers. "Tell me to stop this madness now, my beautiful Mara, because, dear God, I haven't the strength to say it myself."

She couldn't possibly stop now! The very thought of tearing herself away from him at this moment was unbearable. If anything, she craved being with him even more. Placing her hands on either side of his face, she looked into his eyes.

"Please listen to me. I do not want to stop. I do not want you to stop this. Not now. Not ever," she said softly. "I want this. I want this with you, Foster. With all of my heart."

She kissed him then, and they were both lost.

Time seemed to have no meaning while they kissed. They could have been kissing for days or hours or merely minutes for all she knew. A languorous fervor came over her and her entire focus was on Foster and nothing else mattered in the least. She was not embarrassed or awkward or uncomfortable with their intimacy. Everything about the two of them together felt good. In fact, it felt perfect. His hands, his mouth, his tongue, the sound of his breathing, and the feel of his naked skin pressed against hers excited her. As their kiss grew in intensity, the ardent heat between them became almost intolerable.

With an agonized groan, Foster tore himself away from her and climbed out of bed. A short cry of protest escaped her. Then she realized he was removing his breeches. In the dim light she caught a glimpse of his nakedness and instinctively reached for him. He stood naked before her and she was breathless with wonder. Her hand encircled the rigid heat that protruded from his body. Fascinated by the combination of velvety smoothness, rock-hard stiffness, and inviting warmth of this very male part of him, she ran her fingers up and down and around his thick shaft.

He placed his hand over hers and slowly moved it away as he rejoined her on the bed. He positioned his body over hers. Having his naked body pressed against hers left her aching for something she could not identify. She arched her back and lifted her hips against his, relishing the feel of him between her legs.

"Good God, Mara," he murmured.

Every nerve in her body was set on fire with a great need for him to touch her in every conceivable way. And he began to do just that, to her complete and utter delight. It was as if he'd read her mind. He seemed to know what she wanted even before she did.

His kisses moved from her mouth to her cheek, down to her neck and dipped below to her chest. Her breath came in short gasps as he kissed first one breast, then the other, lavishing her with kisses and sucking on her nipples. Her body quivered as his mouth slid down across the taut expanse of her stomach, and liquid heat pooled within her. As she breathed in short gasps with her entire body trembling, he moved between her legs and kissed her.

It was shocking. It was shameful. It was glorious.

An indescribable sensation built within her as his remarkably skilled tongue awakened new pleasures within her. The feelings increased in intensity and he continued to caress her intimately with his mouth. Mara felt she would shatter if he kept on that way, and yet he continued his pleasurable assault on her. She held her breath, her flingers digging into the bedclothes, gasping for release as the pressure mounted within her. It seemed to go on forever.

And suddenly wave after wave of pure bliss washed over her entire body, causing her to scream Foster's name over and over. The unexpected explosion of pleasure left her dizzy and breathless. Before she could even recover and float back down to earth, Foster raised himself over her body once more, placing his arms on either side of her and positioning himself between her legs. In one sure and swift motion, he was inside of her.

She took a deep breath and braced her hands against his chest, as he gently began to move within her body. She adjusted her hips to accommodate him. Although a bit uncomfortable at first, she quickly grew used to the feel of him within her.

"Foster," she breathed, as tears welled in her eyes.

"Have I hurt you?" He instantly froze above her, his voice filled with concern. "Are you all right? Shall I stop?"

Mara couldn't explain to him that she wanted to cry not because she was in any physical pain, but simply because she was overcome with too many emotions to contain them any longer. It was the overwhelming feelings of love, completeness, connection, and again, that sense of belonging with this man, that brought her to tears.

"I am fine. I am more than fine," she managed to say, blinking the tears away. Then she rocked her hips against him to prove it.

With an impassioned sigh, Foster began to move within her, hesitantly at first, then with growing force. Wanting more, Mara wrapped her legs around his waist and matched his thrusts, bracing her hands against his broad shoulders. He groaned and brought his mouth down on hers. As they kissed, the intimacy of what they were doing to each other astonished her, touched her, and fascinated her. The two of them were joined as one this way, and bound together in a passionate rhythm. Her heart beat faster, her skin grew hot, and that wonderfully pleasurable pressure began to blossom within her again.

"Mara, I don't understand what you've done to me," he said in between heavy breaths as he continued to move inside of her. "I've never felt this way about anyone in my life before."

She clasped herself to him as he kissed her again, his motions growing more intense.

"I am so in love with you, Mara, I can't see straight."

Her heart fluttered at his words. She was in love with him too, but was too wracked with delight to speak. She could barely catch her breath because the movements Foster was making against her hips were sending shock waves of pleasure through her entire body but centered most intently at that point between her legs that he was so cleverly attending to.

Another burst of blissful delight raced through her. Again she called his name and clung to him for dear life as his thrusts increased their urgency. As ecstasy flooded her, every muscle in his body tensed and stiffened as he continued to thrust in and out of her, over and over again. She screamed his name just as he called hers. In a slick motion he pulled out, spending himself outside of her body, before he collapsed next to her, breathing heavily and covered in sweat.

They both lay motionless, panting and stunned.

With a heavy sigh Foster lay back on the pillows and pulled Mara alongside of him, so she rested her head on his chest. His heart thudded as loudly as hers. He wrapped his arms around her, holding her as if he would never let go. And Mara never wanted him to.

"That was . . . that was . . ." she murmured through half-closed eyelids. "I never imagined that it would be like *that*."

"It was more incredible than you could possibly realize," he responded. His fingers idly ran through her hair, which was a tangled mess. "It's not always like that."

"It was special for you too then?" she asked, feeling suddenly nervous. "It was definitely special for me, being my first time and all."

He opened his eyes, sat up a little, and cupped her face with his hand. "Look at me." He stared at her as if he still could not believe she was in his bed. "It was extraordinary for me because it was with *you*." His voice quavered as he declared, "I love you, Mara."

Her heart swelled with feelings for this beautiful man.

She had confessed that she was in love with him earlier and now he said it to her. "And I love you, Foster."

He continued to gaze intently into her eyes. "I have never said those words to another woman before in my life."

Tears suddenly welled in her eyes.

"If you cry now, Mara, I swear you will kill me."

She sniffed and blinked back the tears. "It's only tears because I'm overwhelmed with my feelings for you. I'm not the least bit sad."

"Thank God. If you were sad or regretful, I don't know what I'd do."

"No," she promised solemnly. "I don't regret one second of being with you."

"Me either." He released her, and placed a kiss on her lips and lay back down among the pillows.

They both lay there quietly in the pale light, lost in their own thoughts. There was no denying that everything had dramatically and irrevocably changed between them. No, she did not regret lying with him. Not at all. Whatever happened, come what may, she had had this magical night with him.

"What happens now?" she asked after a while. "How did it work with your other mistress?"

"You are not my mistress, Mara!" He was aghast.

She was truly baffled. "Then what am I?"

"I don't know, but you're not my mistress! And don't use that word in reference to yourself again." Foster seemed quite bothered.

"Well, all right, but I don't understand. How does this work between *us*? How often do we meet? Should I come here to your house each time? Do we arrange a secret rendezvous? I've heard that some gentlemen set their mistresses up in a house of their own. I doubt we could do that, considering my parents and I think th—"

"Mara!" Foster interrupted, suddenly sitting up in bed, clearly agitated. "Stop it! I could almost laugh at the ridiculousness of what you are saying, but it is not funny. Not at all. This is very serious and it is your *life* we're talking about."

She sat up too, clutching the bedsheet over her bare chest, and staring at him. His handsome face looked both panicked and appalled.

"I have not a clue how this is supposed to work between us because it wasn't ever supposed to happen!" His voice grew more and more upset. "You're an unmarried young lady from an aristocratic family and you most definitely are not mistress material, and I refuse to treat you as such. Or even use that word in reference to you. Furthermore, I wasn't expecting you to arrive at my house this afternoon and I certainly hadn't planned on bedding you this evening, so forgive me if I haven't worked out the logistics of our forbidden relationship just yet."

When he finally stopped for a breath, Mara asked calmly, "Are you finished?"

"No, I'm not finished! This should never have happened. I should not have laid a finger on you. What in God's name was I thinking? That's just it, I wasn't thinking, not with my brain at least. There's no excuse for it and no denying it. I'm a lowly cad. I should be offering to marry you right now. In fact, I want nothing more than to marry you. Instead I'm shackled to that shrew in Yorkshire—"

Mara put her hand over his mouth. "Stop. May I say something now?"

Foster rolled his eyes and brushed her hand away. "Fine."

Expelling a sigh of exasperation, she began, "I have already told you. I've no wish to get married, even if you were free. I don't want a husband or children, so you see it doesn't mat—"

"There!" he exclaimed in an accusatory tone. "I've been meaning to ask you about that. What exactly do you mean when you say you don't want to be married or have a husband or a family of your own? I've never met a woman who didn't want those things! Explain that to me, please. I'd really like to know."

Mara suddenly froze and her stomach sank in fear.

How could she tell Foster the truth of why she could never marry? She had never told a soul the reason why having a husband and children were out of the question for her.

"I just don't want to be married, that's all," she mumbled a bit feebly.

"There must be more to it than that . . . Tell me the reason why," he demanded.

The real reason was too terrible to utter aloud and Mara feared she couldn't form the words to tell him. The ugly truth of her life had haunted her ever since the night her mother died.

Her real mother, Margaret Ryan Reeves, had been insane, and Mara was quite certain that she suffered from the same malady. The strange premonitions she'd had over the years were proof of her mental instability, and their growing frequency was the beginning of its hold over her. Mara was just like her mother, and one day she too would go completely mad and throw herself into a fire, as her mother did.

Hadn't she heard over and over again, since she was a young girl, that she was exactly like her mother? Hadn't her father told her she was the very image of Margaret and possessed the same mannerisms and traits? She had also overheard the hushed, pitying tones her father used when speaking about Margaret, which alluded to her madness. Why, Mara had even heard her mother's family in Ireland whispering about her mother's odd behavior.

Margaret Ryan Reeves had been mentally ill when she died, and Mara knew without a doubt that she carried that same illness within her and that she was doomed to some tragic end, just as her mother was. It might not be totally evident yet, but she had seen the signs and was quite certain the day would come to pass when she could no longer hide the ugly symptoms of her insanity. Someday, her family would be forced to place her in an asylum, if something tragic didn't happen before then.

So how in good conscience could she possibly marry and risk passing on the madness to children of her own? Mara simply could not do it. She refused to place her own children in the position of seeing their mother lose her mind, as Mara had done.

The memories of her mother were fleeting and few. Margaret Ryan Reeves had been beautiful, with silvery blond hair and blue eyes. The scent of roses clung to her. She sometimes made room for Mara on her lap, where she would stroke Mara's hair and whisper words in Irish in her ear and sing silly lullabies. But her moods were strange and mercurial. She cried frequently, and Mara never knew if she was going to get a kiss or a slap when she spent time with her.

Then there was the terrible night of the fire . . .

Mara had carried the secret burden of this shameful illness for as long as she could remember. She was four years old when she had first heard the conversations of the adults around her who believed her too young to understand what they were saying. Her dear father's fear and dismay when he thought Mara could foresee the future confirmed what she had already suspected. Not only was she different from everyone else, she was also predestined to insanity.

Consequently Mara did the only thing she knew how to do to protect herself and her family. She hid her strange and peculiar visions from them all. Masking the signs of her oncoming madness, she kept to herself the premonitions that haunted her waking hours. She couldn't bear having any of them know and worry about her, for it would only bring them heartache and pain, especially to her father. He'd already lost his wife to the ghastly disease. He didn't need to suffer needlessly for years, knowing that his only daughter would share the same fate. She had vowed to hide it for as long as she was able.

To that end, Mara avoided all prospects of marriage, which was not overly difficult for her to do. Naturally shy, it was not a stretch for her to remain quiet and uninteresting to gentlemen. Years ago she had resigned herself to spending her life alone and unloved by a man.

The role of an unwanted spinster spiraling into lunacy was her fate.

Then Foster Sheridan had appeared and a light was struck within her. When she discovered he was already married, it suddenly seemed to be the perfect solution for her! She could be with the man she loved and be loved in return, without the obligation of marriage or the expectation of having children with him.

Now, he gazed at her with his pleading green eyes, wondering why she did not wish to marry or have children, and she simply could not bring herself to tell him the ugly truth. She would not be able to bear the look of revulsion and pity in his eyes if he knew about the terrible malady she inherited from her mother.

"Mara?" he prompted her.

"It's not . . ." she began slowly. "It's not so much that I don't wish to be married, it's that I don't . . . particularly care for children. A husband would expect his wife to bear his children, therefore I don't want to have a husband." It wasn't entirely a lie, but it was the best she could do.

Befuddled by her response, Foster chuckled a little. "That's it? That's all? You don't like children?"

Mara shrugged self-consciously.

Foster smiled and then laughed heartily. "Well, nobody likes other people's children, Mara! They tend to be dreadful, noisy, sticky little creatures. But I think you would change your mind about children if you had your own son or daughter to love and care for." He looked at her intently and turned serious. "If I were free to marry you, Mara, would you marry me and have my child . . . our child?"

The longing and soulful need in his words touched her heart like nothing she'd experienced in her life. How she longed to say yes! How she longed for it to be true! Imagining Foster as her husband and raising a beautiful little family together almost took her breath away with happiness. Tears suddenly welled in her eyes, knowing it could never happen. Foster was married and she couldn't risk passing along her madness to their children, so it could never be.

In the meantime, she would take what little joy she could with him, while she was able. Perhaps it was terribly selfish of her.

But it was all she could have. It was the best she could hope for.

So it didn't hurt to answer him with the words he wanted to hear. And in actuality, she wasn't lying, because it was what she wanted more than anything in the world. "Yes, I would marry you and have your children if I could, Foster."

"Ah, Mara." He leaned down and kissed her, as tears spilled down her cheeks. "Please don't cry."

"I'm so sorry." She cried for all the things she would not share with him in her life. She cried for the happiness that could have been theirs together. A happy home. A loving family. A life full of love as his wife and partner. Wiping at the tears with one hand, still holding the bedsheet with the other, she pasted another smile on her face and avoided his gaze. "I'm fine."

He placed his hand under her chin and tilted her face toward his, forcing her to meet his eyes. "I know you're not fine, because I am not fine either. But let's not torture ourselves tonight over what we cannot have in the future. It's enough right now knowing that we love each other, and if things were different . . . Well, if things were different I would be waking up every morning with you by my side. For now, we'll figure out the rest as we go, all right?"

She nodded, buoyed by his sweet words.

"As much as I wish I could keep you in this bed with me all night, and every night, it is long past time to get you home." Foster added, with a little wink and a kiss on the tip of her nose, "Let's get dressed first though."

Giggling together, they reluctantly rose from the sheets and stumbled around trying to find all their articles of clothing. Mara enjoyed the newfound intimacy of their dressing together and how they teased and helped each other to mask their sadness at parting. It had been an exquisite, sensual, unforgettable evening together. If nothing else, she had this night to cherish.

"Turn and let me do your gown," he commanded.

Laughing, she presented him with her back, idly wondering how she was going to arrange her hair in some semblance of order. "How did you acquire the skills of a lady's maid, or shouldn't I ask?"

"Don't ask," he said as he kissed the back of her neck. "Now hold still."

Foster was just fastening the buttons on the back of her plaid gown when it started happening . . .

Oh, no! Not now. Not in front of him!

The dizziness came on quickly this time and she gripped

the wooden post at the foot of the bed for support, her fingernails digging into the wood. Her green plaid gown felt as if it were suffocating her.

Oh, God, please, no. Not now. Please don't let it happen now in front of Foster!

Never had she tried so hard to fight the onset of a premonition as she did then. Mortified that he should see her this way, she tried to breathe deeply, to calm herself. She tried to resist what was happening to her.

But it was pointless to fight it. It was inevitable. Then, just as she knew it would, that curiously familiar prickling feeling crept over her skin little by little. Each and every nerve in her body was instantly alight with acute awareness. The blood raced in her veins, her heart beat uncontrollably, and she grew warm, yet she shivered. The soft hair on the back of her neck stood on end and her teeth clenched tightly. Mara held her breath, closed her eyes, and pressed the fingers of one hand to her temple while the other clung to the wooden bedpost.

Seemingly from far away, she heard a muffled cry from Foster, calling her name, his voice filled with alarm.

It was too late. She could not answer him, for she could not speak.

A heavy cloud of silence descended over her, cocooning her. Sharp pinpricks of consciousness lit up inside of her, flashing sparks of light from within.

And then it began . . . Misty images began to appear in her mind and then took the shape of what she dreaded most.

Fire.

Flames everywhere. Blinding bursts of light. Shattering explosions of heat and sound. Flickering curtains of bright orange and golden yellow. Breathtaking, scorching, smoldering heat. Trapped in the burning building, blazing embers and smoky ash filling the air, she heard agonized screams. Someone was screaming for help. Mara was lost and didn't know which way to go, which way was safe. Trapped. She was trapped in the swirling, relentless flames and acrid black smoke. She choked back a sob and recoiled from the smell of imminent death.

Her death. She was going to perish in this raging inferno.

She suddenly fell to her knees. A short breath of cool air and she gasped.

A man was calling her name, frantically calling for her. Foster! Hope raced within her. Through the smoke, he reached for her. She held her hand out to him, trusting him implicitly, knowing he would save her. The terror that held her in its grip disappeared at his touch. She wanted to be with him desperately. He pulled her to him, wrapping his strong arms around her, holding her close. Mara clung to him, filled with a sense of relief and happiness at being with the man she loved. She was safe, secure, and loved. She was his and he was hers. The certainty, the rightness of it was all-consuming. She belonged to him. They belonged together . . .

10

Revelations

"Mara! Mara!"
Foster stared at her in shock, wondering what was happening. One moment she was perfectly fine, teasing him about knowing how to fasten a lady's dress so well, and the next she seemed to be in the throes of some sort of trance. The color had completely left her face. Standing still as a statue, she appeared ashen and deathly cold. Her sharp intake of breath frightened him as she grasped the bed frame to hold herself up. He placed his arms around her, felt her trembling, her body tense with fear. She seemed not to see or hear him anymore, although he kept saying her name, now more as a whispered plea than anything else.

Was it a severe dizzy spell? Was she fainting or gripped by some unknown and terrible illness? She seemed transfixed by something only she could see. He'd never witnessed anyone act this way before. Not knowing what else to do, he continued to hold her, trying to comfort her in any way he could. It was only a moment or two, but it seemed like forever before he finally felt her body start to relax.

Slowly he pried her hand from the bedpost. With the utmost care he lifted her onto the bed and laid her down among the tangled bedclothes. He sat beside her, holding her hand in his.

When her eyelids fluttered open, he whispered, "Mara?"

Disoriented and confused, she stared at him for a moment before she suddenly cried his name, sat bolt upright, flung her arms around his neck, and sobbed.

"Mara, Mara, Mara." He murmured her name over and over, trying to soothe her. He held her tightly against him, rocking her gently back and forth. His hands stroked her back, her head, her hair. "I'm here. I've got you. You're all right. Everything is fine."

Although outwardly he remained calm and in control, inwardly he was very worried and confused. What had just happened? Why was she suddenly crying in his arms? Was she overwrought by their situation and that they had just made love? Had she been stricken by some mysterious feminine malady? Had he inadvertently done something to upset her or hurt her in some way?

As he held her in his arms, comforting this lovely woman who had suddenly come to mean the world to him, Foster experienced something he never had before. He wanted to cherish her, shelter her, and love her. He had the craziest sensation to keep her from ever being sad or scared or upset ever again. A tremendous need to protect her took over him.

This beautiful, passionate, ethereal, sensitive, slip of a girl, with her wide eyes, pert little nose, and sweet smile, had unexpectedly melted the cold, isolated world he had built around himself for the last ten years. Foster would never be the same again. Nor did he want to be. For the first time in his life, he felt wanted. He felt needed. He felt loved.

In a matter of days, Mara had completely changed his life.

He never would have believed such a thing was possible. That such a monumental, life-altering change could happen so quickly. That he could fall in love with a woman so effortlessly. He'd heard of love at first sight, but never thought it would happen to him. He never expected to be loved. Or to love someone else.

And he was in love with her. It was the only explanation for what he was feeling. He was head over heels in love with her. And he never wanted to let her go.

It was inexplicable. It was madness. It was love. Pure and simple.

He loved Lady Mara Reeves.

He belonged to her completely and she belonged to him. Just what they were going to do about this dreadful, tangled, complicated mess they found themselves in, he did not know. He hadn't quite formulated a plan yet, but he was working on it. One thing was for certain. She was not going to be just his mistress, because she deserved far more than that. She deserved far more than he could give her.

Basically Foster had spent his entire life alone, even though he was surrounded by people and friends. In his heart, he'd been alone. He'd felt unlovable and undeserving of love. And now that he'd found her, the woman he belonged with, the woman who had brought love into his life, he'd be damned if he'd ever give her up.

For once in his life he was going to be selfish. He was going to love Mara anyway, even though it made their lives a complex web of lies. He did not care. He'd spent years doing what was asked of him, what was expected of him, what was right. He'd obeyed his nannies and tutors and teachers. He'd acquiesced to his parents' wishes by being an obedient and respectful son. He'd given in to his wife's childish and petty demands, forgoing any of his own rights in their marriage.

And he was miserable.

Well, no more.

As he held Mara in his arms, he vowed to himself that from that moment on, he would do things differently. For once he would fight for what he wanted. And he wanted to spend his life with the woman who loved him in spite of all his weaknesses and failings.

"I'm sorry, I'm so sorry," Mara mumbled into his shoulder.

"There is nothing to be sorry about," he said soothingly, still stroking her back in slow, up-and-down motions, rocking her back and forth. He felt her relax against him and her crying begin to subside. "It's all right, my love. I'm here. I've got you. You're safe with me." And he meant every word he whispered to her. He would keep her safe as long as he was able.

"I didn't mean for that to happen in front of you," she said, her voice full of shame.

"So then it's happened to you before?" he asked. It was somewhat of a relief to know that he had not been the sole cause of her upset if she had experienced these effects before.

"Yes." Her head was still resting on his shoulder.

"What was the matter?"

Slowly she lifted her head and faced him. The sadness and fear in her gray eyes wrenched his heart as she stared at him. "Sometimes I have dizzy spells."

"That was more than a mere dizzy spell, Mara," he countered softly, as he smoothed the tousled hair away from her pretty face.

"No." She shook her head in defeat. "It wasn't just a dizzy spell . . ."

"What was it then?" he prompted.

Looking anguished, she finally blurted out, "Sometimes I see things."

"You see things? What kinds of things?"

She pulled away from him in a panic, avoiding his eyes. "Never mind. It doesn't matter. I should go home now." She scrambled to get down from the bed, but Foster blocked her way.

"Wait. Mara, please stop . . ." He put his hands on her shoulders to keep her from squirming around him. "Wait. It does matter. Look at me." He paused until she raised her wide eyes to his. "What happens to you matters to *me*. Something happened to you just now that worried me and clearly upset you. I love you and care deeply for you. I want to help you. Tell me . . . what things do you see? What do you mean?"

Her delicate brows furrowed. "I've never told anyone before . . ."

"I'm not just anyone." Foster took her hands in his.

She looked at him with the most trusting eyes. "It's difficult to explain . . . but sometimes I get . . . visions of what is going to happen. Little glimpses of the future, you could say. They are not always clear and I don't always understand the images that come to me. I can't explain why it happens to me and I can't control where or when or how often it happens or what I see. Usually it happens in the early morning, just as I'm waking or late at night when I'm alone in my bedroom. It just comes over me without any warning, just as it did now, here with you, and I get very dizzy, and hot and cold . . . and well, you saw for yourself . . ."

"And what did you see just now?" he asked, mesmerized by what she was telling him. Foster had read a book once about people who had the gift of sight and could see the future. It had fascinated him. Had Mara the sight?

"I'm not sure what it means . . . but I saw flames. There was a terrible fire somewhere. You and I were both there and in great danger. I was terrified, and I thought I was going to die. I was lost and separated from you, but you found me. I knew I was safe with you . . ."

"Was it just a bad dream?" he asked. Perhaps she was having a memory of the traumatic events she experienced as a child? Such a ghastly ordeal would scar a grown man, let alone an innocent little girl.

"I wasn't asleep, Foster," she said in an even tone, oddly calmer now. "You saw it happen. I was wide-awake. And it wasn't a dream. And it wasn't the first time this has happened to me. I've had dozens of these kinds of visions since I was a little girl. Everything I 'saw' eventually came to pass, even when I didn't understand what it meant at that time."

"All right then. Let's figure out what the one you had tonight means," he suggested. He hated to see her so distressed.

She seemed rather reticent. "Well, this one was quite different from all the others."

"In what way?"

"Because I've had this same vision once before. It's rather odd, because I've never had the same vision twice. It leads me to believe that what I'm seeing is very important."

"That makes sense . . ." If any of it made sense. Foster was a bit at a loss as to how to help her with this peculiar occurrence. If nothing else, he hoped he could apply some logic and calm her down. "When did you have the first one?"

"It was the night we met at my uncle's party. I had the vision for the first time just before I saw you in the hallway."

"Ah, that explains your dizziness and why you were resting."

She nodded. "Phillip saw me just afterward and insisted that I rest. But you were in that vision, so clearly! I was rendered speechless when we were introduced just a few moments later."

"So you had a vision about me, before you ever met me?" he asked, quite intrigued. There was something rather fatalistic about it and he wanted to know more.

"Can I tell you something?" she asked with hesitation.

"You can tell me anything, Mara."

"In my vision, we had such strong feelings for each other. It was the most incredible sense of love," she said. "And when I met you, I knew then that we belonged together."

As much as Foster hated to admit it, he had felt the same way about her. As an intelligent and rational person, he knew it made no sense whatsoever, but he had heard of stranger occurrences in the world. And the instant attraction he felt for Mara that night? He had attributed that to the old saying, love at first sight.

"Tonight's vision was remarkably similar to the first one I had," Mara continued. "There was the fire and I was trapped. I heard screaming and feared I was going to die. Then you found me. Once you had your arms around me, I knew I was completely safe. That I would always be safe with you."

The trusting look in Mara's eyes in that moment was almost his undoing. Foster knew then and there that he would do anything to keep this beautiful and wonderful woman from harm.

Even though Foster wasn't sure what any of it meant. He'd never personally known anyone who had visions, or possessed "the sight" before, and he didn't know if it was dangerous for her or not. Should he be concerned for her welfare? Was she merely reliving the past trauma with this vision of a fire? That actually seemed to be the most logical explanation, but he didn't believe that.

"I shall always keep you safe, Mara." He took her hand in his.

"I hope so . . ." She smiled sweetly at him. "But I'm concerned. In part of the vision something terrible is happening. There is a great fire and someone is dying. I don't know who it is, but we are in great danger, that much I could see. I know it sounds unbelievable, but I've never had a vision like this before, one that boded ill for *me*. The visions I've had in the past tended to be about others, and they all came true. I saw my cousin Sara marrying the Earl of Bridgeton before she loved him. I saw that my brother, Thomas, would be a boy before he was born. I saw that my cousin Christopher would break his arm . . . I saw ordinary things like that. Those were the types of visions I've experienced in the past. Nothing terribly dramatic and none of them ever involved *me*. So that I've had this vision of a fire that included me, twice now . . . I'm worried that something terrible is going to happen, Foster."

He pulled Mara into his arms, holding her close to his chest. "Nothing bad is going to happen to either of us. And even in your vision it seems the two of us are still together and safe at the end. That is all that matters to me."

"Are you sure?" she asked, her brows furrowed.

"Yes," he said. "And who is to say that any of it means anything? You're probably worrying over nothing at all." He kissed her. "Now it's past time that we get you home."

Reluctantly they both rose from the bed and readied themselves to leave.

A little while later Foster watched from his carriage as Mara made her way in through the servants' entrance to

Devon House. It was with a heavy heart that he returned to his own home.

He had promised that he would keep Mara safe.

Yet making plans to see her again continued to put the woman he loved in great danger.

11

Desolations

Rose Sheridan, Lady Sterling, stared out the window of her bedroom, which overlooked the wide expanse of fields and pastures that surrounded the sprawling estate known as Sterling Hall. The leaves were beginning to turn and dot the verdant landscape with bursts of gold, crimson, and yellow. It almost looked as if little fires were out there, burning in the trees.

She stood still, watching the mist rise and dissipate over the hills, taking no joy in the beauty of her surroundings. No delight in the timeless change of the seasons. No pleasure in the scenic view of the woods that used to bring her so much happiness.

None of it mattered to her. Not after her visit to London.

"I've brought your shawl, my lady. The air has a bit of a chill to it this morning."

Rose looked blankly at her lady's maid, Alice Bellwether, who had been taking care of her since she was just a fifteen-year-old girl and Alice was not much older. With a cloud of red curls around her wide, round face, Alice's chubby frame had given Rose a shoulder to cry on more than once. Alice Bellwether was the closest person Rose had to a friend in all the world.

Humming to herself, Alice draped the soft woolen shawl over Rose's thin shoulders, carefully adjusting the material until Rose was covered to her satisfaction.

Rose continued to stand motionless, her eyes on the soft clouds dotting the morning sky.

"You really should sit down and try to eat a little breakfast, my lady. It will help you feel better," Alice cajoled with a smile.

"I feel fine," Rose responded woodenly.

Alice sighed in resignation. "Well, I'll leave your tray here a little longer."

"You needn't bother."

The servant protested heatedly. "But the doctor said you are to keep up your strength, and to do that, you must eat the meals I bring to you."

"Never mind what the doctor said. I'm not hungry, Alice, so I'm not eating."

With an irritated huff, Alice announced, "I'm leaving the tray there on the table and I insist you eat something before I leave. At least have some toast. And then perhaps you might go for a walk today. It's a lovely day and the air will do you good." Her heavy frame bustled around the ornately decorated bedroom, putting things to rights.

Rose stared out the window, listless and disinterested. Ever since she came back from London she had been this way.

Her life was not her own anymore. Not that it ever really had been.

Not even thirty, Rose didn't recognize her own reflection in the mirror. She'd never been what anyone would describe as a beauty, but she had once been passably attractive.

Attractive enough to catch the eye of a handsome and

charming young footman who worked in her family's home, Brookwood Manor. Andrew Cooper had just been hired the summer she was seventeen years old and Rose was instantly smitten with the tall, blond, blue-eyed and laughing young man. She'd never seen anyone so devastatingly handsome. In his presence she seemed to come alive for the first time in her life.

For Rose Davenport had led a very sheltered existence.

The only daughter of Henry and Elizabeth Davenport was a disappointment to them in every way from the moment she was born. Henry Davenport, an extremely successful textile merchant, had made quite a fortune for himself. He married the beautiful and elegant Elizabeth Carroway, the daughter of a baron, in an attempt to raise his social status. Then they bought Brookwood, a large Tudor-style manor house, from the struggling estate of James Sheridan, the Earl of Sterling. After years of trying to have a child, the birth of their son John was the true highlight of their marriage and they pinned all their hopes on their bright and handsome boy.

Over ten years later, Rose was born, and as she understood it, she had not been an expected or wanted child. The pregnancy was exceptionally difficult on her mother, and the delivery was so harrowing it almost cost Elizabeth her life. When it was revealed that Rose was a girl, and not a particularly pretty baby at that, Henry and Elizabeth were less than delighted. They took little interest in her, lavishing all their attention on their only son and heir. While John was given the best of everything and sent to the finest schools in London, Rose languished at Brookwood Manor, left to the care of a succession of nannies as her parents lived their lives in London, with only sporadic visits back to Yorkshire to visit their daughter.

Each time they visited, Henry and Elizabeth Davenport

discovered more about their daughter to disappoint them. Nothing about her compared to their son, and he outshone her in every way possible. Ten years older than Rose, John Davenport was handsome, intelligent, popular, charming and well liked by everyone who knew him. He was quick-witted, athletic, and poised to take over the family's thriving textile business.

To Henry and Elizabeth Davenport's increasing dismay, Rose was not pretty enough, not smart enough, and not charming enough to warrant their time or affection. Their only daughter was too slow, too plump, and too plain. Her mother would shake her head in frustration at Rose's lack of charm and grace.

Must you stomp when you walk, Rose? It's a shame you have such an ungainly figure. Perhaps if you smiled more often you could appear more attractive. Try to tone down the pitch of your voice, Rose, you sound like a squawking goose. If you keep eating sweets, you'll become even fatter than you already are. Why can't you be more agreeable and pleasant to be with, like your brother? Everyone loves John. You're such an odd, depressing, and morose child!

After each visit her parents would invariably return to London even more dissatisfied with her than when they arrived.

For the most part Rose was left to her own devices, which was not saying much. Her education was sketchy at best. Not having a natural aptitude for academics nor any interest in pursuing it, she left the schoolroom lacking in any real knowledge of the world around her. Instead, Rose spent her days walking the grounds of the estate and sketching the beautiful flowers in the garden and the pastoral landscapes that surrounded her.

Drawing had become a passion of hers and it filled her solitary days. Rose could lose herself for hours, trying to sketch a perfect yellow daffodil or tender blades of green grass or the spidery veins on a maple leaf. She was mostly self-taught, for her father thought drawing a frivolous pastime and denied her repeated requests for an art teacher when she was twelve years old. And thirteen. And fourteen . . . So she saved her pin money on sketchbooks and pencils that she would purchase in the village nearby. Rose hid all her sketches in a wooden trunk in her bedroom and she had never shared them with anyone.

Except Andrew.

Andrew Cooper came into her life like a thunderstorm after a drought and she fell in love with him with a white-hot passion and blind devotion that was almost her ruination. And in fact, it was.

Loving Andrew Cooper had most definitely ruined her life.

The summer Rose was seventeen her parents were excitedly preparing for John's upcoming society wedding to Lady Anne Carlisle, and they had decided to put Rose's debut on hold for another year. They were so preoccupied with planning their son's nuptials in London that they did not take any notice of the very handsome young footman employed at their country estate, Brookwood Manor.

One afternoon, while Rose was out sketching in the east garden, where the white roses were fragrant and lush, Andrew happened upon her. Admiring her sketches, he confessed that he also loved to draw. It all started from that shared small moment, that simple bond over a love of pencil and paper. Placing his hand over hers, Andrew showed her how to hold the pencil just so, to create shading and add depth to her pictures. His skills surpassed her own and she learned from him. Mesmerized by his charm, golden looks, and the attention he lavished upon her, Rose was immediately enraptured.

When he touched her, an exquisite thrill raced through her entire body. That someone as beautiful as Andrew Cooper would find her interesting or want to spend time with her was a breathtaking novelty to her.

Rose and Andrew began to meet in secret, out in the woods on the edge of the grounds where they wouldn't be seen together. They would draw together under the trees, talking and laughing, and of course, kissing. Living in a state of suspended bliss since Andrew entered her life, Rose could think of nothing but him.

It was only a few weeks later that he asked if he could sketch her in the nude.

"True artists are skilled at drawing the human body," he explained in his sweet and charming way. "We both should practice sketching and modeling for each other."

Rose had finally shed the extra weight when she sprouted up in height that spring, and with her lustrous brown hair falling over her naked body as she posed for Andrew, for the first time in her life she felt beautiful and loved and wanted. She was not self-conscious or embarrassed as she stood barefoot in the grass, her dress thrown carelessly on the ground, her back against the rough bark of the tree, and her arms wantonly stretched above her head.

"My pathetic drawing can't begin to capture how beautiful you are, Rose," he'd marveled at her, dazzling her with his golden smile. But his drawings were splendid. They stunned her. In his pencil sketches, through his blue eyes, she looked like a beautiful woman.

Her heart was irretrievably lost to him in that moment.

When it came time to sketch his naked body, she was in awe of the magnificence of the male form, especially *his* male form. The muscles in his arms and legs, the breadth of his shoulders, the contours of his broad chest, and the smoothness of his skin left her weak with a fledgling desire.

As she attempted to do his masculine beauty justice with her unskilled pencil, she knew she had failed miserably.

"I'm so sorry, Andrew," she apologized with a giggle. "It looks as if you have the arms of a gorilla!"

"Let me see," he said, joining her on the blanket where she sat sketching in only her plain white chemise and stockings.

Andrew never looked at her drawing.

Instead he brought his mouth down over hers in a kiss that left her breathless and shaking. They made love for the first time that day, there in the quiet of the woods that she loved, with the man that she loved, and for the only time in her life, Rose was completely happy. She gave herself to him without reservation or regret and he was sweet and tender, telling her over and over that he loved her.

It was a magical time that summer. They spent every moment they could together. Andrew had even taken to slipping into her bedroom each night when the house was quiet. They made love and slept with their arms around each other, then Andrew would sneak out of her room before dawn. Deliriously in love, they began to make plans for the future. Knowing her parents would never approve of her marrying a lowly footman, they talked of eloping and running away together, perhaps to Scotland. They knew money would be an issue, as would finding a way to support the both of them. Yet all those unpleasant little details could wait. As summer turned to fall, nothing else mattered but their bodies pressed against one another, their passionate kisses, and their sketches of each other.

Then the great tragedy happened.

Rose's brother, John, was killed in a carriage accident during a rainstorm. The carriage overturned and his body was flung into a ravine. When he was finally found, his neck had been broken. Devastated, her parents' sudden return to Brookwood Manor bearing the terrible news and the subsequent depression and anger that followed, put a decided pall over the entire house. Oh, Rose was sad about her brother's death too. She and John had never been close, since he was ten years older than she was, but he was kind to her on the rare occasions they saw each other, such as holidays. But for most of John's life, his younger sister was merely an afterthought to him.

However, her parents took his death very hard, retreating to Brookwood Manor and giving up the life they used to live in London. They were broken and beyond devastated at the tragic loss, and being forced to see Rose every day did not bring them any consolation. They had lost their bright, golden son, the pride and joy of their hearts, and were left with only their rather plain and unexceptional daughter. The bitterness ate them alive. With John's death, Henry Davenport grew angry and belligerent, while Elizabeth became even more distant and self-centered.

The unexpected return of her parents to her daily life was upsetting to the intimate world Rose had created with Andrew. Reduced to even greater precautions to safeguard their affair, it became more and more difficult for the two of them to be alone together. Yet they kept their secret plan to run away together in the spring, when the weather would be better for traveling and they would have saved enough money for the journey to Scotland.

But, oh, it was hard to wait! Every day Rose longed to be free, free of Brookwood Manor and free of her parents. Every night she yearned to be with Andrew. She counted the days until they could live together out in the open as husband and wife.

But fate had other plans for Rose Davenport.

The night her father caught Andrew as he was leaving Rose's bedroom changed everything. She could still feel the sting of humiliation at being called a whore by her father as he dragged her naked from her bed and threw her to the floor, screaming at her and kicking her. Andrew tried to restrain him, but Henry's rage proved too powerful, for he punched Andrew in the face, breaking his perfect nose. The altercation drew the attention of all the servants, and her shame was complete.

Still, Rose didn't care about herself. She only worried for Andrew.

Andrew had declared his love for her before her father had him removed from the house and locked Rose in her bedroom. She watched from her window, tears streaming down her face, as the love of her life was placed in a carriage and driven away to she knew not where. She only hoped that somehow Andrew would get word to her and come back for her.

After a week of being confined to her room in disgrace, Henry and Elizabeth sat their daughter down and told her that they had arranged a marriage for her. She was to marry Foster Sheridan, the only son and heir to the Earl of Sterling. Apparently Lord Sterling was eager to regain the Brookwood land that had once belonged to his family and Henry had generously offered the earl a great deal of cash to persuade his young son to marry Rose.

Rose was being sold off to a man she did not know.

"I won't do it!" she cried out. "I'm going to marry Andrew. I love him and he loves me!"

"You have no say in the matter," her father said angrily. "This is a once in a lifetime chance to redeem yourself, Rose. Lord Sterling is unaware of what you look like or what you've done. He wants his family's land back and the money to bail himself out of debt, so you'll marry his son, Foster, and become a countess one day."

"I don't want to be a countess!" she protested.

"Really, Rose, you have humiliated yourself enough," her mother began sternly. "If word about your bedding a footman gets out, there isn't a man out there who would have you! For once in your life don't be a great fool. We must act quickly. Foster Sheridan is a good-looking man your own age. He's just finishing Cambridge and his father wants him settled down. When his father dies, he'll become the earl and you'll be the countess. Which is more than we ever hoped for the likes of you. Be grateful! Many girls would be thrilled to marry him. Consider yourself fortunate, because you are!"

"I don't care who he is or what he looks like or if he were the Prince of Wales himself. I'm not going to marry him!" Rose sobbed hysterically, unable to stop the enraged tears that sprang from her eyes.

In a swift motion, her mother slapped her across the face. "Not another word. After all your father and I have been through with losing our darling John, you will not disgrace us with a public scandal now. You should count your blessings we haven't thrown you out in the street, as you so rightly deserve after your vulgar display with that worthless footman. Your father was kind enough to arrange this marriage for you, and you turn up your nose? You ungrateful, wretched girl! You *will* marry Foster Sheridan as soon as Lord Sterling sets the date."

"I only hope it's not too late," he father grumbled, as he held a glass of scotch in his hand. He'd been drinking a lot more often since John had died.

Her hand still on her stinging cheek, Rose stood up for herself for the first time in her life. "It is too late. I cannot marry the Earl of Sterling's son and I won't do it." She paused only a moment before announcing, "I'm having Andrew's baby."

Her mother froze, a look of utter horror on her face. "Oh, dear God in heaven."

Rose had suspected she was carrying Andrew's child for some time. Just before they had been discovered in her bedroom by her father, Rose had whispered her suspicions to Andrew as they lay naked together in her bed. Smiling with happiness, Andrew had placed his hand over her stomach in awe, promising to marry her and vowing to love and protect her and their baby forever.

Now that another week had passed, Rose was quite certain she was with child.

"Get out of my sight, you disgusting, little whore!" Her father flung his glass of scotch across the room, the crystal shattering against the wall.

Rose fled to the safety of her bedroom, sobbing hysterically. She hated her mother and father. She truly hated them and wanted nothing more than to leave their house forever. Longing for Andrew, she wished she knew where he was and if he was coming for her. She'd gotten no message from him and had even sent her lady's maid, Alice Bellwether, into the village to make inquiries about him. No one knew his whereabouts and that made Rose worry.

What had her father done to him?

For weeks she agonized over her plight, and as her pregnancy progressed, her parents kept her hidden from the world. She wasn't even allowed out of the house to walk in the gardens anymore. Only Alice was permitted to wait on her. Her father postponed the wedding until spring, explaining to Lord Sterling that Rose had taken ill with a consumptive-like cough.

Henry then declared to Rose that as soon as her bastard child was born, he would have it sent away to a foundling home.

But Rose knew she would die before she let that happen.

One way or another, she was keeping her child. Andrew's child.

All through the cold and lonely winter, Rose focused her attention on the baby growing inside of her. She vowed to herself that she would be a loving, kind, and understanding mother, unlike her own parents. Just before the baby was due to be born and the snow was finally melting, Rose finally received a message from Andrew. His letter had been addressed to Alice.

Andrew was in New York! Her father had had him beaten, tied up, and tossed on a ship sailing to America. After recovering, Andrew worked some odd jobs in the city before finally finding a position as a clerk at a large bank. He said he was doing well but her father threatened to kill him if he ever came near Rose again, and Andrew believed him. He wasn't coming back for her and he didn't ask her to join him in New York. There were no words of love or mention of their baby. He wished her well and said goodbye.

Rose was so heartbroken by the letter from Andrew that she barely noticed her first labor pains. By the next morning, she was writhing in agony. It became a hellish nightmare of pain. Something was terribly wrong, but her father refused to send for a doctor or a midwife. With only poor, terrified Alice to tend to her, Rose labored for three days and was losing so much blood that even her mother, haunted by her own dreadful experience giving birth to Rose, begged Henry to relent and send for a doctor at last.

That was when the horror truly began.

When it was finally all over, Rose was so scarred from the inexperienced doctor's ham-fisted procedures that she would never be able to bear another child. But worst of all, her sweet baby boy was dead. The cord had been wrapped around his little neck and he was blue. Not that Rose recalled any of that. She had long passed out from the excruciating pain. When she awoke and discovered what had happened, she was so distraught that she wished she had died with her baby.

She named him Andrew after his father, and after touching his perfect little face with a kiss, she and Alice buried her sweet infant son out in the woods.

All hope died within Rose the night she lost her baby and she was never the same again. Any spark of life or glimmer of hope within her was permanently dampened. Barely a month later, she reluctantly married the Earl of Sterling's son, a young man she met for the first time on the morning of their joyless wedding. A man who had no desire to wed her either and was completely unaware that not only was his new bride not a virgin, but she was also barren and pining with heartbreak for another man and her dead baby boy.

Foster Sheridan had not known that he had married a hollow shell of woman who would resent him for something he had nothing to do with. Poor Foster. He had been spectacularly duped by her family. He and the earl were sold a bill of goods on that wedding day ten years ago.

At the time Rose hadn't cared. She had been too broken-hearted and full of spite and hatred for the world to bother with Foster's feelings. In spite of his kindness and initial attempts at making the marriage work, she had cruelly rebuffed him. In her eyes, no man could compare to the golden handsomeness of Andrew Cooper.

Besides, after what she'd been through in delivering her son so soon before her marriage, her body had barely recovered. The thought of anyone touching her made her recoil in horror. Her tears on her wedding night were not forced or playacting. She truly never wanted any man to touch her again.

Rose's life was ruined and the only way she could lash out, as powerless as she was, was to ruin someone else's.

Foster Sheridan became the object of all her anger and rage. And she had taken it out on him for ten long years.

Yet he hadn't deserved any of it.

"Please eat something, my lady," Alice begged her, jostling Rose from her reverie as she stood staring out the window of Sterling Hall.

What did it matter if she ate or starved to death? Nothing in her life mattered. It never had. For the first time in many years, Rose Sheridan began to cry for all the pain and wasted time.

12

Relations

"Well, I'm of two minds. On the one hand a large, airy, open space would be perfect for children. But on the other hand, the charm of this smaller, cozy space is truly difficult to resist," said Colette Hamilton Sinclair, the Marchioness of Stancliff, as she turned around slowly, surveying the small, empty shop.

"I think this is definitely the one, Aunt Colette," Mara whispered, feeling in her heart that this would be an ideal location for a children's bookshop. "This is it."

It was a small redbrick building covered with ivy, not far from the original Hamilton's Book Shoppe in Mayfair. The interior was mostly dark wood, probably oak, along the floor. Twin wooden staircases on either side of the room ascended to a lovely balcony that ran around the entire shop. An intricately carved wooden balustrade edged the interior balcony. A quaint spiral staircase graced the back brick wall, offering another route to the balcony above. The entire space inspired warmth and security.

"Uncle Quinton was right," Mara said. "It's quite perfect." She and Colette had stopped by the small shop that morning on the recommendation of Aunt Lisette's husband, Quinton Roxbury. He had thought this might be what they were looking for.

"Do you really think so?" Colette asked, eyeing her closely.

"Oh, yes!" Mara exclaimed. A sense of excitement grew within her as she pointed above. "I can see beautiful book-shelves lining the walls along the balcony up there. And with brightly colored carpets, perhaps some whimsical art-work here and there, and children's furniture, it will be an enchanting space."

Colette smiled in agreement. "I do believe this could be a very special shop. It's not too large in that we would have a difficult time filling it with books, but it's not too small either. And the location is practically perfect."

"It *is* perfect. I can see it and feel it. It will be a shop that children will want to come to." She beamed at Colette. "It will be a shop that children will beg their parents to take them to. It will be the first and only children's bookshop in all of London."

"I can't even explain why I love this idea so much," Colette continued. "Yvette is completely skeptical of it and I think even your mother has her doubts, although she gave her consent to go forward with our plans. But I think you and I shall prove them all wrong."

"We shall." Mara nodded emphatically. "And I've been thinking . . . It might be best to remove all the children's books from both our shops and bring them here."

"Yes!" Colette instantly understood her meaning. "That way when someone asks for a children's book, we can send them here. Mara, you're quite brilliant!"

"What shall we call this shop?" Mara asked.

"I suppose something like the Hamilton's Children's Book Shoppe. But we have time to consider that yet. However did you come up with this idea in the first place?"

"I'm not entirely sure . . ." Mara thought for a moment. "I suppose I've always had the idea in my head. I just remember thinking how wonderful Hamilton's was when I was a little girl. I loved coming to the shop then. It was such a special place, filled with wonderful stories that made me forget about how terrible things were. I felt safe and happy there. And when you and I were talking that afternoon a few weeks ago when I came to stay with you, it just popped out of my mouth. Even though I've had the idea for years, I never mentioned it before. Perhaps I thought no one would think it was a good idea."

"It's a wonderful idea!" Colette hugged her. "And I'm happy you finally told me about it. I love the challenge of having a new project. And this is so exciting! I shall have my solicitor draw up the contracts so Hamilton's can purchase this building." She sighed with satisfaction. "When my father, Thomas Hamilton, began his little bookshop before I was born, I doubt he ever imagined that his daughters would be carrying on the tradition and expanding in such a grand way. But I know he would be proud of not only his daughters, but his granddaughters as well."

"I'm not truly a Hamilton," Mara said softly. It surprised her how much that fact used to upset her. That she wasn't related to this wonderful family by blood.

"Of course you are!" Colette looked at her in surprise. "Mara, of all the Hamilton granddaughters, you love the bookshops the most! You have more 'Hamilton' in you than Yvette's three little girls, who haven't shown the least bit of interest in the shops as of yet, or Lisette's daughter, Elizabeth, who has merely tolerated her time working with us. And you certainly possess more dedication than Juliette's daughter, for Sara has no more than a passing curiosity in how the shops are managed. I have no daughter of my own to pass down my love for our bookstores, but I have been so proud of my beautiful niece over the years. I look upon you as my little kindred spirit."

Mara blinked back tears as her aunt continued to speak.

"Even though we always include all our sisters in the major decision-making, Paulette and I have been the only ones who truly love working in the bookshops. It's in our blood and our hearts. It's been that way ever since we were young girls." Colette gave a little laugh. "Paulette and I both married extremely well for the daughters of a shopkeeper. She is a countess and I am a marchioness. We've no need to run three bookshops, for heaven's sake! And most people are surprised, and by turns appalled, that we do. But she and I love working and we built these shops into a success from the run-down little store we inherited from our father. We improved the business when everyone doubted us. That is, all the men we had to do business with, doubted us. Why, even our own mother thought we were foolish to want to keep our father's bookshop going and she tried to sell the store out from under us! And if it weren't for Lucien believing in me, we would have lost it altogether."

Mara listened to her aunt with rapt attention. She'd never really known this about the family.

"Paulette and I work hard because we love the bookshop," Colette continued. "There's very little in this world a woman can truly call her own, and we had a chance to create a place where it is safe for women to work. We hire women only, for a reason. We wanted to prove that women can be successful in business, and we have, all the while hoping someday we would have daughters to carry on the tradition. Now I love and adore both of my sons, and I would be thrilled if Phillip or Simon ever took more than a half-hearted interest in Hamilton's. But it's not to be. As it is, neither Paulette nor I gave birth to a daughter. But then there was you, Mara . . . A gift. A true Hamilton granddaughter."

Mara could no longer hold back the tears. To hear the words from someone other than Paulette somehow made a world of difference. "Aunt Colette . . . That means so much to me."

Colette hugged her again, placing a kiss on her cheek. "Your mother and I have talked about it often. About how very lucky we are to have you in our lives, Mara."

Wiping her eyes, Mara murmured, "Thank you. You have all changed my life for the better by making me part of the family."

"Of course you are part of our family! And it certainly wasn't my intention to make you cry." Colette smiled and hugged her again, attempting to soothe her.

"I realize that." Mara laughed a little and took a deep breath. "I'm sorry I'm such a watering pot."

Colette patted Mara's shoulder. "There is nothing to apologize for, Mara. Everything is fine. And didn't we just discover the perfect location for our new shop? Now let's hurry back or we shall be late for supper. All the family will be at Devon House tonight."

Later that evening, a chorus of raucous voices greeted Mara when she entered the third-floor schoolroom where her younger Roxbury and Eddington cousins had gathered.

"Mara, come join us!"

"Yes, please, Mara! Play with us for a little while."

The whole Hamilton family was in attendance at Devon House for their monthly supper together. Mara had been attending these large family dinners for as long as she could remember. Looking around fondly at the brightly painted walls, trunks full of toys and games, and shelves bursting with books, she recalled the dozens of happy memories of playing in this very room with Sara and Phillip and Simon

when they were children. Now the younger Hamilton cousins
had taken over the schoolroom.

"We're playing pirates!" shouted little Vivienne Eddington, the youngest of all the cousins at six years old. "And
the girl pirates are winning!"

Vivienne's pretty blond curls, usually neat and tidy, were
a tangled and tousled mess and her large pink hair bow was
askew, dangling over one eye in an effort to be a patch. The
incongruous sight of the usually demure-looking girl attempting to appear ferocious made Mara smile.

The twins, Christopher and Charles Roxbury, who were
closer in age to her brother, Thomas, stood behind a large
table turned on its side, brandishing sticks like swords.
They gave Mara helpless smiles, for at sixteen they were a
little too old to be playing in the schoolroom, but they had
obviously been wrangled into placating Vivienne, whom
they all adored. They were caring and good-hearted young
boys, who would readily play with their younger cousin if
it made her happy.

Elizabeth Roxbury, the twins' younger sister and the
other two Eddington girls, Violet and Victoria, were shout-
ing pirate terms and swinging their own sticks.

Violet, the eldest Eddington daughter, ran to Mara's
side. She grabbed her arm, tugging Mara farther into their
area of play, and handed her a "sword."

"We have the boys trapped on the island. They have no
way to get off," Violet explained excitedly.

"And they will most likely die there!" Vivienne shouted
with wicked glee. "And then . . . And then we shall throw
them to the sharks and take their treasure!"

Giving in to their requests, Mara gamely took the stick
that Violet handed her, held it up, and exclaimed in her best
pirate voice, "You must forfeit your treasure to us or forever
remain on the island!"

Christopher yelled, "We shall never surrender!" as he

leapt over the table and began to chase his little cousins around the great room. Shrieking and some heated sword fighting ensued.

Feeling more lighthearted than she had in years, Mara played at being pirates with her cousins, yet her mind was with Foster and all that they had shared the other night. It was still difficult to believe any of it had really happened.

As she had rightly assumed, she returned from Foster's house that evening without being detected, and for that she was very grateful. She had worried that someone would notice the change in her, for surely her sudden happiness was radiating from her. She felt as if she couldn't stop smiling. But no one mentioned a word. Not even Aunt Colette, with whom she had spent most of the day.

Mara could think of nothing but how happy she was!

Foster Sheridan loved her and she loved him. Buoyed by the exquisite feeling of being loved and wanted in spite of her flaws, Mara had floated on a cloud of utter delight since the first evening they had spent together.

Mara hadn't seen Foster since last week, when he had discreetly taken her back to Devon House under the cover of darkness, but they had exchanged a few notes and were planning to meet again. Tomorrow afternoon, in fact. Mara was to come to his house via the back entrance, so as to avoid anyone seeing her enter his home. She'd even purchased a new cloak with a deep hood, which would cover her head and face, making it difficult for anyone to identify her.

A loud voice suddenly echoed through the room. "I am the Pirate King and this pirate war is now over! I claim all the rewards and treasures for my own!"

"Papa!" Vivienne yelled in delight at the tall and handsome man with laughing eyes who stood in the entryway, a mischievous smile on his face.

Uncle Jeffrey walked in and swooped his youngest

daughter up in his arms. "I shall hold this vicious little pirate hostage unless you all get ready for dinner!"

Vivienne demanded, "Play with us first, Papa!"

And he did, jumping right into the fun. He took Vivienne's sword in his hand, and still carrying her in his arms, Uncle Jeffrey dueled with each of them, while little Vivienne shouted insults at them. One would never guess that he was the Duke of Rathmore.

A rousing duel ensued, with perilous chases around the large schoolroom leaving chairs overturned and books and games knocked over. However, it all came to a sudden halt when Aunt Yvette arrived, staring at the chaos in the room with utter disbelief.

"It sounds as if you're about to come crashing through the ceiling," Yvette said, surveying the state of disarray around the room with a wry look. "And we're two floors below you! Honestly, Jeffrey. And you too, Mara." She shook her head and laughed. "I didn't expect to see the two of you involved in these shenanigans."

"Just a bit of fun with my darling daughters, nieces, and nephews," Jeffrey explained, out of breath and winded from his exertions. He winked at his wife with a wicked smile. "I'm the Pirate King."

Yvette laughed in amusement, her eyes adoring. "Of course you are."

Uncle Jeffrey set a reluctant Vivienne down on the floor and Mara too tried to catch her breath.

"Come along now, all of you, supper will be ready soon, and since you insisted on dining with the adults this evening, then you must behave accordingly. Yes, you too, Vivvy!" As Yvette expertly shooed all the children from the room, Mara and Uncle Jeffrey stood behind, looking a little sheepish.

"That was fun though, wasn't it?" he asked her when everyone else had gone.

"Yes, it was," Mara agreed with a smile.

Her uncle was always great fun. Over the years he had been the one ready and willing to play with her and Sara, Phillip, and Simon when they were young. Uncle Jeffrey had a gift for bringing levity and diversion wherever he went. He was adored by all his nieces and nephews, and Mara was no exception.

"I've been meaning to talk to you, Mara," he said, as he righted a chair that had been knocked on its side on the schoolroom floor.

"Oh?" she asked, as she began to pick up some of the toys that had been scattered around during their pirate war. "Have they sent you to try to discover the *secret* reason why I haven't gone to Ireland with my parents?"

Uncle Jeffrey burst into a wide grin. "Guilty as charged."

"I suspected as much."

"How did you know?" he questioned, picking up another chair.

Mara shrugged and tossed a few more stuffed animals into the large trunk of toys against the wall. "Just a feeling I had."

He gave her an admiring glance. "I don't think anyone gives you enough credit, Mara."

"Enough credit for what?" she asked.

Wordlessly they each took an end of the large table that had been "the island" and together they turned it to rights. They both sat upon it, Mara's feet dangling because she couldn't reach the floor.

"As long as I've known you, your parents have worried about you and treated you as if you were made of glass," Jeffrey explained. "I understand why, of course. I more than likely would have done the same, if I were Declan. You suffered a terrible tragedy at a very tender age. When I first met you, Mara, you hadn't spoken since the fire. Do you recall that?"

Oh, yes, Mara could never forget the year she didn't utter a single word. It hadn't been a deliberate or defiant act on her part. The fear and horror of what she had seen the night her mother died had quite literally left her speechless for months on end. "Yes, I remember that time quite well."

"I always thought you were the most remarkable child," he said. "The night Paulette and I rescued you from your father's cousin, you were so calm and ran off with us without a complaint."

Mara hadn't thought of that strange night in quite a long time. She did recall the secrecy and urgency of leaving Cashelmore Manor with Paulette and being carried by Uncle Jeffrey to safety. He had been so kind to her, while she waited with Paulette to see her father again. It was all such a long time ago.

Jeffrey continued. "I just think that because of everything that happened, Declan and Paulette, and all of us, feared losing you again or upsetting you in any way after all you'd been through. Because you are undeniably sweet, thoughtful, and quiet, everyone in the family felt the need to protect you. Myself included." He gave her an appraising look. "But I think we all underestimated your strength, Mara. There is no need for us to tiptoe around your feelings. You are a lot stronger and resilient than we give you credit for."

"So what are you saying, Uncle Jeffrey?"

He sighed in defeat. "That you are correct. Your mother and father, out of their great love for you, have asked me to talk with you. They are worried about you, and for some reason, probably because I'm the favorite uncle"—he grinned devilishly—"they believed you would confide your secrets to me."

Mara had known her parents were concerned about her, and her aunts as well. She was not at all surprised that they sent Uncle Jeffrey to check on her. It almost made her laugh. She loved her uncle, but she could never bring herself to tell him about her relationship with Foster Sheridan.

"Well, dearest Uncle, I appreciate your caring and concern, but there is nothing to worry about. I am perfectly fine," Mara said in a matter-of-fact tone. "There is no deep, dark reason that I stayed in London. What everyone seems to forget is that London is just as much my home as Ireland is. I simply wanted to stay home. That is all. So please relay the message back to my mother and father and all my aunts, that I am completely fine and perfectly happy."

"I guessed you'd say something along those lines, and I told everyone as much. But as I said, they all love and care for you." He gave a helpless shrug. "And I suppose I had to try."

"Thank you," Mara responded and planted a little kiss on his cheek. "You're quite a good uncle."

"You're very welcome." He smiled at her warmly. "And just remember, sweet Mara, that if you *do* ever need my sage advice or heroic assistance in any way, you can always come to me. I shall even keep what you say in the strictest of confidence, if that is the case."

"Again, thank you, and I promise that I will come to you if ever such a need arises," Mara said. He really was a dear. She slid down off the table.

"Well, then, that's settled," he said, clapping his hands. "I suppose we should go dress for supper as well."

And then it happened. Mara inwardly groaned.

Oh no! Not now. Not in front of Uncle Jeffrey!

It was starting and there was no way she could stop the dizziness once it started. She swayed and almost fell over.

"Mara?" her uncle called out in alarm, reaching out to grip her shoulders and steady her. "Mara!"

She could not answer him. She was powerless to move or speak.

And so it began . . . Again . . .

That peculiarly familiar tingling sensation slowly crept over her flesh, awakening each and every nerve in her body. Her heart beat wildly in her chest and she grew hot and yet she shivered at the same time. The hair on the back of her neck stood on end and her teeth clenched. Mara closed her eyes and held her breath. Everything around her receded into a dark cloud of silence. Sharp pinpricks of awareness lit up inside of her, flashing sparks of light from within.

Misty wisps of images began to take shape in her mind, presenting themselves to her . . . whether she wanted them to or not . . .

Fire. Glints of flames. Blinding bursts of light. Shimmering walls of golden orange and brilliant yellow. Breathtaking, scorching heat. Trapped in the burning building, blazing embers and smoky ash filling the air, Mara didn't know where to go or how to escape. Where was she? How was she to get out? Gut-wrenching, tormented screams echoed against the rush of flames. Someone was in great agony. Someone needed her help. A woman. But where was she? Mara could not see, did not know where to go. Her own panicked, terrified cries reverberated around her.

Scalding tears, knowing it was her fault, knowing it was too late. Blinding heat and black smoke and swirling flames, the vicious sting of fear and the horrific smell of imminent death surrounded her. It was too late. Too late.

Her death. She was going to die in this raging inferno.

Swirling darkness. A short breath of blessedly cool air. She gasped and fell to her knees.

Foster. He was there.

Frantically calling to her, his hand outstretched, reaching for her, a look of love, mixed with anguish and horror, awash on his handsome face. She held out her hand to him, trusting him implicitly, the terror that engulfed her dissipating at the touch of his fingers. Flooded with relief and elation, buoyed with happiness and hope, Mara clung to him, his strong arms embracing her, carrying her away.

Foster held her tightly to his broad chest and she was safe, secure, loved. In spite of their dangerous surroundings and the acrid smell of smoke thick around them, she could breathe easily within his sheltering embrace. A profound peace enveloped her.

She belonged to him. They belonged together.

"Mara!"

Her eyes fluttered open. Uncle Jeffrey stared at her with a worried expression on his face. She closed her eyes again and breathed deeply, trying to calm herself. Struggling to understand what had just happened.

This was the *third* time she had experienced the same premonition in the last three weeks. She didn't know what to make of it. She'd never had her visions come to her so frequently and so strongly before. And never, ever, had she had the same vision repeated once, let alone twice. The urgency of it frightened her.

It was bad enough she had experienced one in front of Foster, but at least he would keep her secret. Now she feared what Uncle Jeffrey would do.

Once again she opened her eyes, facing him.

"Are you all right?" he asked, guiding her to sit on a nearby chair.

"I'm fine," Mara said, but she knew he didn't believe her because she *wasn't* fine. She was still trembling as she sat down.

Uncle Jeffrey gazed at her. "Are you ill?"

She shook her head. "No, it was just a dizzy spell. I get them from time to time."

"I don't know what that was, but it wasn't just a dizzy spell, Mara." He crossed his arms over his chest. "I'm not a doctor, but you seemed to be having some sort of attack or seizure of some kind. Have you seen a doctor?"

"I don't need a doctor," she said, feeling a bit panicked. The last thing she needed was for Uncle Jeffrey to make a great fuss over what just happened, and tell her parents and everyone else that Mara was ill and call for a doctor. She would be confined to bed and made to rest and everybody would worry and she would have to miss her visit with Foster tomorrow. She wasn't having that. There was only one other choice.

She had to tell him the truth. "It's just that sometimes these things happen to me."

"What things? What was that?" His brows drew together in confusion.

"Once in a while, I can't explain how or why, and I cannot control when these visions come to me, but I can see things." She held her breath, waiting for his reaction.

"You have visions?" Oddly enough, he didn't sound appalled, just intrigued.

"Sometimes I can see things that will happen in the future."

Uncle Jeffrey stared at her for a long moment, as if carefully considering his words. She was infinitely grateful that he didn't overreact and treat her as if she was crazy, even though she was.

He asked, "What did you see just now?"

"I saw myself almost die in a fire."

Uncle Jeffrey let out a long, low whistle, surprising her. "That's a loaded vision, my dear."

"It's not a memory, if that is what you're thinking, Uncle Jeffrey. The fire in my vision is very different from the fire that killed my mother," she said softly.

"I believe you."

"It's not as if these visions come to me all the time. I've experienced them my whole life, and everything I have foreseen has come to pass. I saw that Aunt Yvette would have three daughters even before Violet was born. I saw

Sara marrying Christopher Townsend. Those are the kinds of visions I've had."

"You saw that I would have three daughters?" He seemed quite impressed by this development. "That's quite remarkable. Anything else?"

"Nothing important." She gave a little shrug.

"It's happened your whole life?"

"Yes, since I was a little girl, but I've never told anyone about it. Not even my parents."

"Why not?" he asked gently.

"I didn't want them to ever worry about me."

He eyed her closely as if assessing her. "Do your visions scare you?"

"No. Not at all." At least not until this latest one. But she kept that bit of information to herself.

Beaming at her, Uncle Jeffrey smiled broadly. "And that's a perfect example of what I meant when I said that no one gives you enough credit, Mara. Visions would terrify most people. But you've taken them in stride, since you were a small child no less, and never told a soul, because you didn't wish for anyone to worry about you. You, Lady Mara Kathleen Reeves, are a marvel."

She felt her cheeks grow warm at his compliment.

He paused before asking, "Would you like to talk to someone about your visions?"

Her heart raced with sudden fear and dread. Not doctors! She hated doctors. "What do you mean?"

"I mean, sweet girl, that I can see that these visions cause *you* to worry, even though you say otherwise. But I believe you may have a tremendous gift," he explained calmly. "I can make some discreet inquiries and see if I can find an expert in the field, whom you can use as a resource. Someone who knows more about the subject than you or I do. Someone who can answer the questions you must have about your visions."

"No." She quickly shook her head. "No. That won't be necessary."

"Are you quite certain?"

"Yes, and will you promise that you won't tell anyone about me?" she asked.

Mara didn't want anyone to know what was going on in her head. Especially her parents. They would be heartbroken to discover that she had inherited her mother's madness. One day, when Mara could no longer contain the symptoms, they would learn the terrible truth, but she hoped to postpone the inevitable for as long as she could. And that included being questioned, poked, and prodded by doctors. She had had enough of that when she was a child.

"I promise not to breathe a word to anyone." Uncle Jeffrey moved to place his hand on her cheek. "And you must promise me that you will let me know if you feel you are in difficulties or if you need help, or change your mind and want to learn more about your amazing gift. Do you promise me that?"

So touched by his concern for her and fearing she might cry, she could barely speak. "Thank you, Uncle Jeffrey. I promise."

He removed his hand. "You are a very loved and cherished member of this family, Mara."

"So are you," she whispered.

He grinned wickedly. "I'm a rogue, that's why they love me. Now. I think it's time we headed downstairs. Are you ready?" He held out his hand to her.

Feeling terribly guilty, Mara rose from her chair and took Uncle Jeffrey's arm as he escorted her from the schoolroom.

Her uncle seemed proud of her and wished to help and protect her. He offered advice and did not seem appalled by her visions. He promised to keep her secret and reminded her that she was loved by her family. He thought she possessed a gift.

Mara blinked back tears of shame.

He did not know that her supposed *gift* was actually a curse.

Today certainly seemed to be her day for family declarations of love.

That afternoon she'd had the conversation with Aunt Colette about carrying on the family tradition of running the bookshops, and now with Uncle Jeffrey . . .

Well, Aunt Colette and Uncle Jeffrey and everyone else in her family would not be so proud of her, or continue to love her, if they knew that she had willingly begun an affair with a married man . . .

And didn't that hopeless and insane act in and of itself prove that Mara was afflicted with madness, just as her mother was?

13

Obstructions

Foster surprised her. She was not expecting his arrival, so he had the element of surprise on his side. Just as she had when she'd gone to his townhouse in London unannounced last month.

"Good afternoon, Rose," he said as he stood in the doorway of one of the smaller parlors at Sterling Hall, which she had adopted as her own private retreat.

There was no denying the shock on her face, and for the slightest moment he thought she was happy to see him. "Foster!" she cried. "What on earth are you doing here?"

Rose looked a mess, worse than he recalled ever seeing her before. As she sat rocking in a chair near the fireplace, she looked like someone's grandmother, certainly not a twenty-eight-year-old woman.

"Can't a husband come home and visit his lovely wife?" It was a sarcastic retort and he knew it. But he hadn't come all the way home to Yorkshire because he wanted to visit Rose. He had some serious business to attend to.

Her face fell and that brief glimpse of a welcoming Rose vanished. Her usual bitter façade took its place instantaneously. He regretted his words as soon as he said them. But it was too late. The tone had been set.

"What do you want?" she flung at him before resuming her rocking, a woolen shawl draped around her thin shoulders.

"Are you ill?" he asked. He'd never seen her like this before.

"I have a headache, not that you would care." She kept her eyes averted. "You still haven't told me the reason I'm graced with your company this afternoon."

He took a seat on a gilt-edged chair near her. It was odd to think he married this woman ten years ago and she was still a complete and utter stranger to him. By law, Rose was his wife. Yet she had never really been his wife in any sense of the word. Not in the least.

Again, he marveled at the drastic change in her appearance. She looked worse than she had when he had seen her in London a few short weeks ago. That was the very same night he met Mara for the first time.

Lady Mara Reeves. She was the real reason for this visit.

Ever since Mara had spent the night with him, Foster knew what he must do. He had to release himself from Rose in any way that he could so he would be free to marry Mara. There was no other option. He was in love with Mara, plain and simple. He could not relegate her to the role of his mistress when she was so much more than that to him. She *deserved* more than that from him.

He wanted Mara to be his wife. He wanted a life with her, a home, and a family. There was only one obstacle to his happiness, and to Mara's happiness, and to a hope for a real life together. And that obstacle sat in front of him now, glaring at him.

"I don't see the point in beating around the bush, Rose. So I shall come right out and say what I came here for." He straightened his shoulders. "I've come to tell you that I want to dissolve our marriage."

After a sharp intake of breath, Rose stilled and did not say a word. A heavy silence grew between them.

"Rose?"

She pulled the shawl tighter around her shoulders and looked at him, her blue eyes filled with anger. "Why now?"

"There are many reasons." He was not going to tell her about Mara. "The primary one being that we are miserable together and do not share a life or a home or anything together for that matter."

"And the others?"

"To be frank, I would like to have the chance to have children." He waited, letting his words sink in. It was the truth. Even she could not deny that she had deprived him of that opportunity.

Rose began rocking slowly again, back and forth, as she stared at the fire blazing in the fireplace. She would not look at him.

"Listen, Rose," he said, keeping his voice calm. "We both know this marriage was a mistake from the start. You didn't want to marry me and I didn't want to marry you. This was our parents' doing and none of them are still living. After all this time, you and I haven't been able to make it work or find a common ground. We have wasted ten years of our lives. Let's stop punishing each other for something neither of us ever wanted, and set each other *free*."

She scoffed sarcastically, "Free to do what?"

How could she not understand? He wanted to scream at her, but he held himself in check. "We could set each other free from this eternal bitterness. Free to find happiness. Free to find love."

Rose turned sharply and stared at him. Slowly, a scornful smile spread across her haggard face, and she laughed. It was a brittle-sounding cackle, dripping with derision.

"So that's it. That's the real reason you came here. Foster Sheridan is finally in love."

Normally he would become angered by Rose's petty taunts. This time he did not feel angry. He simply felt sorry for her. He pitied her inability to love. Rose was so swept up in nursing whatever desperate wounds had scarred her, she would never understand his feelings for Mara or why he needed a different life, and he wasn't about to explain it to her.

"You're not denying it, so it must be true! Who is she? Some bright-eyed debutante in her first Season? A true, highborn lady? An earl or a duke's daughter, perhaps? Has a little blond china doll caught your fancy, Lord Sterling? Being your mistress isn't good enough for this one, is it?" Her words dripped with cynicism.

Ignoring how close to the mark her words actually were, Foster allowed her to vent her anger. It was the least he could do. He wasn't going to engage in a sparring match with her, because if it came down to it, he would win. He could afford to be kind to her because the marriage was over, whether Rose liked it or not. He'd already met with his solicitor about how to proceed. The only thing that remained to be decided was whether to divorce her or annul the marriage.

But being a gentleman, he would allow her to choose.

"You didn't think I knew about your mistresses, did you, Foster?"

Again he didn't rise to her petty bait. She was only guessing anyway. He said nothing.

"Let's see," Rose began, making a show of counting on her fingers. "There was Sally Winters, the dancer from Whitechapel. You were with her the longest, I believe. Three years, wasn't it? Feel free to correct me if I'm wrong, Foster." She waved her hand airily, as if she hadn't a care in the world.

Foster remained silent.

Rose continued counting on her fingers. "But Sally wasn't the first and certainly not the last of them. Then there was Daisy Bradshaw, the domestic from Sussex. You dipped quite low with that one. Really, Foster, a parlor maid?" She gave him a look of utter contempt. "And let's not forget Lady Penelope Barrington! The fetching widow who spent a year or so visiting your bed after her husband died from pneumonia, before she married that wealthy American banker. And what is the name of your most recent one, the buxom little actress with the dark hair? The one from the Imperial Theater? Oh, yes, Annie Blake, that is it! There were others, but let's not get into them. They are not worth mentioning. Have I left out any of the truly significant mistresses?" A vicious smile played across her gaunt face.

Foster had to admit he was surprised, stunned in fact, by just how much Rose knew. All these years he thought he had been quite discreet while he carried on his affairs in London and Rose lived over a hundred miles away in Yorkshire. He had not realized that she'd been so aware of what he'd been doing or how he spent his time. Not that it mattered in the end either way. Rose had left him no choice.

Smug and self-satisfied with her knowledge of intimate details of his life, Rose gloated at his shock. "You see, Foster, I'm not as oblivious as you thought I was. I have had you watched and followed all these years. I know all about the so-called 'ladies' you entertained and then bought extravagant gifts in exchange for *services* rendered. And in some cases, you even paid them in the form of real estate. Sally Winters and Daisy Bradshaw warranted elegant houses in London when you were through with them. Oh, they must have been quite talented indeed! But all of them were rewarded most handsomely. Such a gentleman my husband is . . . I am so very proud."

He still had not uttered a word. He had no reason to defend himself. What he did was none of Rose's business. When she turned him out of her bed, she gave up all expectations of him to be a faithful husband, as far as he was concerned.

Foster was not ashamed of any of the women he spent time with over the years. They had all been quite lovely and pleasant. He had, however, just ended his most recent relationship with Annie Blake, an actress he'd been seeing for the last year or so. He concluded that affair the day after Mara spent the night with him. Annie had been great fun, but since he met Mara, Foster had no desire to be with any other woman. He doubted he would be with anyone but Mara ever again. Just before he left for Yorkshire, he'd instructed his solicitor to purchase a house for Annie Blake as a token of his affection.

"What do I get as my parting gift, darling?" Rose's voice dripped with sarcasm. "Now that you're finished with me, do I get a new house too?"

"Finished with you?" Foster scoffed. "We never had anything to start with, let alone finish."

"That's not my fault!" she cried.

"Isn't it?" He folded his arms across his chest, pleased that she had played right into his next move. "You know, Rose, I don't need your permission to divorce you."

"You have no grounds to divorce me."

Foster smiled smoothly. "You do recall the necessity for all my mistresses, don't you, Rose?"

Saying not a word, she pulled her shawl tighter around her, her nose in the air.

"Our marriage was never consummated," he said in a cool tone. "I could seek an annulment. Something I should have done ten years ago."

"You can't prove that."

"Of course I can. We have no children. And you know perfectly well the truth of our marriage bed. Or lack thereof."

She rose suddenly from the rocking chair, leaving it swaying wildly without her. "I refuse to let you disgrace and humiliate my family and me like this."

"What family? Your parents are dead. My parents are dead. There is no one left to disgrace or humiliate," Foster railed. "And if anyone should be humiliated, it should be me for allowing this ridiculous farce of a marriage to continue for ten long years."

"Exactly!" she cried. "It's been ten years! If it was so terrible, you would have left at the start. And you can't divorce me, you've no grounds! I've been a model wife, while you've been off in London entertaining all those loose women. I've kept up Sterling Hall. I've done my part. And you can't possibly get an annulment after all these years, no one would believe you."

"Oh, I will. Watch me. I have the grounds and the power to go through with either. I'm the Earl of Sterling."

She flinched. "I won't have it. You can't do this to me. I am your wife."

"No," he pointed out. "You are not my wife and you never have been. You don't even know the meaning of the word *wife*."

The color rose on her cheeks as she grew angrier. "You cannot do this, Foster. I am your wife. My whole life was ruined because of my marriage to you. I never got to marry whom I wanted to marry and live the life I wanted. My punishment was marrying you. You married me and I will die as your wife."

For the first time Foster looked with surprise at Rose. *I never got to marry whom I wanted to marry and live the life I wanted.* What did she mean by that? It had never occurred to him that Rose might have been in love with someone else before they wed. They had both been young, and she had only been eighteen years old. He had not been given the opportunity to court her or to get acquainted with her before they married. Hell, he only met her on the morning of their wedding day!

Foster had been away studying at Cambridge when his father had unexpectedly shown up at school and unceremoniously announced that marriage plans had been arranged for him. James Sheridan, Earl of Sterling, was not a man who took no for an answer, especially from his twenty-year-old son. Foster had learned very early on not to cross his father. Whatever James Sheridan's reasons were for wanting his son to marry Rose Davenport, Foster did not question him at the time. At least not to his face.

With no say in the matter, Foster was hastily packed up and brought home to Sterling Hall to be married. He did not even meet his intended bride until she appeared, looking dazed and just as unhappy as he felt, in the little chapel the following morning.

Rose Davenport had been better looking than he expected, but not as pretty or charming as he had hoped for on his journey to Yorkshire. She was trim, with a decent figure, and lustrous brown hair hanging down around her shoulders. At first glance she looked young and appealing. But on closer inspection, she was not even the least bit friendly or inviting. The icy blue eyes, pallid complexion, and sour expression did not conjure any hope for joy in their future together. Nor did her frosty demeanor induce much sympathy.

Instead of looking at him as an ally placed in the same uncomfortable situation, Rose regarded him as an enemy. As if he'd forced her into this marriage himself. Nor did she seem particularly pleased with him. Now Foster knew he was an attractive-looking man, having been told so too many times to count, and any young lady would have been pleased to look upon him as her husband. As the young and handsome heir to an earldom, he was a catch. Yet Rose Davenport gazed at him with scorn and hatred.

It did not bode well.

Before they both uttered their vows and wooden responses, Foster remembered wondering if their arranged marriage had been as much of a surprise for Rose as it was for him. Or had being told of the marriage only the night before been a special degradation that his father had reserved just for him? Had Rose had any forewarning of the arrangement? For who else learned of their wedding the night before and had no idea who his bride was?

Still, Foster had felt sorry for Rose. She looked far more miserable than he felt. And that was quite a lot. As their marriage was declared official, he could not ignore the awful knot in the pit of his stomach. He was now tied to this woman, a complete stranger who clearly did not wish to be with him, for the rest of his life. It happened so quickly he could hardly believe it. It seemed like a bad dream.

There were no warm congratulations or celebrations afterward with well-wishing friends and family. There was only a small wedding breakfast with awkward and stilted conversations between his parents and Rose's parents, who made their departure shortly afterward. He'd been struck by the abrasiveness of Henry Davenport and thought he was remarkably like his own father. Two self-centered, strong-willed men who dominated and manipulated the people around them, had bound their son and daughter together in a life of misery so they could each get whatever it was they wanted.

Meanwhile, his bride could not muster even a forced half smile, an understanding glance or inviting gesture for him. Foster's heart sank.

Later that evening, in his bedroom at Sterling Hall, he knew what was expected of him. It was his duty to procure an heir for the earldom, which would one day belong to him. Yet he recognized that Rose was young and scared. He did not make advances toward her or attempt to kiss or touch her. Foster had no desire to frighten her or force her to consummate the marriage. In his mind they needed time to at least become acquainted with each other before engaging in such an intimate act. When he said as much to her, Rose burst into tears. She spent the night sobbing on the divan, while he slept in the bed. Being a gentleman, he had offered to sleep on the divan instead, but she would not go near the bed. Not only that, but she refused to speak to him or answer his questions, denying his attempts to get to know each other.

During the interminable days and nights that followed, the cold and empty pattern for their wretched marriage was set. Rose spent each day holed up in her bedroom, rejecting his offers to walk in the garden, or to dine together, or to simply talk about their situation and their future. Each evening Foster would invite her to his bedroom, where Rose would become hysterical, crying and sobbing and begging him not to touch her.

So he let her be.

Confounded by her behavior, for arranged marriages were not at all unheard of, and as far as husbands went, Foster thought Rose was very fortunate to have one as understanding as he was. And he understood what the problem was, or at least he thought he did. In the beginning, Foster truly believed that Rose was simply a naïve and sheltered young girl, who needed time to warm up to the idea of having a husband and sharing a marriage bed. As time passed, however, he knew that she couldn't still be skittish because of an arranged marriage.

There was more to it than just that. Something was truly troubling Rose.

As the days turned into weeks, then months, he knew his cold and withdrawn wife needed more than time. Yet he did not know how to help her. She completely shut him out; rebuffing his overtures of friendship, rejecting his attempts to comfort her, ignoring his inquiries to get to know her better.

Another man might have asserted his husbandly authority over her. Whether Rose liked it or not, it was her duty as a wife to procreate.

Yet Foster Sheridan was not that type of man.

He left her alone.

After that first disastrous month at Sterling Hall with Rose as his wife, who was still a virtual stranger to him, he gave up. He went to London, thinking to give her some distance from him, and hoping it would make her more relaxed. She could come to him. Eventually, like all women, she would want children. They were still young and had plenty of time to sort out their situation.

But Rose never did come to him. And in spite of his regular visits to Yorkshire, which grew less and less frequent over the years, their relationship never warmed. In fact, Rose hated him even more, if such a thing was possible. She tolerated his visits but still never allowed him in her bed.

At first he was foolish and naïve enough to think that eventually Rose would change. He hoped that she would mature and realize he was a decent man, and they would have children together and create some semblance of a life together.

Then before he knew it, ten years went by. Rose had only become more spiteful, while he grew more indifferent, and they led completely different lives.

As he stared at her now, he wondered, not for the first time, what had happened to her to make her so angry and bitter at the world. Lord knew, Foster hadn't had a happy childhood, but it didn't prevent him from taking happiness when he could find it. Rose never seemed to grasp that fact.

She was happier and infinitely more comfortable being miserable.

"I'm sorry your life was ruined by marrying me, Rose. There was a time years ago when I would have been sorry to hear that and I would have cared about why you're so unhappy," Foster said. "But *my* life was also ruined by this marriage. The difference between us is that I want to change that. I want out of this dreadful mess. I want to be happy. You don't."

"You cannot dissolve our marriage, Foster. You simply cannot," she protested, tears of frustration glinting in her icy-blue eyes.

"Watch me." He stared at her, and for the first time in their ten-year marriage he felt that he was the one in control.

Foster turned and left the room.

14

Impressions

On a chilly October evening, once darkness had fallen, Mara quietly made her way to Foster Sheridan's townhouse, which was becoming something of a familiar routine for her by now. She knew exactly where to go and what to do. The intrigue of it all was rather exciting. They could not meet too frequently and they had to be very discreet. The consequences of being caught were too terrible to contemplate, but not enough to dissuade her from coming to him this way.

She and Foster chose their nights together with the utmost care, and Mara went to great lengths to ensure they were evenings when Aunt Colette and Uncle Lucien had plans to go out and she would not be missed. Only Brighton, her lady's maid, knew exactly where Mara was going, but she was devoted to Mara and would never divulge her secret. If her family inquired, Brighton was instructed to tell anyone that Mara was merely under the weather and staying in her room. Mara could be sleeping, or suffering a headache, or any other vague malady that would cause her family no undue worry and allow them to leave her in peace.

So far, Mara was certain no one at Devon House suspected anything unusual in her behavior.

When Mara was coming for the night, Foster dismissed all his servants except his butler, Preston, and even he was out of sight for the evening. It had been almost a week since they had last seen each other and Mara missed him terribly. As she tiptoed along the back path and quietly let herself in through the kitchen door, her heart beat with excitement. Once inside, she flung back the hood of the dark blue cloak that kept her face hidden. She unfastened the clasp at the throat and removed the cloak, tossing it carelessly over the back of a kitchen chair.

With quick footsteps she made her way through the quiet and dimly lit house, anxious not to waste a precious moment of their time together. She practically flew up the staircase to Foster's bedroom.

He was waiting for her.

Foster stood before the fire, wearing only black trousers and a white shirt, which was open at the neck and the sleeves rolled up nearly to his elbow. His brown hair was combed back from his clean-shaven face, and he had no shoes on his feet. There was something incredibly intimate about seeing a man dressed so casually.

A grin lit his handsome face when he saw her.

They ran into each other's arms, their mouths meeting in a passionate and hungry kiss. Mara's heart immediately felt at peace. All the pangs of guilt she suffered during the week when she thought about what they were doing dissipated as soon as she was with him again.

"You're early," he whispered, his hands carefully undoing the pins in her hair, allowing it to spill around them in silvery blond waves.

"I'm afraid I'm always early."

"I love that about you. And it means we have more time together." He smiled at her adoringly. "I've missed you."

"I missed you too," she murmured into his mouth. The heat from his tongue sent shivers of anticipation through her body.

Foster suddenly lifted her off her feet and carried her to the bed, laying her among the pillows. He continued kissing her for some time. Then he paused and asked, "Supper first?"

"After," she said, pulling him back down to kiss her. Mara loved the feel of his mouth on hers and delighted in the passion that grew between them whenever they were together. She loved him and wasn't shy about showing him just how much.

Foster gazed at her. "I have an idea you might like . . . a bit of a surprise for you," he whispered, his eyes twinkling with mischief. "Something we can try together."

"What is it?" Their secret evenings had proven to be quite an education for Mara and she had enjoyed every moment with him. Each time they were together, Foster lovingly introduced her to some new way to give or receive pleasure. She was certain that this evening would be no different.

"Well, you will have to remove your clothes to find out."

Mara laughed. "Isn't that what we were planning to do anyway?"

"Yes, but this is rather different."

She was intrigued. "Only if you remove yours as well."

Foster lifted his white shirt over his head, revealing his muscled chest. "Oh, I was planning on it. Now you."

"Well, if I must, I must," Mara replied gamely, and then began unlacing her boots.

"Aren't you even going to try to guess what I have planned?" he teased, as he continued removing his clothes.

Mara laughed. "No, I couldn't even begin to guess."

Foster had shown her so much pleasure during their nights together that she trusted him implicitly and whatever designs he had for them this evening. "I shall let you surprise me," she added.

"Very well."

She kicked her boots to the floor and began to remove the puffed-sleeve jacket that matched her claret-colored skirt. She then unbuttoned the front of her high-necked black blouse, and her skirt followed. When she had only her black corset and garters left, she looked up to see that Foster stood before her completely naked.

He was glorious. The male form fascinated her. His broad chest, lightly dusted with dark hair. Muscular arms. A trim waist and hips . . . Powerful legs, and of course, the most masculine part of his body, which displayed itself quite proudly.

The very presence of him, standing there, staring at her with his green eyes and an irresistible smile, left her a little breathless.

"You are quite handsome, Lord Sterling."

"And you are so beautiful, Mara. I can't think of anything but you and I've been counting the hours until we could be together again." He stepped toward her and pulled her into his arms.

She stood on her tiptoes and reached around his neck, meeting his kiss with her own. Heavens, but she could kiss this man all day and not get enough. His kisses consumed her.

"As much as I adore how you look just wearing the corset, let's get you out of that contraption." With skilled hands, he released her from the confines of the undergarment in record time. He placed soft kisses along her neck and shoulders, moving down to her breasts. He knelt before her and ran his hands along her stocking-covered legs, unhooking the black garters that held them in place.

Slowly he slid the stockings down her thighs, kissing her skin as he went.

When she was finally as naked as he was, Foster took her hand in his. "Are you ready?"

Suddenly feeling a little nervous, she nodded anyway. What on earth was he planning for them? "I suppose so."

"Then come with me."

He led her across the expanse of his bedroom, which had the same sleek feel as the rest of his house. Mara had come to love this place and thought of it as *their* bedroom. They'd spent all of their time together there and it felt like a luxurious cocoon, where she was safe and loved and nothing else mattered except the two of them. It had become their cherished space where they could be alone and shut out the rest of the world.

Her eyebrows rose in surprise when he brought her into the bathing room.

Granted, Foster's bathing room was the most magnificent one she had ever seen, rivaling even those in her own house or her aunts' houses. It was definitely the most modern one, possessing the very latest innovations in plumbing. The room was decorated with smooth white tiles on the floor and walls and beautiful stained-glass windows. A very large canopy bath stood against one wall, wrapped in a majestic mahogany frame. The room had been lit with beautiful beeswax candles instead of the usual gaslights.

Foster led her to the canopy bath.

"Foster?" she questioned, suddenly beginning to understand what he had planned for them.

He didn't answer, but let go of her hand. He moved quietly to turn the faucet on, allowing the water to run hot and begin to fill the large enameled cast-iron bathtub. He turned around to face her, his expression one of excitement, and held his hand out to her. She knew it was an invitation to join him in the luxurious tub. Giggling with nervousness at the erotic idea of bathing with a man, Mara slowly stepped toward him and took his hand. She pressed her body against his as he kissed her.

Carefully he helped her step into the tub and followed in behind her. They both sank into the warm water. Foster sat with his back against the lower edge of the tub, while Mara sat between his legs, resting her back against his chest. The sensation of the warm water on her skin and Foster's naked body against hers was exquisite.

"I've always wanted to do this," he whispered in her ear, kissing her neck.

She smiled with satisfaction. "You are quite clever to have thought of it." Settling into her position, she relished the intimacy of the two of them together this way, never dreaming that doing anything like this was even possible.

He took a cake of soap from the little tray beside the tub and began to create some lather with it. His hands then moved slowly over her body, through the warm water. With infinite care, he lathered her breasts, circling and massaging each one with the sandalwood-scented soap. Mara sighed at the deliciousness of it all. The warm, soapy water, the woodsy scent, and the mind-melting pleasure of his caresses sent her into a languorous state of relaxation. It was quite extraordinary. Never had her senses been so heightened while her body was so utterly lethargic.

As he continued to kiss the back of her neck, whispering in her ear sweet words, his hands slid lower, across her abdomen, down between her legs. Desire swept through her like flames at his touch. Her own hands wrapped around his knees for support as his fingers began moving, arousing that familiar aching pressure within her that demanded to be released.

"Oh, Foster." She breathed his name as the tension began to build with each stroke of his fingers.

Mara closed her eyes and rested her head against his

broad chest. Time ceased to exist and she gave herself over
to his delectable ministrations. Thrilling waves of pleasure
began to build within her and her breathing began to
quicken as his hand moved faster and faster against her.
Every nerve in her body tightened, anticipating the deca-
dent sense of bliss that was sure to come.

And it did, bursting upon her like an explosion of little
fireworks. Awash in pure sensation, she lost herself in the
sumptuous feelings that flooded her body.

When she could breathe again and floated back down to
earth, she found herself still cradled within Foster's strong
arms. A sense of peace and belonging overcame her and
she sighed deeply in contentment. She could stay like this
forever.

Instead she squirmed around so she was facing him.

He grinned at her in satisfaction. "I love making you feel
that way."

"I love that you can make me feel that way." She smiled
back before kissing him on the mouth. His tongue entered
her mouth and they lost themselves in the passion of their
kiss. He pulled her tighter against him and she thrilled to
the feel of his body against hers.

"You're like a beautiful mermaid in here with me," he
teased.

"A mermaid who is here to serve you," she replied with
a saucy tilt of her head, while fishing around in the tub for
the lost cake of soap. She made a show of looking for it by
touching just about every part of him in her search, splash-
ing and causing them both to laugh. Finally she found the
errant soap near the drain. She positioned herself between
his legs. "I think you need a little cleaning up, sir."

"If you must," he admitted with feigned defeat.

Practically floating across the length of him, hovering
over him, the water in the deep tub covered almost all of her.
Indeed, she did feel a bit like a little mermaid. She certainly

didn't feel like herself. Yet nothing she had ever done in her life felt more real than being with Foster like this. She began to run the soap along his chest, her fingers splaying through the dark hair that lightly covered him. She'd never been this intimate with anyone, and the act of cleansing someone seemed almost sacred, pure somehow. Her eyes were drawn to his. He looked at her with a mix of adoration and desire. How she loved to make him happy!

"Well, I believe you're cleaner now." She playfully kissed the tip of his nose.

Skimming her hands across the expanse of his chest, she then moved lower, down his abdomen, to the protrusion between his legs. Slowly she ran her fingers over the smooth shaft, encircling him, caressing him with the soap. He groaned with pleasure and closed his eyes while she stroked him, up and down, down and up. Being a quick learner, she knew how to touch him now and it excited her to make him feel as wonderful as he made her feel.

She noticed that with a flick of his foot, he pulled the chain that held the stopper in the drain and the water began to slowly recede from the tub. She continued to stroke him with her hands, admiring the contrast of silky softness and firm rigidity at the same time.

As the water continued to empty, he opened his eyes. "Stand up," he commanded, his voice a bit raspy.

With shaky legs and careful maneuvering, they both stood in the tub. He turned some of the knobs and suddenly warm water began to rain down upon them from the shower nozzle above the canopy. He pulled her close to him as the water rinsed the soapy suds from their bodies. She wrapped her arms around his neck, clinging to him.

The water cascaded over them, binding them together. They kissed as the stream washed over their faces. The pleasant sensation and the warmth of the water, the press of their naked skin, created a new wave of desire coursing through her. She loved him so much. Loved that they were sharing this experience together. She wanted to love him as he had loved her.

Mara pulled away, wiping the water from her eyes, grinning. Carefully she lowered herself until she could take him in her mouth. As the water spilled down her back, soaking her hair, she began to run her tongue along the length of his shaft.

"Mara." He groaned her name as he held the walls of the canopy to support himself. His entire body tensed.

Loving the power she felt at giving him pleasure, she continued to move her mouth over him, in and out, as the water fell over them.

"My God," he cried, pulling away from her, breathing heavily. He reached for her, bringing Mara to her feet. Holding on to her, he turned the water off. He pulled her close for a hard, passionate kiss. "I need to be inside of you. Now."

His words caused her heart to pound and her body to grow tense with desire. "I want you inside of me," she whispered back.

He stepped from the tub and grabbed a thick towel from the hook on the wall. He wrapped it around her. She soaked up the warmth of the towel and his arms around her. He lifted her easily from the tub and carried her to the bed with quick steps. They were both still wet and slick as he laid her down on the covers, tossing the towel to the side. He climbed on top of her, positioning himself between her legs.

Foster brought his mouth down over hers, possessing her, claiming her in a heated kiss. He entered her quickly and with hard, need-driven thrusts. She was ready for him, greedy for him, and eager to feel him within her. This was what she had wanted all night, what she had craved all week, and what she had longed for all the time they had been apart. Mara needed this connection with him.

She gripped his muscled arms, holding on as he drove himself in and out of her. Again, time slipped away and her whole focus became the two of them alone and the passion that they shared. The passion that consumed them both.

Words were unnecessary now. They knew what the other desired. They knew what they needed and how to get it. She raised her hips to his, meeting his thrusts, as her need for him grew. That deep ache within her demanded its release as the pressure mounted.

In a frenzy of clasping hands, slick bodies, eager mouths, hot breath and driving thrusts, they both gave in to the surging passion that overwhelmed them.

Mara cried out as the waves of pleasure poured over her once more. Foster continued to move against her with forceful thrusts, becoming more frantic, before he called her name and pulled out from her just as he found his own release. Collapsing beside her in the bed, now damp from their bath, he breathed heavily.

Mara's breath too came in gasps. She slowly regained her senses as she lay on her back. Luxuriating in the sated feeling that now enveloped her, she could not move a muscle. She was content to stay in that bed with him forever.

"Well, the bath and the shower were a wonderful surprise," she whispered.

"I thought so," he said with great satisfaction.

After some time, he raised himself and rested on his elbow, his head against his hand, looking down at her. "You make me happier than I ever dreamed I could be, and I love you more than you know, Mara Reeves."

Mara reached her hand up and touched his cheek, which was rough with the beginning of stubble. She slowly ran her fingers along his jawline, admiring the coarse feel against her skin. "I love you so much, Foster. And I'm glad that I make you happy, because you make me happy."

"You deserve more than I can give you, sweet Mara." He smiled at her. "But I'm changing all of that."

"What do you mean?"

"Never mind, for now," he answered. "I'll let you know when the time is right. Now let's finish drying off and get some food into you."

"I couldn't eat a bite," she said, rolling over and snuggling into the blankets. She didn't want to move from the bed. "I'm completely sated."

"Well, I'm starving, missy." He grinned wickedly. "Being with you works up my appetite."

"For more than food, I would imagine."

He swatted her bottom playfully. "Yes, my appetite for you is much greater than food. But I'm a man, and a man must eat sometime. Come join me."

"I suppose so." She sighed heavily, reluctant to leave the warmth of the bed. The room was chilly and her hair still quite damp. But she draped a small blanket around her and made her way back into the bathing room to clean herself up a bit.

"I'll stoke the fire and warm up the room for you," he called to her.

Alone in the bathing room, Mara stared at her reflection in the mirror. With her dripping hair and wearing nothing but a blanket, she thought, *I am a mistress.*

Although she didn't look as she imagined a mistress would look. A gentleman's mistress would be very sophisticated and worldly. She would be beautiful and seductive. Mara was none of those things. She looked rather like a plain woman with wet hair and wide eyes. Albeit a well kissed, thoroughly loved woman with wet hair and wide eyes.

She looked a bit mad, actually. But then, she would

have to be more than a bit mad to knowingly enter into this relationship, to willingly become Foster's mistress, wouldn't she?

So this was it. This was to be her life. Secret nights, clandestine meetings, skulking around under the cover of darkness. Never being out in the open together. Never introducing Foster to her family. Never sharing how much she loved him with them. Never being with him out in the daylight. Never going to the theater or dining with friends or attending parties together.

She would only ever have a half-life with Foster. They would never live together or share a home. They would never raise a family. She would be relegated to the shadows of his life.

Wiping a tear from her eye, she knew this would be her life until the madness completely took over and he didn't want her anymore. It would have to suffice. Being Foster's mistress would have to compensate for the life she could never have. She had to grab happiness with him while she was able. For now she and Foster loved each other and were happy with each other.

That would have to be enough.

With a brisk shake of her head, Mara splashed cool water from the basin on her face and attempted to fix her hair, which was quite hopeless. With a last look at her reflection, she resolved not to waste their precious time together now worrying about things she could not change. It was what it was.

After finishing her ablutions, she returned to the bedroom. True to his word, Foster had a blazing fire going and had laid the food out on a blanket in front of the mantel, creating an indoor picnic.

"Come get warm," he called. He brought one of his thick quilted robes to her and she gratefully put it on. Mara sat on the blanket near the fire, letting the heat absorb into her body and dry her hair. Foster poured her a glass of wine.

"Well, this is much better." She sighed contentedly after a sip of the fine cabernet.

"I thought you'd like that." Foster, wearing a robe also, sat down on the blanket beside her.

As they ate bread, cheese, and fruit and drank the wine, they talked about everything going on in their lives. She updated him on the plans for the children's bookshop and described the perfect building they had found.

"I have some news too," Foster said. "I went to talk with my solicitors the other day."

"Did you?" she asked idly, staring at the flames. They always mesmerized her. That fire could invite warmth and comfort and then suddenly wreak havoc was a constant mystery.

"Yes, and I don't want to get your hopes up too soon, but . . ." He paused dramatically. "I'm getting an annulment for my marriage with Rose."

Mara sat bolt upright. "What did you say?"

"We cannot continue on as we have, and I cannot keep you as my mistress, Mara," he explained matter-of-factly. "We're bound to be discovered if we keep this up, and I refuse to let you be ruined. You deserve better. We both deserve more than this. *We* deserve a real life together. A marriage. A family. I want those things with you. I wish to marry you as soon as I can."

The blood rushed from her face and her heart felt like it stopped. What was Foster saying? What was he thinking? This wasn't supposed to happen! He wasn't supposed to end his marriage. Oh, God, she couldn't possibly marry him!

"Mara? Did you hear what I said?"

She stared at him and nodded her head.

He smiled broadly, his excitement evident in his manner. "I've left you speechless! I knew you would be happy. Lord knows *I'm* happy to finally end my marriage. I only wish I had done it years ago! I even went to Yorkshire this week to tell Rose."

"You told her about me?" Mara was horrified. Mortified. This was not how things were supposed to go.

"I didn't tell her about us or you specifically, but she did guess that I had met a woman I wished to marry. I informed her that I am seeking an annulment."

"Whatever did she say?" Mara asked.

Foster hesitated. "Well, she was not pleased, as you can imagine. But I don't need her permission or her consent. It's out of her hands completely. My solicitor said I have grounds for an annulment and is putting the case together. I'm not sure how long it will take, but rest assured it will happen, Mara. And then we won't have to hide in secret. We can be married and spend our lives together as we've longed to."

Mara's heart sank. This was what she had wanted to avoid from the start. Marriage. Children. She could never have those things, and she had believed she was safe with a man who was already married! Why couldn't he be content to let things alone?

Foster, when faced with Mara's inevitable insanity, would only grow to resent her. In spite of his sympathetic words after witnessing her premonition that first night, she knew it was only a matter of time before he would be embarrassed and ashamed of her peculiarity. And as her madness took more of a grip upon her, one day he would look at her in revulsion and pity. That she could not bear. And she simply could not risk passing on her illness to their children.

Mara could not speak.

"Aren't you happy?" he asked.

He looked at her with such joy, such hope, and so much love that she did not have the heart to deny him. She smiled faintly, wishing her life were different, and nodded her head. She would gladly marry him if she could. In truth, what he was doing was for her truly touching. She never expected him to end his marriage to be with her. The fact that he wanted to marry her was quite honorable, but he would never marry her if he knew the ugly truth.

She leaned over and gave him a kiss on the lips. Then she whispered, "It's getting rather late. I should get home."

"I hate that you have to leave." He kissed her back. "One day soon, when we're properly married, we will never have to part at night."

Again, she said not a word, for there was nothing more to say. She could never marry Foster.

Silently they both dressed and followed their routine to get her back to Devon House. He drove her in his carriage, and they kissed good night, before dropping her at the back gate of her aunt's house.

Mara unlocked the door and slipped cautiously in through the dark kitchen, and with silent feet tiptoed up the servants' staircase and down the hallway to her bedroom. The house was quiet, but being that it was close to three in the morning, everyone was sound asleep.

Noiselessly Mara opened the door to her bedroom, relieved to have arrived home once again without being caught. Especially looking as disheveled as she did. That shower with Foster had ruined her hair, but it had been worth it. As usual, Brighton left a small lamp burning for her. Carefully she closed the door behind her, sighed heavily and closed her eyes, leaning her back against the door.

Leaving Foster became more difficult each time they were together. She loved him so much, yet tonight he left her quite worried. If he were truly seeking an annulment, their affair was going to have to end sooner than she would have liked.

And she most definitely did not want to end things with him. Not yet.

Wearily she opened her eyes and almost jumped out of her skin when she suddenly noticed her cousin, Phillip Sinclair, sitting in a chair by the mantel, his arms folded across his chest. He did not look happy with her at all. In fact, he looked quite furious.

"Where the hell have you been?"

15

Instigations

R ose Sheridan simply would not stand for it.
She seethed with anger as she sat in a hired carriage, staring out at the large white mansion, waiting and watching.

Arriving in London a few days ago, she'd checked into the Hotel Savoy, not wishing for Foster to know she was in town. She had left Yorkshire the day after he had been to see her and tell her his shocking news. If he thought he was going to end their marriage after ten years, he was sadly mistaken. With all Foster's forward-thinking ideas and visions of progress, a divorce would not be among them. Not even an annulment. Rose would not abide it.

So she devised a plan to stop him from obtaining an annulment. It was a simple plan. It was classic blackmail. She only needed to find something to blackmail him with. So she hurried down to London after him. She despised the city and it cost her quite a bit of effort to venture there. It had been an exhausting few days, but she finally believed she had something to use against him.

Rose had been correct in her assumption that he'd fallen in love with a lady!

The first order of business when she arrived in town was to meet with Briggs, the man she had hired to spy on her husband all these years.

"He's keeping this one very secret, my lady," Briggs said, after telling Rose he had had some trouble discovering who Foster's current paramour was, if there was one.

Bailey Briggs was a lanky man in his late thirties with a nondescript face and average coloring, which made him an ideal investigator. No one noticed him, and if they did, they never remembered what he looked like. He used to work on the estate in Yorkshire as a coachman, but Rose had hired him to keep an eye on Foster while he was in London. He wasn't the brightest man, but he'd done a good job for her over the years. She paid him well and he was loyal to her. Being a countess had its privileges.

And she was not about to give those up.

Briggs continued his report. "I've seen no woman going to the townhouse. Lord Sterling hasn't been doing any of his usual activities, like attending the theater or out publicly with a lady. It seems he ended his affair with the actress, Annie Blake, and he purchased a townhome for her recently. Are you quite sure he's already taken up with someone new?"

"Yes, I'm positive," Rose snapped, irritated with his lack of information. "But this is not his usual type of harlot. I think this one is a true lady. I want you to find out who she is. Find out everything you can about her and what their plans are. I shall pay you handsomely." She paused. "More than I usually do."

"I'll see what I can do," said Briggs, looking thoughtful. "But I did hear about one thing today that seemed a little odd. One of Lord Sterling's housemaids, Nellie, tells me things from time to time, if I buy her a pint at the King's Head. She was how I found out about his last mistress.

Nice girl, Nellie. Pretty, too. Anyway, Nellie told me just this morning before I came to see you, that lately Lord Sterling has been giving the entire staff the night off."

Rose's interest piqued. "How often does he do this?"

"Nellie says about once a week for the last month or so." Briggs shrugged his shoulders. "Says he never gives them much notice, just tells them all to leave for the night. Only the butler stays. But I've tried talking to him before. That guy is shut up tighter than a nun's—" He cut himself off, slightly embarrassed. "Anyway . . . Nellie says it's all very mysterious and no one knows why he's been doing this."

"Well, *I* know why!" Rose declared with great annoyance.

Briggs looked at her with a mystified expression.

"Honestly, Briggs!" Rose snapped. "If I can figure this out, surely you can!"

He scratched his head, looking uncomfortable. "Well, my lady, like I told you, I only just learned about it before I saw you, so I haven't had as much time to mull it over as I'd like to."

"Must I spell it out for you, Briggs?" Exasperated, Rose took a fortifying breath. "When Lord Sterling dismisses his house servants, he is obviously having a secret rendezvous with a woman. A woman whose honor he wishes to keep protected."

The man raised his eyebrows and nodded slowly. "You may be right about that, my lady."

"Of course I'm right about that!" she barked, biting her tongue before she called him a fool. Talking to him was causing her head to throb more than usual. "Now this is a different kind of assignment than the others. This one will require you to use all your wits. What you need to do, Briggs, is find out exactly who Lord Sterling is entertaining on these nights."

"Yes, my lady."

Rose reached into her reticule and gave him a pound

note. "Go buy Nellie a few drinks at the King's Head and make her promise to tell you right away the next time Lord Sterling dismisses them for the evening. And then you sit yourself outside that townhouse all night and watch who comes and goes. I want to know every detail, no matter how insignificant you may think it is. Do you understand me?"

"Yes, my lady, I do." Briggs pocketed the money and tipped his hat. "I will report back to you the moment I discover anything of note. Good day, Lady Sterling."

Rose then spent the next two days at the Hotel Savoy, waiting for news from Briggs. Furious that Foster wished to end the marriage because he wanted to marry someone else, Rose was beside herself. She had not cared a whit that Foster had kept mistresses over the years. In fact, she gladly welcomed their presence in his life. These cheap women had kept Foster happily occupied and away from her, and that had been her main concern. It was the only reason she had her husband watched.

As long as Foster had a woman in his bed, Rose could rest easily in hers.

Rose's life had been nothing but a series of disappointments, despair, and heartaches, and she would be damned if Foster was going to leave her with nothing after everything she had been through. Being the Countess of Sterling was all she had left, and she refused to give up what rightfully belonged to her.

What made him think he could simply walk away and cut her out of his life, as though she never mattered or never existed? How *dared* he? She simply wouldn't have it. Not now. Not after everything that had happened to her.

"You haven't eaten yet today, my lady," Alice Bellwether reminded her as they sat in her hotel suite. "Shall I bring you some biscuits or tea cakes?"

Rose didn't want to eat anything. She was too angry and too tired to eat. Alice meant well, of course, but Rose was growing weary of her constant hovering. Yet she could not alienate Alice. That woman was the only person in the world who cared about her.

Rose placated her. "I promise that I'll eat something a little late—"

A sudden knock at their hotel room door caught her attention.

It was Briggs and he happened to come calling with some important news, a vital piece of information, which cheered Rose greatly.

"When Nellie gave me the word, I spent all night, as soon as it was dark, watching Lord Sterling's house." Briggs smiled triumphantly as he spoke. "You were right, my lady. I saw a woman wearing a dark cloak enter the back of the townhouse in the early evening, just past six. So I waited and watched until Lord Sterling took her home in his carriage in the wee hours of the morning."

And wasn't her home just the clue they needed to identify her? Devon House. That large, white monstrosity of a house in Mayfair that belonged to the Marquis of Stancliff was where the girl lived. At first Rose thought that perhaps Foster was having an affair with Lady Stancliff, but that didn't quite fit. Colette Sinclair had a grown son only a few years younger than Foster. Besides being the wrong age for Foster, it was well-known that Lord and Lady Stancliff were besotted with each other. It took some further digging to discover the probable identity of the mystery woman, but Briggs had come through for her yet again.

It seemed Lord and Lady Stancliff had their pretty, young niece staying with them. A Lady Mara Reeves, and by all accounts she was a sweet, quiet little thing. Just the sort of lady who would need her honor protected. The daughter of the Earl of Cashelmore would not want her name and reputation sullied and would certainly not want the world to know that she was carrying on an illicit affair with a married man.

Thrilled by the discovery, Rose gave Briggs a large bonus, told him to buy Nellie another drink, and instructed him to keep up his surveillance of Foster's residence as well as Devon House, and continue to report back to her daily. In the meantime she could not resist a little peek at the new lady in Foster's life.

So there Rose found herself, seated in a carriage outside Devon House with Alice Bellwether by her side, hoping and waiting for Lady Mara Reeves to appear. It was a damp October afternoon and she shivered, in spite of the hot bricks at her feet and the thick woolen blanket wrapped around her.

"It's so cold! I can't feel my toes." Rubbing her hands together, Alice asked impatiently, "How much longer should we wait here?"

"Until I see what I came for." Rose prayed it would not be much longer. Her whole body ached, her head was splitting, and she was just as cold as Alice claimed to be. But she needed to see the girl with her own eyes. She needed to be sure. She had to know. Who was this girl who thought she could simply waltz in and take Rose's husband from her? Who was this woman that Foster intended to marry after he got rid of Rose?

Suddenly her heart leapt when Alice cried, "There! Look!"

Rose peered out the carriage window in anticipation. Was it her?

The large front doors of Devon House opened and down the marble steps came two ladies. Both were attractive and elegantly dressed. Rose focused her attention on the younger one, following her hunch that this was Lady Mara Reeves with her aunt.

The girl was petite and very fair and seemed quite delicate. Her silvery blond hair was visible under the stylish little bonnet on her head. Rose had to admit there was an aura of fragility and innocence about the girl. But she barely had time to notice more than that before the two women climbed into the large carriage waiting for them out front.

"Was that her?" Alice asked breathlessly, her red curls bouncing with excitement under her hat.

"I'm not entirely sure, but I believe it may be." Rose instructed her coach driver to follow the carriage with the two women. "Let's see where they go."

They didn't have long to find out. Both carriages made their way through the London streets until they stopped outside what seemed to be a bookshop.

Alice could barely contain herself. "They must be shopping! Shall we go in too?"

Catching some of Alice's enthusiasm, Rose had a burst of energy she hadn't felt in years. Why not go in? The girl had no idea who Rose was. She'd get a better glimpse of her this way. So with some effort, Alice and the coachman helped Rose down from the carriage and the two of them made their way into a store called the Hamilton Sisters' Book Shoppe.

It was a fairly modern, large building with a handsome façade. The bell over the door jingled as they walked in. The inside of the shop was lovely, actually. Rose had never set foot in a bookstore before, since reading had never interested her, but the place surprised her. It was light, airy, and inviting. Wooden bookshelves were attractively arranged and there were pretty displays of sundry articles, such as stationery, notepaper, inkpots and writing implements. Comfortable seating areas and tables with light refreshments of fragrant teas and freshly baked scones were available for the enjoyment of their patrons.

Rose and Alice meandered slowly around the shop. Rose

nearly forgot to keep an eye out for the girl, so entranced
was she with the bookstore. It almost made her wish she
enjoyed reading books. A heavy sigh escaped her. Why
hadn't she ever visited a bookshop before? Or spent her
days reading a book or two from time to time? There had
been so many lost opportunities in her life and so many
things she would never do. Sadness enveloped her.

"Where did they go?" Alice whispered.

"I'm not sure," Rose replied. The store wasn't so large
that they could easily lose two people. Granted, there were
other customers browsing and some salesclerks were walking about, but there were no signs of the two women. How
could they just disappear? It made no sense.

"May I help you, ma'am?"

Rose spun around at the sound of a soft, pleasant voice
with a trace of an accent and came face-to-face with *her*.
At this close range, Rose could see how stunningly beautiful the girl was. Soft ivory skin, a pert little nose, silky
blond hair, rosebud lips, and those eyes! She had the most
remarkable eyes. They were wide and thickly lashed, but it
was the color. Were they soft green or misty gray? They
were mesmerizing.

Well, the girl certainly didn't seem to be a seductress, or
even particularly sophisticated. There was a sweet innocence about her. Surely she could not be the one who was
visiting Foster's bed at night! Rose just could not see it!

"Is there a particular book I can help you find?" The girl
smiled at her, radiating kindness. "Or would you prefer to
just browse on your own?"

Rose suddenly lost her voice.

Confused by the girl's words, Rose didn't know what to
say. Was the girl working here? Was she employed to work
in a bookshop? It made no sense whatsoever. Young noble

ladies did not *work*! In shops! Rose grew a little dizzy, trying to comprehend the situation.

A look of genuine concern came over the girl's pretty face. "Ma'am, are you sure you are quite well? Would you care to sit down? Can I get you a glass of water, perhaps?"

Rose cleared her throat. "Yes, please. Thank you. That would be most appreciated."

"Of course, please come this way." She guided Rose a short distance to a chintz-covered armchair, while Alice scurried behind them. The girl then instructed another employee to fetch some water for her.

Actually grateful to sit down, Rose hadn't realized how tired she was. She sank into the comfortable flowered cushions, trying to catch her breath. Alice began to hover over her. However, the girl simply stood there, remaining calm and handing the glass of water to Rose when it arrived.

"Please just rest for a moment or two," she suggested kindly, her voice full of earnestness and sympathy. "Can I get you anything else?"

Rose shook her head before taking a sip of the cool water. It did help revive her somewhat. "Thank you," she managed to utter. "You've been quite kind. Please tell me your name . . ."

"I'm Mara Reeves."

It *was* her. Lady Mara Reeves. This lovely woman was the one. Foster was leaving her for this pretty young girl. This was the woman who was sneaking over to Foster's house in the dark of night. *This* was whom he wanted to marry. Rose could easily understand Foster's desire to wed this woman. In spite of her reckless behavior at night, there was nothing tawdry or cheap about Lady Mara Reeves. Unlike the other types of women Foster consorted with.

"And please feel free to rest as long as you like," Mara

said with a little smile. "I'll be over by the counter up front if you have need of me." She then moved to leave.

"Have you worked here long?" Rose couldn't help herself from asking, not wanting the girl to leave just yet.

Mara turned to face her with a contented air. "Yes, I've worked here since I was a little girl. My family owns this shop. If you are looking for anything in particular or would like some help choosing a book, please don't hesitate to ask me."

Rose didn't know what to say to that, aside from the big question she was dying to ask. *Why are you trying to steal my husband?*

The situation was not at all what she expected. This woman was not what she had envisioned as the type to be having an affair with Foster.

Rose suddenly hated this sweet, beautiful girl, who seemed lovely, kind, and well loved and cared for by her family. This young woman had her whole life ahead of her. A life that she apparently wanted to share with Rose's husband.

It was the kind of life that Rose had once wanted for herself years ago when she too had been young and hopeful. A life that Rose could never have. Would never have. Ever. Not now. It was over for her. It was far too late to change anything.

But she certainly wasn't giving up her husband to this girl who could still have whatever she wanted.

Absolutely not. Rose was not having it.

In that moment every single ounce of bitterness in her life, resentment of her parents, heartache over her lost love and dead child, and anger at Foster that dwelled within Rose boiled over into a deep and overwhelming hatred that was now directed squarely at this young girl who seemed to have everything. The girl who had the happy and fulfilling life that Rose should have had.

Her head began to ache again and she desperately wanted to lie down. It was time to go. She had seen what she'd come for.

With a heavy heart, Rose murmured her thanks to Foster's harlot and motioned for Alice to help escort her from the shop. She had work of her own to do.

She had to execute the next part of her plan.

16

Ramifications

As Mara watched the sad, rather sickly looking woman leave the bookshop, an odd feeling settled over her chest. There was something strange about the woman, almost eerie. The way she looked at Mara, with a curious mixture of interest and dislike and surprise. Mara wondered who she was, even as she felt an incredible sense of relief at her departure.

With a determined shake of her head, Mara gathered the heavy leather-bound ledger from behind the counter. She had more pressing matters to attend to than worrying about a peculiar woman who wandered into the shop.

"Can I get you anything else, Mara?" asked Anna Hastings, a tall brunette. She was one of Hamilton's most trusted managers and had worked there for years.

"The ledger was all my aunt wanted to see, but thank you, Anna. We'll be upstairs if you need us." Mara made her way from the front counter to the staircase that led to the suite of private offices above the main shop.

She had come to Hamilton Sisters' Book Shoppe with

Aunt Colette to go over the books and continue with the plans for the children's bookshop that afternoon. But Mara was still reeling from her encounter with Phillip the night before last.

That nightmare kept repeating over and over in her mind.

Finding her cousin waiting for her in her bedroom gave Mara the shock of her life. The worry and anger on Phillip's face was enough to bring her to tears. In fact, she did cry.

Where the hell have you been?

His question saw all her worst fears realized. And Mara had no reasonable answer that she could give him. Truly, where on earth could she safely say she had been until three o'clock in the morning? There was nowhere. Instead, she simply stared at him, unable to speak or move. The horror at being found out had paralyzed her.

"So you're not going to answer me. I couldn't get anything out of Brighton either," he'd said as he scrutinized her.

He was quite irate and justifiably so. Mara realized it was an anger born from his worry and concern for her welfare.

Phillip had continued to rant at her. "Brighton claimed not to know where you were, only insisting that I not worry. She said that you were safe and not in any danger but managed to let slip that this was not your first venture out during the evenings when you'd led all of us to believe you weren't feeling well."

Mara needed to give Brighton a wonderful bonus. Her lady's maid was indeed a treasure. Brighton knew exactly where Mara had been, but she hadn't revealed Mara's secret, even under duress from her cousin. Brighton's loyalty was exceptional. Although the poor girl must have been frightened by Phillip questioning her in such a manner.

"So I've been sitting here for hours, wondering where my sweet little cousin could be all night . . ." Phillip began to pace back and forth in front of her. "Wondering where she has been spending more than a few nights. I've racked my brain trying to think of a logical and sane reason that would justify my lovely, unmarried cousin being out alone in the city until all hours. And do you know what, Mara?"

Phillip had glared at her. Her heart slamming against her chest, Mara swallowed, but she had still not uttered a single word. She stared mutely at Phillip.

"I could only come to one conclusion," he continued explaining his thought process. "Care to take a guess as to what I came up with?"

Very slowly Mara shook her head, her heart in her mouth. She wished she could just crawl into a hole in the floor and hide.

He paused for a moment, standing still, eyeing her closely. "You're involved with a man, aren't you?"

Mara remained motionless at his accusation. He was absolutely right. Her cheeks flamed in embarrassment and shame. The answer was written all over her face. Mara didn't need a mirror to know what she looked like in her disheveled outfit, from her well-kissed lips to her tousled hair. She had just showered with Foster, for goodness' sake!

"I gather from your lack of protest that I am correct," he'd gone on to say. Then he'd raked her with an appraising look. "Not to mention your current appearance . . . like you just tumbled out of bed." Phillip shook his head in disbelief. "I've given this a lot of thought, Mara, since I had plenty of time to think while I was waiting here, sick with worry over you. Aren't you the least bit interested in what I have to say?"

Again Mara shook her head.

"I'd shake my head too, if I were you," he acknowledged ruefully. He resumed pacing back and forth. "With all this time on my hands waiting here the last few hours, I began to ask myself what kind of man entertains a well-bred young lady secretly at his home in the middle of the night? Certainly no respectable gentleman would do such a thing. But I thought, Mara has no contact with disreputable fellows and she's not one for rough or coarse men. So it would have to be someone from our own ranks. A gentleman . . . But only a gentleman who had something to hide. Perhaps a gentleman who didn't want *his wife* to discover what he was doing." He stopped pacing and looked at her knowingly. "I'm correct, aren't I?"

Mara barely nodded her head in acknowledgment. She held her breath, afraid to make a sound.

"Mara! What in God's name are you thinking?" he cried in anguish. His face was aghast with horror. "A married man?"

Feeling faint, the entire room spun around her. She had not moved an inch from where she had stood with her back against the door, and now she pressed herself against it to keep herself upright. What on earth had brought Phillip to seek her out this evening? Why was he even in her room? How had this happened?

"Who is he?" Phillip demanded, his eyes flashing angrily.

Mara could not respond.

"Do I know him?"

Unable to stop herself from nodding her head, she cringed. Mara had never been a good liar. She could keep others' secrets and she could easily remain silent, but she had a terrible time lying when it came to herself. Especially when asked a direct question.

"Who is he?" Phillip repeated. His face grew red with outrage. "When I find out who he is, and believe me, Mara, I will find out, I shall kill him!"

The threat of physical violence finally spurred Mara from her horrified stupor. She flung herself from the doorway. And once she started speaking, the words came out in an unstoppable torrent.

"Stop! Please stop it, Phillip! I'm very sorry to have worried you. That was never my intention. But there is no need for you to kill anyone. I'm fine. I am safe. I'm not in any danger, nor have I ever been. I am a grown woman, not a child, if you haven't noticed. I can think for myself and make my own decisions. No one is responsible for my actions but me. And what I happen to be doing with my life is of no concern to you. Yes. I'm involved with a gentleman, and yes, he happens to be married. I'm not going to tell you his name, only that there are extenuating circumstances to his marriage and that his wife lives hundreds of miles away. But I will tell you that it was an arranged marriage when he was very young. It's a dreadful marriage. He has not ever lived with his wife and they haven't any children."

Phillip was stunned into silence at her unexpected outburst and remained still while she spoke.

Mara continued to explain, for she had no other choice but to defend herself. "Imagine that life for yourself, Phillip, before you pass judgment on him or me . . . Being forced to wed a girl you don't even like because your parents made you, and you are then tied to her for the rest of your life, and you are miserable together. Yes, I'm quite aware that being with a married man goes against everything that is right and moral in our society, but that is something I have reconciled with myself. That he is married doesn't matter to me. He is a gentleman. He's wonderful and kind and caring. We are not hurting anyone. His wife doesn't care. We are being very careful. He loves me and I love him very much, and unfortunately, this is the only way we can be together. No matter what you think of me, I shall continue to see him in secret and there is nothing you need to worry yourself about. What I am doing has nothing to do with you or anyone else. It only concerns him and me and we've worked out things between us. So I don't need your help or your protection or your righteous anger. But I do know you love me, and out of that love for me, I would ask that you keep this information to yourself and not share it with your parents or mine."

Mara finally stopped to take a breath. Phillip stared at her with a look of utter disbelief on his face.

"This is why you stayed in London, isn't it? To be with him?" he asked calmly, her words having had a softening effect on him.

Mara nodded.

"It's late," said Phillip with a defeated sigh. "And I'm rather shocked and exhausted, but relieved to see that you are finally home safe." He paused and shook his head before adding, "Well, I'm not quite sure if you're *safe*. But we'll not talk about it anymore tonight. However, know this . . . You've been like a younger sister to me, Mara, and I care very much about what happens to you. Even though I ought to tell your parents, I won't tell anyone about what you've been doing, but I would caution you to rethink how you have been behaving."

Mara could hardly believe his benevolence. "You really won't tell, Phillip?"

Shaking his head wearily, he answered her with great reluctance. "No, I won't tell. At least not for now. But I reserve the right to change my mind at any time."

"Thank you," she whispered. A wonderful sense of relief flooded her.

"I'll go, but before I do, I must say this." Phillip stared at her with sadness in his eyes. "Be very careful. You could ruin your entire life, Mara. Good night." He placed a kiss on her cheek and then Phillip left her bedroom.

His parting words still haunted her. *You could ruin your life, Mara.*

Phillip was quite right, of course. But he was also very wrong. She couldn't ruin her life, for her life was already ruined. It was just that no one realized it yet but her. Mara was only trying to live and be happy while she was still able to. Was it wrong to grab love and happiness with both hands before it was too late for her?

Since the night of his discovery of her affair with Foster, Mara had kept her distance from Phillip and tried to behave normally around him when she did see him. She wondered whether to tell Foster that her cousin had discovered that she had been sneaking out to see him at night.

But as much as she worried about Phillip informing his parents and her parents about what she'd been doing, she was still more worried about Foster telling her that he was going to end his marriage. That saddened her most of all. She loved Foster and was honored that he wanted to marry her. She frankly wished with all her heart that she could marry him.

But it was not to be. She could never marry Foster, even if he managed to end his marriage. He would want children. And that she just could not allow. Nor could she abide for Foster to watch her lose her mind little by little in the coming years. He didn't deserve that.

With a long sigh of regret, Mara made her way up the stairs of the bookshop, carrying the heavy accounting ledger in her hands. Suddenly the image of that strange woman came into her mind again. Something about her made Mara feel uncomfortable and quite sad. The woman had looked at her so intently with very troubled eyes.

And then it started.

It came on so quickly this time that Mara dropped the leather-bound ledger and sank to her knees on the steps. With one hand she gripped the railing, as she grew dizzier and dizzier.

An icy, tingling sensation slowly crept over her skin, and every nerve in her body became acutely aware. The hair on the back of her neck stood on end and her teeth clenched. She grew hot and yet she began shivering. Her heart thumped erratically against her chest. Mara closed her eyes and held her breath, pressing her fingers to her temples. Everything around her receded into a dark fog of silence. Small pin-pricks of consciousness lit up inside of her, creating flashing sparks and light within her mind.

Misty images began presenting themselves to her . . .

Fire. Glints of flames. Blinding bursts of light. Shimmering walls of golden orange and brilliant yellow. Breathtaking, scorching heat. Trapped in the burning building, blazing embers and smoky ash filling the air, Mara didn't know where to go or how to escape. Where was she? How was she to get out? Gut-wrenching, tormented screams echoed against the rush of flames. Someone was in great agony. A woman's desperate cries pierced the smoke-filled air. But where was she? Mara could not see, did not know where to go. This place was unfamiliar to her. Her own panicked, terrified cries reverberated around her.

Someone needed her help. A woman called to her, pleading with her, begging her. Through a break in the smoke, Mara glimpsed the face. The face of a woman with sad, troubled eyes filled with hatred, stared at her. The woman was trapped by the fire, her thin frame engulfed in orange and gold flames.

Scalding tears, knowing it was her fault, knowing it was too late, Mara fled. Blinding heat and black smoke and swirling flames, the vicious sting of fear and the horrific smell of imminent death surrounded her. It was too late. Too late.

Her death. She was going to die in this raging inferno. They were both going to die there.

Swirling darkness. She gasped and fell to her knees. A short breath of blessedly cool air. She crawled forward, reaching for the hand that would save her. Foster grabbed her and lifted her into his arms. She was safe within his embrace. She could breathe again . . .

"Mara! Are you all right?"

Mara opened her eyes, feeling quite faint and dizzy. She was seated on the steps and Aunt Colette was sitting beside her.

"You must have fallen," Aunt Colette said, concern in her voice. "I heard a noise and looked down and there you were. Are you hurt?"

"I tripped, that's all. I'm fine." Mara attempted a smile, as Aunt Colette helped her to her feet. "Just a little embarrassed."

But she was truly shaken. This premonition frightened her.

It was now the fourth time she'd experienced the same premonition about a fire since she'd met Foster. But this one was quite different than the others in one respect. There was a third person in this vision. A woman.

The very same woman who had visited the bookshop just a short time ago.

Mara wasn't sure what alarmed her more; the growing frequency and intensity of her visions, or the fact that a strange, sickly woman had so spooked her and then presented herself in the vision she'd been having for the last month.

17

Visions

Paulette Hamilton Reeves reread the letter for the third time. Her heart sank and she knew something had to be done. Never one to put things off, she rose from the chair where she had been sitting at her little desk in her morning room and made her way into her husband's large study within Cashelmore Manor.

Cashelmore was a beautiful home and, as the Countess of Cashelmore, Paulette had worked hard over the years transforming it from a vast, overly ornate and uninviting house into a warm, beautiful, and more welcoming home for their little family. She had grown to love the house, the estate, and the rolling Irish hills that surrounded it.

"Declan," she called, after knocking briefly and opening the door to his study.

He looked up as she came in and grinned happily when he saw her. "To what do I owe the pleasure of my wife's company this morning?"

After seventeen years together, Declan still managed to make Paulette's heart skip a beat whenever she saw him. His handsome face had aged well, with few wrinkles around his green eyes. His dark hair had some sprinkles of gray, but his smile still made her weak-kneed. Their love for each other had only grown stronger over the years.

"But from the look on your pretty face, I can tell something is wrong," Declan continued, immediately rising from his seat and coming toward her.

Paulette headed for the wide mahogany desk. "I think we should return to London."

Declan placed a sweet kiss on her lips before she handed him the letter she had received from London that morning.

His dark brows drawing together in puzzlement, Declan took the letter from her and returned to his seat behind the desk. He gave her a pointed look before he began reading. Paulette stood by, watching the man she loved as he read, wondering how he would react to the news about his daughter. Their daughter. For Paulette loved Mara as if she were of her own flesh and blood.

And the letter she had received from Jeffrey Eddington had raised her concern over their daughter's welfare.

With a heavy sigh, Declan put down the letter and turned to her, his eyes filled with doubt. "I'm not sure what to do."

"We should return home," she insisted. "Aren't you worried about her?"

"I've always been worried about Mara. I didn't wish to leave her alone in London in the first place, if you recall." Declan shrugged. "But I don't know that our going home now will change anything."

"But clearly Jeffrey is worried about her! He states that she seems distressed about something and he has concerns about her well-being," Paulette pointed out. If anything happened to Mara while they were gone, Paulette would never forgive herself. "And I realize that I am totally to blame for allowing her to stay in London without us. I pushed you into agreeing with me, when you would have preferred that she come with us to Ireland."

Declan reached over and pulled his wife onto his lap, wrapping his arms around her, holding her close. "I'm not blaming you, my love. I admit that I was reluctant at first. But we made the decision together to let her stay there. I agreed with you, especially when you said that Mara never asks for anything and that it was important to her to stay. There was nothing wrong with Mara wanting that or for us to allow it. You were absolutely right. After everything the poor girl has been through in her life, I tend to be over-protective of her and she probably needed some time away from us. Especially me. She's twenty-two years old and in the care of Colette and Lucien, who love her almost as much as we do . . . So there is no blame to be placed any-where." Declan kissed her cheek.

"But Jeffrey's letter," Paulette protested.

"There's nothing in that letter to alarm us." He attempted to calm her. "Jeffrey simply wanted us to be aware that he had spoken to Mara."

"Read between the lines, Declan! When was the last time we received a letter from Jeffrey? He's almost as bad as Juliette when it comes to correspondence. I know he doesn't blatantly write that he's worried about her or that strange little 'episode' she had while she was with him. But it's the reason why he has written to us. We should go back," Paulette said, biting her lip.

"To do what? If something were truly wrong with Mara, Jeffrey would have come right out and said so."

"It's what he's *not* saying that worries me." Something in Jeffrey's carefully worded letter didn't sit right with Paulette. He was alluding to the fact that he was worried about Mara because she was distressed about something.

"I think you're reading too much into it, my love."

"Well, just what does he mean by *episode*?" Paulette rested her head on his chest, listening to his heartbeat, feeling secure and loved in her husband's embrace, as she always did.

"I'm not entirely sure." Declan ran his hand up and down Paulette's arm, soothing her. He grew thoughtful. "I wonder if he means what I think he does . . . I suppose he may be referring to something that happened when Mara was quite young. She had an episode of sorts then."

"Why do I not know about this?"

"You do. I told you years ago when it happened, remember? Mara had a kind of premonition . . . I guess you could call it, about Thomas. I was walking with her in the gardens and she told me that she had 'seen' Thomas falling down the marble steps overlooking the garden and that we should take care not to let him out there. I thought she was being fanciful and brushed it aside. And not a week later, do you recall what happened?" he asked softly.

"How could I forget that?" she cried. "Thomas escaped from his nanny and fell down those very steps and hit his head. I thought he was dead! And he very nearly was. That was a terrible day."

Paulette shuddered at the memory of finding their mischievous three-year-old son, lying motionless at the bottom of the marble steps. He had fully recovered, thank the heavens! But it had been a terrifying ordeal nonetheless. The doctor had been sent for and for days they had kept little Thomas in bed, which was no easy feat. Had Declan told her that Mara had a foreshadowing of Thomas's fall? Paulette supposed he had, but she had been too preoccupied taking care of their son at the time to pay much attention to it.

"It was a terrible day and Mara was more distraught than you were," Declan recalled. "She kept crying, 'I told you, I told you.' She blamed herself for allowing Thomas's fall to happen in the first place. I had quite a time calming her down and dissuading her from taking the blame. It was no one's fault, just an accident. But she kept telling me she had *seen* it happening before it happened. A full week before Thomas fell, and it wasn't as if Thomas ever played there."

"You're saying Mara has the sight?" Paulette asked on a whisper.

"Possibly. She never really talked to me about it again. I thought perhaps she'd grown out of it. But you know Mara, she always had her *feelings* about things and would often tell us what would happen before something did. I just believed her to be very observant and intuitive."

"Yes, that's always been her way since she was a little girl," Paulette agreed. "Mara is a deep thinker, a watcher and a feeler."

Ever since Paulette had first met Mara, the child had been a silent observer of the world around her. Traumatized by the horrific death of her mother, the child had not spoken a word in over a year, instead watching with her wide gray-green eyes, taking in everything around her. Little Mara had gravitated to Paulette right from the start. That alone touched Paulette's heart as she grew to love Declan's daughter in that moment.

Declan sounded remorseful. "I thought because she didn't talk about it again, that she didn't have any more of those visions. But looking back now, I may have been wrong. Perhaps I should have discussed it with her, pressed her a bit more to let me know what was happening with her."

"How could you have known?" Paulette kissed his cheek. "Mara knows how much you love her, how much we both love and adore her. If anything was seriously troubling her, I believe she would have come to one of us."

"I'd like to think she would. Yet her letters to us have

revealed nothing unusual. She seems quite pleased with the plans for the children's bookshop and working on the preparations with Colette." Declan's face grew pensive. "Maybe we're wrong to think things are fine, though."

"What are you suggesting?"

"I'm not sure." He shook his head. "I've just always worried about Mara. Not that she ever caused trouble or anything like that. She was always so sweet, loving, and thoughtful, and had been through such an awful ordeal that I worried about it haunting her and the effects it had on her. She's always been so reticent to marry, that I fear that maybe she remembers things."

"What things?"

"The night of the fire"—Declan closed his eyes—"and the awful things I screamed at Margaret, not knowing that Mara was there. Just all of it."

Paulette hesitated for a moment. "I've given this a lot of thought, Declan. Whatever horrors Mara witnessed the night of the fire are one thing. And obviously watching her mother burn to death was the cause of her not speaking for a year. But she was so young and those memories fade over time, and it's been close to twenty years now. If you're worried about what happened between you and Margaret and you're thinking that relationship has somehow caused Mara to fear marriage, I think you're wrong. If anything, our marriage has set a wonderful example for her."

"Then what do you think the matter is?" he asked, looking perplexed.

"I don't know." A weary sigh escaped her. "We've talked about her lack of interest in marriage many times, and I know you would be relieved to see her happily married to a man she loves, but that may not happen for her. Or it may not have happened yet. Mara is a very special girl and she deserves a very special man to love her. She has not met him yet. But I wouldn't worry about that. She will be fine either way. She has your resilience."

Declan frowned. "But she also has Margaret's blood in her, and that's what worries me."

"But we've been the ones influencing her all these years, giving her a stable home and lots of love," Paulette offered. "Mara isn't capricious and moody or reckless like Margaret was, from all your accounts of her."

"I know, but I still worry about her. My daughter is not like everyone else."

Paulette knew what her husband meant. There was a fey-like quality about Mara. At times she seemed almost otherworldly. And it was true that Mara had a sense about things happening sometimes.

"Do you think maybe Mara's sight has lain dormant all these years because she was safe and loved?" Paulette asked. "And for whatever reason, now, as an adult, it has resurfaced and she just hasn't told us about it? Do you think she had another vision about something terrible happening? To her? Or to one of us? Is that why Jeffrey thinks she's distressed?"

Declan nodded reluctantly. "That could be."

"You know, Declan," Paulette continued, thinking aloud, "she never did tell us the reason *why* she wanted to stay in London. She said it was just a *feeling* she had, that she needed to stay for a little longer. But it's been almost two months and she has made no mention of wanting to join us here. Perhaps she felt that something terrible would happen if she came to Ireland with us."

"Maybe you're right, Paulette," Declan said slowly.

"About what?"

"We should go back to London," he announced.

"Right away?" she asked. Paulette knew in her heart that going home was the right thing to do.

"Yes," he said with an emphatic nod. "Let's tell Thomas together. Then I'll start making arrangements to sail home."

Paulette flung her arms around Declan's neck and kissed him. She was flooded with a great sense of relief. "Oh, I was hoping you'd say that! Let's leave as soon as we can! We'll surprise her!"

18

Interpretations

Mara lay exhausted in his arms, their naked bodies entwined beneath the tangled sheets of his large bed.

Foster still could not believe that this exquisitely beautiful woman loved him. He didn't deserve her, but it would take more than moving heaven and earth for him to give her up now, for he couldn't imagine living without her in his life. He kissed her forehead tenderly as she snuggled into him. Lord, how he loved the feel of her in his arms!

After her cousin Phillip Sinclair had discovered that she had been sneaking out at night, he feared she would no longer come to him. But she had shown up tonight, just as they had planned. Although a little early, as she always did!

He was now more resolved than ever to end his marriage to Rose.

He needed, wanted, to marry Mara. As soon as he possibly could.

The past week had been a blur of meetings with his solicitor, and things were on track with the annulment going through. If all went well, Foster would be able to marry her in the new year.

The thought of marrying her, of having Mara as his wife, made him incredibly happy. Happier than he thought he had a right to be. Happier than he ever dreamed possible. He wanted to shout from the rooftop his joy at having her in his life. He wanted to walk out in the daylight with her. He wanted to dance with her at a ball. He wanted to sit with her at the theater. He wanted to exclaim to the world that she was his wife and that they belonged together.

But even more than that, he wanted to share a home with her. He wanted her beside him in bed at night, and wanted to see her pretty face when he woke up each morning. He wanted a house full of beautiful children with her. He wanted to grow old with Mara by his side.

In order to do that, he had to end his marriage-in-name-only to Rose.

Rose.

He hated to hurt her. Truly. He would provide well for her, making sure she was cared for financially. And who knew, perhaps she could even find love in her life and marry again? Rose was not even thirty years old yet. She could still find happiness for herself and maybe have a family of her own one day. Foster just knew that the two of them would never find happiness together. It was far too late for that. Even if there had ever been a glimmer of hope for them, it had been permanently doused the moment he met Mara.

Mara.

She had come to mean the world to him in such a short amount of time.

"Foster?" she whispered through the darkness as the clock on his mantel chimed two o'clock in the morning. They had just made love, yet again, and both were dreading when the time came to take her home. "Can I ask you something?"

Idly his hand stroked her back, thinking how lovely it

would be when she could sleep with him the whole night through. Up and down, his fingers gently caressed her back. Mara's skin was impossibly smooth. He asked, "What is it, my love?"

"You mentioned ending your marriage . . ." Her voice was oddly tinged with worry.

"Yes, I did," he answered. "And I am."

He sensed the hesitation in her before she spoke. "Well, I . . . I just wanted to tell you . . . that you don't have to end your marriage simply for my sake."

"Mara, love, I'm ending that marriage for both our sakes, for both of our futures together. You must know that. I can't bear being married to Rose for one more day. Not only that, I want to marry you the moment I am free to do so." He suddenly paused, a terrible sense of dread creeping over him. "You do wish to marry me, don't you?"

The long silence that ensued caused his heart to stop. She was not saying yes. How was such a thing possible? What on earth was going on inside that pretty head of hers?

"Mara?" he questioned, becoming alarmed at her lack of response. Why was she not answering him?

"I told you," she began reluctantly, her voice trembling a little. "The day we met in the park. I told you that very first day that I had no interest in ever getting married and having a family with anyone. That I was content to have things just as they are between us."

The woman lay naked in his arms, yet she didn't want to marry him? It made no sense. "I thought you were simply putting up a good front, Mara, because I was already married and you knew that we could not wed. I assumed you were being a good sport, as it were. I certainly didn't think you truly meant what you said!"

"Well, I meant it then." She sniffed with a bit of an injured air. "And I still mean it now."

Abruptly he sat up, lifting her with him, and reached over to turn on the lamp on the bedside table. It cast a hazy glow around them, so at least he could see her face, her expression. He needed to look at her, because he couldn't believe what she was saying to him.

"Mara?" He gazed into her misty green eyes. "I don't understand what you're saying to me."

She looked flustered, a bit panicked even, as she clutched the bedsheet over her breasts. Taking a shaky breath, she said once more, "I don't wish to marry anyone, Foster. So please, I beg you, there is no need to go through all the trouble of ending your marriage, whether through a divorce or an annulment, just for my sake. You'd be wasting your time."

Foster shook his head in disbelief. "We love each other, Mara. I love you and I thought you loved me."

"I do love you, truly I do," she said hurriedly, her eyes wide. "I love you more than anyone. I've only ever loved you, and I know I shall never love anyone but you for my entire life, Foster. You must believe that."

"Then I don't understand." His heart began to race and a knot formed in his gut. What was going on here? If they loved each other, then what was the problem?

Loving Mara Reeves had irrevocably changed him. Loving her had filled his empty life with hope and happiness, making him want things he had previously thought impossibly out of reach. Being loved by her had made him feel like the luckiest man in the world. The thought of losing her . . . he could not bear it. If he lost Mara's love now, he would fall into a deep pit of dark despair and loneliness from which he was certain he would never be able to escape. He would never be able to recover from the loss of her.

"I'm sorry that I can't explain it to you better than this . . ." she said helplessly. "But I simply can't marry you. I don't wish to get married. Ever. No matter how much I love you.

I thought you understood that when we started this . . . affair."

"So is this all you want, Mara? To continue to meet like this, in secret, forever? To spend the rest of our days only seeing each other when we can arrange to be alone without arousing suspicion? Do you wish to be nothing more to me than my mistress? Shall I set you up in a house of your own? Let your family disown you with your reputation in tatters? Is that what you really want? Because that is the future that awaits us if we continue like this."

Mara looked horrified, but she remained oddly silent.

"Well, that's the best you can hope for if I don't end my marriage, Mara," he said coldly, trying to impress upon her the severity of their situation. "You, the daughter of an earl, a well-bred lady from a distinguished family, you will be reduced to the humiliation of being my mistress, creating a scandal the likes of which this town hasn't seen in decades, when word gets out. And it will. You would face public scorn and ridicule. You would be ostracized. Is that what you want? Because I certainly don't want that. Not for you. Not for us. What I want is for you to become my wife so I can love you for the rest of my life."

He suddenly saw that she was crying. Tears were streaming down her sweet face and it just about killed him to see her like that. He pulled her to him, wrapping his arms around her again.

"It doesn't have to be that way, Mara. Please, let me make this right, for both of us. I love you. Let me marry you." He whispered into her hair over and over that he loved her, while she sobbed against his shoulder, her delicate body shaking.

Foster knew a thing or two about women. He wasn't completely clueless, given his relationships over the years. But never had he been with a woman who seemed so devastated and wracked with grief. Mara's anguish was undeniable, but he didn't know how to soothe her, how to make it right. His overwhelming desire to protect her and take care of her left him feeling ridiculously helpless. How had the simple and honorable question of asking her to marry him reduced her to this sobbing, hysterical mess? How had a proposal become such a problem?

"Mara, my love, help me understand, please," he pleaded with her. "You're breaking my heart here. I deserve a real explanation. Why don't you want to get married?"

"If I told you why, if I told you the real reason, you wouldn't ever want to marry me," she mumbled through her tears.

"My sweet, sweet Mara, there is absolutely nothing you could have done that would possibly change my feelings about making you my wife." He was stunned by her words. Had she lost her wits? What on earth was the woman thinking? He attempted to tease her out of her sadness. "How can you think such things? Have you gone crazy on me?"

At his words, Mara released a cry of sorrow. She suddenly pushed herself away from him. She scrambled out of the bed before he could stop her. Frantically she began dressing, pulling on her stockings and undergarments faster than he thought possible. Stunned by her actions, Foster too rose from the bed and began putting his clothes on.

Wordlessly he helped to fasten her dress. He didn't know what else to say to her. Whatever he did say was wrong, or set her to crying. It was late and probably best that they call it a night. She seemed too distraught to talk rationally anyway. He had professed his love for her over and over and she didn't seem to believe him. Although he hated for her to leave while she was so upset.

When they were both dressed, she moved toward the bedroom door, but he reached for her hand. "Mara," he called softly.

"Please just take me home now." She would not meet his eyes.

"Listen to me," he pleaded, hating himself for what he was about to say. "We can't go on like this much longer. If you don't want to marry me, I can't keep risking your reputation this way. It's your whole life we're talking about. If your cousin already knows, it's only a matter of time before others find out as well . . ." He took a breath, feeling a weight crushing his chest. "We shouldn't see each other anymore, Mara."

She flinched, but still she would not meet his gaze. Her eyes were glued to the door. She looked like a frightened deer that would startle and flee at the slightest movement.

"I'm going ahead with the annulment, Mara. I can't bear to be married to Rose, whether you and I are together or not. So if nothing else, I thank you for inspiring me to do that. But if you have no intention of marrying me"—he pointed to the two of them—"then this, whatever *this* is, is over between us."

Mara remained silent. He still held one hand while her other hand reached for the doorknob.

"You need only say the word, though, and I am yours. I will wait for you to change your mind, Mara, however long it takes. I love you and I will marry you anytime you say."

She gave a brief nod of her head, pulled her hand from his, and opened the door to the bedroom. She squared her shoulders and walked into the hallway.

Foster's heart sank as he watched her go.

Mara didn't sleep a wink when she returned home from her night with Foster. They had not spoken a word to each other while he escorted her home in his carriage, for there was nothing left to say.

The evening had not ended the way she had wanted. She

thought he would love her enough and want her enough to continue seeing each other the way things were. She had not expected him to end their affair.

The loss paralyzed her.

The devastation left her without tears. It was as if she were frozen. She lay in bed until the sun came up, just staring at the ceiling and feeling an enormous hole open up inside her heart.

Foster loved her and she loved him, yet circumstances beyond their control kept them apart. Mara could never live a normal life, nor could she explain to Foster the reason why she couldn't marry him.

Those damned visions were haunting her and she couldn't figure out what they meant. All the other visions she'd had in her life had come to pass relatively quickly. She had always understood what was going to happen to someone she loved, whether it was her little brother falling down the stairs or her cousin Sara getting married. Yet this one, this one with the flames that terrified her, was becoming more vivid and more horrifying each time she experienced it. The fact that this vision was reoccurring was especially terrifying, for that had never happened to her before either.

Did the increasing frequency mean that the event was growing closer to happening? Was she to be involved in some sort of fire? Or was it as Foster believed, a discarded memory from the fire in which her mother died?

It frustrated her not to know what any of it meant. Or when or if it would even happen. Was she in grave danger? Was Foster? Was there something Mara needed to do to prevent this calamity and the sense of death in the vision?

She didn't know what the vision foretold. Were she and Foster meant to be together or not? Now she was confused by the images. And that strange woman! Who was she and what was she doing in her premonition?

Nothing made sense to her anymore.

But suddenly Mara knew what she needed to do and where she needed to go to get the answers to figure out just what was happening to her. Her mother's family would know. Her aunt Deirdre and aunt Ellen. Her mother's sisters would know about the madness in the family. Perhaps talking to them would shed some light on what would happen to Mara in the years to come.

When Brighton came in to wake her, Mara was already up and packing her things.

"My lady, can I help you?" Brighton asked, rather perplexed at the clothes scattered around the room.

"Yes, Brighton," Mara answered hurriedly. "Can you please finish packing while I go speak to my uncle Lucien about making arrangements so we can leave as soon as possible? You'll need to pack your things as well."

The young maid's freckled face appeared confused. "Of course, my lady. May I ask where we're going?"

"We're going back home," Mara declared. "To Ireland and Cashelmore."

19

Complications

Foster Sheridan could not wait any longer. He missed Mara too much and he was afraid if he didn't do something soon, he would lose her forever.

Steeling his resolve, he rang the bell to the front door of Devon House. He'd made up his mind that he had to go to her, and at this point he didn't care if her family wondered why he was standing on their doorstep. In fact, he hoped they would ask. It was time to have everything out in the open.

Quite simply, he was determined to marry Mara one way or another.

"Good day," the Devon House butler asked. "How may I help you?"

"I'm the Earl of Sterling and I was hoping to speak to Lady Mara Reeves, although she is not expecting me."

The butler raised an eyebrow very slightly. "I'm afraid Lady Mara is not at home today."

Disappointment surged through him. On an impulse, Foster asked, "Is Lord Waverly in, by any chance? Might I speak with him?"

With a nod, the butler showed him to a drawing room to wait. Too anxious to sit, Foster paced the length of the room. He idly wondered where Mara was. Thinking she might be working at the bookshop, he chided himself for not visiting there first. He also wondered how she would react to his calling upon her this way.

"Lord Sterling?" Phillip Sinclair, the Earl of Waverly, entered the drawing room, a perplexed expression on his face. "Good afternoon."

Foster and Phillip Sinclair were not complete strangers. They'd met on numerous occasions and frequented the same clubs and social functions. However, they were not friends and he knew Phillip thought it was a bit strange to have Foster call upon him at home. "Good afternoon, Waverly. I apologize for coming by unexpectedly and I thank you for taking the time to see me."

"It's no trouble at all." Phillip smiled agreeably, although Foster could tell that he was still confused by Foster's presence.

"I hope not to take up too much of your time," Foster said. "But I'd like to discuss something rather important with you."

"Yes, of course. Can I offer you a drink first?" Phillip asked with a winning grin. "Something stronger than tea?"

"That would be wonderful." Foster could definitely use a drink. This was not going to be easy.

"Scotch?"

"Perfect."

Phillip went to the sideboard and poured two glasses of scotch from a crystal decanter. He handed one to Foster and motioned to the sofa. "Have a seat, please."

"Thank you." Foster sat down and Phillip took a chair across from him. They raised their glasses to each other.

"So," Phillip began after he took a sip of his scotch, "what can I do for you, Sterling?"

"Well, it's a bit of a delicate matter, which I think you are already aware of . . . but I actually came here today to see your cousin, Lady Mara." Foster paused, waiting for the meaning of his words to sink in.

Phillip's eyes widened. "You?" He sounded incredulous. "You're the one?"

Foster nodded wordlessly. Their secret was most definitely out now.

Phillip downed his drink in a swift motion. Then he stared at Foster. "You've got a nerve, Sterling, coming here like this, because you know I may have to kill you."

"I wouldn't blame you if you did. In fact I would be surprised if you didn't," Foster said, "but please hear me out first. There are things you should be aware of."

"I don't know what you could say that would make what I believe is going on between you and Mara any better, but you can go ahead and try." Phillip glared at him through narrowed eyes.

Foster had to give Phillip Sinclair credit for controlling his anger. Foster didn't know if he would have been so calm and forgiving in the face of a man who had seduced his innocent cousin.

"First of all, I apologize. I know there is no excuse for any of it. None whatsoever and I take full responsibility for it. I am a married man and Mara is an unmarried young lady."

"Don't remind me," Phillip growled.

"I am quite aware that this is a dreadful situation," Foster began. "But I need your help, Waverly. I love your cousin. And I know she loves me too. My marriage will be annulled soon and I wish to marry Mara. But she's got some ridiculous idea in her head that she doesn't want to get married. Ever. To anyone. I need someone to help me talk some sense into her."

Completely baffled, Phillip stared at him for a long

moment. "I need another drink." He stood abruptly, went to the sideboard and refilled his glass. He took a swig and came back to his seat. "Do you want to explain that to me again, Sterling? Because that made no sense whatsoever. Did you say that my cousin refuses to marry you when you're a free man?"

"That's what she said, and quite adamantly too, I might add." Foster finally took a sip of his own drink. He needed it.

"I don't understand any of this," Phillip grumbled, rubbing his hand against his forehead. "First of all, I'm still going to have to deck you for not being a gentleman with my cousin. But that can wait until later. Secondly, you *are* getting an annulment? Truly? Mara didn't mention that bit to me at all."

Foster nodded. "Yes, proceedings have already begun to have the marriage annulled. You should know that my marriage was arranged by my parents, when I was younger than you are now. It was forced upon the both of us. I was not even given a chance to meet my bride until the morning of our wedding. If you can imagine such a thing. It was a miserable union from the start, and to be quite blunt, it was never consummated. Since the start we have lived separate lives for the entire ten years of our marriage. Rose lives in Yorkshire and I live in London. We've no children because there was never the possibility of conceiving any."

"My God," Phillip muttered in disbelief.

"Meeting Mara that night you introduced us—"

"I'd forgotten all about that night!" Phillip interrupted. "That was when all this mess began?"

"Yes, and I can assure you that neither Mara nor I have forgotten it. That night has changed both our lives for the better. Yes, in spite of the dreadful circumstances. I know it sounds ridiculous," Foster confessed, "but I fell in love with Mara the first time I saw her that night."

Phillip ran his hand through his hair in astonishment. "What a tangled predicament."

"That's an understatement," Foster continued, wishing it was all settled. "As I was saying, meeting Mara inspired me to finally end my charade of a marriage to Rose. The process has already started and I shall be free to marry her in the new year. Mara is the one I want to spend my life with. I want her to be my wife. Not my mistress. But for some inexplicable reason, Mara says that she would prefer to keep things as they are . . . She'd rather be my mistress than my wife."

"That can't be!" Phillip rose from his seat, his expression befuddled. "If you are both in love and . . . and, well . . . you've already done the deed, so to speak, and you're more than willing to marry her, why won't she agree to it? She really has no choice but to marry you now. I don't understand her reticence. She already told me that she loves you. Because of that fact and because I believe you really do love her, I'm going to cut you some slack, Sterling, and I'm not going to beat you to a bloody pulp here in my mother's drawing room."

"Thank you, Waverly. I appreciate your trust in me, given the awful circumstances." He was beginning to like Mara's cousin and hoped they could be friends one day. Phillip Sinclair was a good man.

After taking another swig of scotch, Foster continued his explanation. "So I'm in a quandary. I told Mara that I couldn't see her again unless she agreed to marry me . . . and so we haven't seen each other since. You can see why I need your help."

Phillip flopped back down onto the chair. "I shall never claim to understand women."

"No one can," Foster quipped lightly. He certainly didn't understand Mara. As much as he loved her, their last conversation left him completely at a loss. "I actually came here today to speak to her, to try to talk some sense into her. When I discovered that she isn't home, I thought I'd try talking to you. I know I am taking a risk in coming here in the first place, and speaking to you in the second. But I'm desperate. Maybe together we can get her to see reason. Perhaps this afternoon."

"But Mara's not here." Phillip sat up.

"Is she working at one of the bookshops?"

"No." Phillip shook his head. "I assumed you knew already. Mara has left London."

Suddenly Foster's heart began to beat faster, and there was a tightening in the pit of his stomach. "What do you mean Mara has left London?"

"I mean," Phillip explained, "that my cousin Mara left for Ireland two days ago."

Foster rose to his feet. *"What?"*

"Yes, to everyone's surprise, Mara suddenly said she wished to be with her parents. My father made arrangements for her and she left for Ireland the day before yesterday."

Foster was speechless. Mara had gone. She had left England without a word to him. He didn't know what to think. Was her intention to never see him again? What was he to do now? He hated how they had left things between them and now he regretted telling her that they could not see each other anymore.

"I take it she didn't tell you she was going?" Phillip asked not unkindly, rising to his feet as well.

"No," Foster ground out, feeling rather put out. "She did not."

"Had you an argument?"

"Yes," Foster shot back. "I wanted her to marry me and she said no."

"Women." Phillip gave him a rueful smile and shook his head. "What will you do now?"

Foster sighed heavily. "It looks like I'm headed to Ireland to convince your beautiful but stubborn little cousin to marry me."

"It seems the only logical course, Sterling." Phillip reached out his hand. "I'd put in a good word for you if she were here, if that helps."

"It does, thank you very much," Foster replied, shaking Phillip's hand. "I know my marriage creates the worst sort of circumstances and I'd like to avoid as much scandal as possible, for Mara's sake. So I would appreciate any way that you and your family could support us. We may need it."

"I'll do what I can, but I can't vouch for her parents and the rest of the family. I don't know how they'll react to your situation, but I do believe your intentions are as honorable as they can be, given all the facts. I'm impressed by your character, Sterling. Coming here and explaining your situation to me took courage. And I've been thinking about your circumstances, trapped in a marriage like that. I don't know what I would do if I were in your position, so I'll reserve judgment. I've issues about Mara getting involved, but again . . . if your marriage is being dissolved and you both love each other . . . it should work out."

"Thank you, and I know I don't deserve it, but I am most grateful for your support."

Phillip nodded. "I wish you the best of luck with her in Ireland."

But Foster feared he would need more than luck to get through this ordeal.

When he got home that afternoon, he was still upset that Mara had left town without telling him. What if he hadn't stopped by Devon House? How would he have ever known that she had left? Maybe he was wrong to want to go after her. What if she truly never wanted to see him again?

But in his heart he knew that was not the case.

Mara loved him. They loved each other. There was no doubt in his mind on that score. Their connection to each other had been too strong, too deep, and too real to be anything else but love.

No, what Foster needed to do was to get to the bottom of what was bothering Mara. What was it that was keeping her from him? He had no choice but to go to Ireland to talk to her. He loved her far too much to let her just walk away.

"Excuse me, my lord." Preston entered the study. His butler looked more than a little annoyed. "But one of the housemaids seems quite agitated and wishes to speak with you."

"Which one?" Foster asked distractedly. He'd been at his desk, already making travel arrangements to go to Ireland.

"Nellie Smith."

Foster recalled her as an agreeable young girl who by all accounts performed her duties well. "What is the matter and why does she wish to see me?"

"I'm not entirely certain, my lord." Preston looked thoroughly disgruntled by the situation. "But she is very distraught and said it was a private matter and it was urgent that she speak to you."

"All right then," Foster said with a resigned sigh. "Send her in, Preston." As if he didn't have enough to contend with, he had to add troubled housemaids to his list.

A few moments later, Preston ushered in a young woman, who stood nervously in front of Foster's desk. Her young face was blotchy and streaked with tears.

"Thank you, Preston," Foster said. "You can leave us now." Then he turned his attention to the anxious housemaid. "Good afternoon, Nellie. How can I help you?"

The girl burst into a fresh round of tears. So much so

that Foster rose from his seat to give her one of his handkerchiefs. What on earth could the girl want to discuss with him that couldn't be handled by Mrs. McCafferty or Preston? His housekeeper and butler usually dealt with the servants' issues. He guided the girl to a chair and patted her shoulder.

"There, there, Nellie. I can't help you if you don't tell me what the matter is, and you need to stop crying in order to tell me." Foster gave her an encouraging smile and returned to his seat behind the desk.

Nellie wiped her eyes and sniffled. "I didn't mean to do it, and I came to tell you how very sorry I am, my lord."

His brows drew together. "Sorry for what?"

"I know that I'll be sent packing for what I've done." Nellie's voice trembled and caught on a sob now and then. "Your lordship has been a good employer, fair and kind, and I like working here, so I thought you should know what happened. Because I have a bad feeling about it now, and I'm awfully sorry for doing it."

Foster was trying not to lose his patience. "Doing what, Nellie?"

"I told the man about us having the nights off and I shouldn't have. I didn't know he was spying on you until yesterday."

He looked sharply at her. Spying on him? What on earth did the girl mean? This wasn't some trivial household problem she was upset about. "You say someone was spying on me? Who?"

"I thought Bailey was my fellow, flirting with me the way he was. We were stepping out together now and then. He would buy me a drink at the pub and we'd dance and talk together. He asked a lot of questions about the house and your lordship. I thought he was just curious about me and my work. But then yesterday . . ." Nellie burst into a fresh round of tears.

"What happened yesterday?" he asked when she had taken a few breaths to calm down. Foster was starting to get a very bad feeling about this situation.

She wiped at her eyes with the soaked handkerchief. "He told me that he was working for your wife. For Lady Sterling. That it was his job to tell her everything you were doing, especially on the nights you sent us away."

Rose had hired someone to spy on him! Of course she had, which is how she knew so much about his past mistresses. Under normal circumstances Foster would not have cared that Rose knew what he was doing. But these were not normal circumstances. Not with Mara involved. He hadn't wanted Rose to know about Mara.

Nellie's speech was punctuated by sniffles. "I thought I was his girl and when I said so, he laughed at me. He said it was over between us and he wouldn't be seeing me anymore. He was leaving for Ireland with Lady Sterling—"

"Did you say Ireland?" Foster interrupted her. That could only mean one thing, and it alarmed him.

"Yes. He left with her yesterday for Dublin. But he called me a foolish girl and said I had betrayed your lordship and that he could never trust me . . ." The crying started all over again.

So Rose had had him followed and discovered that he'd been seeing Lady Mara Reeves. Foster was more than a little surprised by her gumption. He didn't think Rose had it in her to travel all the way to Ireland. But he was also worried now. It was one thing for Rose to know about Mara, it was something else entirely that she was following Mara to Ireland. Why? What was Rose planning? That uneasy feeling within him grew stronger.

"I'm ever so sorry, my lord. I didn't think I'd done anything wrong. I'd only tell him when I had my nights free so I could see him, that's all."

And that was enough, Foster realized. If the man knew

which nights Foster dismissed his staff, then he knew what nights to watch the townhouse to see who came and went. And that must have led the chap to follow Foster's carriage when he took Mara home. It was simple enough to discover her identity after that. And that was apparently just what Rose's spy had done.

"Is that all you told him, Nellie?" Foster asked.

"I swear, my lord. I don't know anything else to tell."

He didn't doubt that. He'd been very discreet. Although apparently not discreet enough. "Did he happen to say why he was going to Ireland?"

She shook her head balefully, her red-rimmed eyes sad. "I think he just wants to get away from me."

"I doubt that, Nellie. You're a fine girl and any young fellow would be lucky to have you." He forced a smile. "Thank you for telling me this. I'm going to instruct Preston to give you a little bonus in your wages."

"Thank you!" she cried, looking flabbergasted. "But, Lord Sterling, I thought you would dismiss me for being disloyal to you."

"No, I'm not going to dismiss you, Nellie, so please stop crying. You've actually done me a great favor by coming to me today and telling me the truth. I wouldn't have known that Lady Sterling was having me watched if you hadn't told me. I appreciate that."

"You do?" Her teary blue eyes widened.

"Yes, I do. Now go and have a bit of a rest and recover yourself. And do try to stay away from unscrupulous gentlemen in the future, Nellie."

She rose to her feet, a hesitant smile on her face. "I promise I will, my lord. Thank you."

As she made her way to the door, Foster called after her. "Nellie?"

"Yes, my lord?" She turned back around.

"What is the name of this man? Your supposed fellow?" he asked.

"His name is Bailey Briggs."

"Thank you, Nellie."

As the housemaid left, Foster tried to remain calm. Why was Rose following Mara to Ireland? Rose had never been any farther from Yorkshire than London. She despised traveling and avoided doing so at all costs. She had always been quite satisfied staying at home. He couldn't imagine why she would go all the way to Ireland unless to confront Mara and cause trouble. It didn't bode well for any of them. Foster decided to leave for Dublin right away.

There was no time to lose.

20

Connections

Mara was home again.

As she walked along the rocky stream that edged the Cashelmore estate, she pulled her dark cloak tighter around her shoulders to ward off the autumn chill. It was an overcast day and the clouds hung low in the sky. A slight mist began to gather over the fields and hedges, but she did not care. Mara always loved the misty days best. She breathed deeply of the fresh air, thinking how good it was to be away from London. She needed to clear her head, and there was something about being back in Ireland that eased her soul and made her feel calmer.

She'd arrived at Cashelmore Manor that day only to discover that her parents and her brother, Thomas, had gone back to London to surprise her. It seemed they'd been at cross purposes. Mara had smiled at the sheer absurdity of it all when Collins, the butler, had informed her that she'd missed Lord and Lady Cashelmore by a day.

In a way it was a relief to not have to face her parents, for she was not proud of what she had begun with Foster Sheridan. Yet with her parents in London, Mara was free to visit her mother's family without having to answer her father's questions about why she was doing so. The first thing Mara planned for the morning was to travel to visit her aunt Deirdre, who had moved to Galway.

Mara continued walking along the stream, stepping over the mossy rocks and stones at its edge. The beauty of the lush landscape inspired her, and the pastoral surroundings filled her with peace. Only the babbling of the stream, the twitter of birds, and her own footsteps could be heard. Such a change from the constant noise and bustle of London!

She came to a rocky outcropping and climbed upon one of the larger gray stones. The quiet perch afforded her an expansive view of the estate with the impressive sight of Cashelmore Manor in the distance. Since she was a little girl, she had always come to this place to be by herself and think. Which she desperately needed to do just then.

Mara needed to sort out her life.

During the journey to Ireland, she had done nothing but think about Foster and her future. She desperately wished she had someone she could talk over things with. Her lady's maid, Brighton, was sweet, but not the best confidante or adviser.

She needed her cousin Sara Fleming—or Lady Bridgeton, now that she was married. Sara would know exactly what to do. Sara would be able to help her make sense of this foolish mess that Mara had gotten herself into. However, wishing Sara would magically appear did not help her situation either.

But talking with her mother's older sisters might. And that would take some courage.

Mara had feared her aunts when she was younger. Aunt Deirdre especially. Mara had vague memories of her mother's sisters trying to take her from her father after the fire. They wanted her to live with one of them, which Mara did not wish to do. She supposed their intentions were good, of course, but they had both been rather stern and exacting women and they had scared her.

Even as Mara grew older and realized that they could not take her from her father any longer, she did not spend much time with either of her mother's sisters. Aunt Deirdre and Aunt Ellen had, in fact, been rather distant and cold. They were quite unlike her Hamilton aunts, who were warm and welcoming to a fault.

But Deirdre and Ellen could help her now. They might be able to tell her more about her mother. At least Mara hoped that they would.

The more she thought about it, the more she realized that she actually knew very little about her mother, Margaret Ryan. Perhaps because everyone had been too afraid of upsetting Mara by mentioning her mother, fearing it might scare or worry her, Mara had grown up only over-hearing things about her.

Lord knew her father never wanted to talk about his first wife and avoided doing so at all costs.

Mara reached into the pocket of her cloak and took out the small picture she had of her mother. It wasn't as clear a photograph as the types available nowadays. This one was rather grainy. Aside from the formal portraits in the gallery, it was the only image Mara had of her mother, and she kept it in a special box in her bedroom at Cashelmore Manor. She had retrieved it this morning.

Holding the photograph in her hands now, Mara stared at the sepia-toned oval image of a laughing woman. She was quite beautiful. Slender and fair, with her long blond hair spilling around her, Margaret Ryan Reeves wore a simple white gown with long sleeves. She stared into the camera lens with a look of . . . what? Impertinence? Defiance? Mischief? Mara was not sure.

Mara definitely resembled her mother. Everyone always said that they looked remarkably alike. But just how deep did their likenesses run? Yes, Mara had inherited her mother's fair looks. But had she inherited more from her mother than she wished for?

Had the madness been passed on to her as well? Mara feared it had.

A sudden sound startled her. Mara turned and looked around her, but didn't see anything or anyone. Still, she couldn't shake the feeling that someone was watching her. The grooms knew where she walked and would have announced their presence. No one else would be wandering the Cashelmore estate.

Since it was growing dark and she was feeling a bit spooked, she decided to walk back to the house. With more traveling ahead of her in the morning, Mara needed her rest.

She didn't know what she would discover at her aunt's house.

"What is it that brings you here, Mara? It's such a surprise to see you. I can't even recall the last time you paid me a visit."

Deirdre Ryan Hollingsworth was every bit as intimidating as Mara remembered her being when she was a little girl. Mara had not spent a great deal of time with her mother's older sister over the years, but her aunt had always had a severe look about her then, just as she did now.

Deirdre's ash-blond hair was tinged with gray and her thin face was more creased than before, but there was still a faint resemblance to Margaret. She more than likely was never the beauty that her younger sister had been, but she was not an unattractive woman. Her features were good, possessing a fine nose and clear blue eyes, but her expression always seemed dour, with her lips pursed in displeasure.

Aunt Deirdre was a widow now, her husband having died about ten years ago. She was left well-off, and her children had grown and married.

They sat together at a tea table in her aunt's house. It was a pleasant and comfortable drawing room with a wide window overlooking the rolling green fields outside and a cozy fire burning to ward off the damp chill of the rainy afternoon. The table was covered with an elaborate lace tablecloth and set with lovely Belleek china. Aunt Deirdre loved her tea.

"I came because I wanted to speak to you, Aunt Deirdre. About my mother." Mara paused, waiting for a reaction. No one ever seemed to want to talk about Margaret Ryan.

"That's truly the reason?" Deirdre's face continued to look impassive. She didn't even raise an eyebrow at Mara's request.

"Yes. I would like to know more about my mother."

Aunt Deirdre suddenly smiled. It changed the whole appearance of her face. Her eyes lit up and she looked almost happy and pretty. Astonished by the transformation, Mara tried to recall if she'd ever seen her aunt smile before.

"Well, I have been waiting for this day," she said triumphantly. "It's about time."

"What do you mean?" Mara asked.

"I mean that you're twenty-two years old and you have never come to me before to learn more about your mother." Reaching across the table, Deirdre placed her wrinkled hand over Mara's younger one. "Mara, you were practically a baby when Margaret died. Of course you didn't know her. I doubt if you can even recall much about her at this point. Oh, I've wanted to talk to you about your mother for years."

"You have?" Incredulous, Mara stared at her aunt, whom she had been so fearful of for her entire life.

"Of course, my dear. I was much older than Margaret, and our parents were not in the best of health, so I practically raised my sister. When she died so tragically, I wanted to raise you as well. But your father wouldn't hear of it. He wanted to keep you himself."

"Yes." Mara recalled that battle between her father and her aunts. She was very grateful for staying with her father and she shuddered to think how different her life would have been if she had been made to live with Aunt Deirdre.

"I suppose it all worked out for the best, but I always thought it sad that you didn't spend more time with Ellen and me instead of becoming all involved with your stepmother's family the way you did." The smile had disappeared from Deirdre's face and the austerity had returned.

Mara grew defensive, thinking of her lovely Hamilton aunts and how good they were to her. "Paulette's family was very welcoming to me."

Deirdre put on an injured air. "I'm sure they were. But they're not your blood relatives. They didn't know your mother."

"No, they did not." That was the truth and Mara could not deny it. But she loved her Hamilton family as much as if they were her blood relatives.

Deirdre poured hot black tea into the fine china cups. Mara spooned some sugar into hers and let it cool a little.

"Your mother was an incomparable beauty. Men would fall over themselves for her." She eyed Mara. "You do have a strong resemblance to her."

"Thank you. I shall take that as great praise." Mara knew she wasn't half as beautiful as her mother was, but it was compliment enough to know that she resembled her.

"As a child Margaret was delightful. A prettier baby you

couldn't imagine! Our parents, everyone who met her, all of us were captivated by her. We doted on her every whim and, I suppose, we all spoiled her terribly. But no one could refuse her. As she grew, she blossomed into a stunning young woman. She was renowned for her beauty and we had arranged a fine marriage for her. To the Duke of Kilcarragh, no less, and he was head over heels in love with her. But then Margaret met Declan Reeves, and that was it. Declan was young and terribly handsome, and a fine catch too. It was no wonder that Margaret threw over the old duke and ran off with your father."

"My mother and father eloped?" Mara was stunned and fascinated. She had never heard this story before. It was the most intriguing thought that her parents had run away together!

"Oh yes. She was only eighteen and Declan not much older than that, and they ran off to Galway just before she was to marry the Duke of Kilcarragh. He was fit to be tied when he found out Margaret jilted him, let me tell you. Such a scandal, that was! But that was our Margaret. She never thought things through. She never thought about the consequences of what she was doing. But the main trouble with Margaret was that once she finally got what she had been longing for, she completely lost interest and didn't want it anymore. Which is what happened with Declan."

"What do you mean?" Mara asked, a bit confused. How could her mother lose interest in her father after marrying him?

"Margaret, God rest her soul, was a flighty girl. She could never settle on one thing for long and she always wanted what she couldn't have. What was out of reach or denied to her . . . that was what she wanted most! She didn't want to marry the duke, because he was much older and not nearly as handsome as Declan, of course, but also because she was being *told* to marry him. But the duke would have been able to manage her better, I believe. Declan never knew how to handle Margaret properly. He was not the right man for her, as he soon came to realize after it was too late. But there was no talking to her, and before we could stop her, Margaret ran off and married Declan anyway. She was in love with the romance and adventure of eloping and all that. She adored doing things she shouldn't. As soon as she defied us all and married Declan, she was then expected to behave as the proper wife of an earl. But oh, our little darling wasn't having any of that!" Deirdre shook her head ruefully.

"What happened?" Mara couldn't imagine her mother acting the way Aunt Deirdre depicted her.

"Well, after we discovered Margaret's marriage to Declan, we were trying to have it annulled, but then she discovered she was having his child. *You.* So we accepted Margaret as the Countess of Cashelmore, which was the next best thing to being a duchess. But if Margaret didn't like the duties of being a wife, she really despised the responsibilities of being a mother. Oh, she loved you!" Deirdre said when she saw Mara's expression. "You were a beautiful child and a credit to her, Mara. Your mother loved you as much as she was capable of loving anyone. But motherhood was not exciting to her. To be sure, she was a sweet and loving girl, and when her love shined upon you, it was a glorious thing. It's just that it didn't shine on one thing for very long. I suppose Margaret was rather vain and flighty, and she wanted other men to love and adore her. And, Declan . . . Well, Declan was also very young and very jealous. It all added up to tragedy." Deirdre sighed heavily and took a sip of her tea.

Mara quietly considered all that she'd just been told

about her mother. It was quite a surprise and it was no wonder her father was reluctant to talk about her. But Mara kept waiting for her aunt to mention something about her mother's madness. Perhaps she was too ashamed to bring it up? "The tragedy of the fire, you mean?"

Deirdre nodded sadly. "I know you were there the night of the fire, Mara dear, but I don't think you know what led to it. Margaret always confided in me through her letters. She was terribly unhappy with your father, she said. I know Declan had been besotted with her at the start, but after you were born, he began to see Margaret for what she was. Spoiled and selfish. It gives me no pleasure to say that about my sister, but it is the truth."

It was rather disconcerting to discover that her mother and father had such troubles. She had always imagined them happy together up until the night of the fire, although she recalled the two of them having a terrible quarrel that night.

"Margaret grew more restless and demanding, as Declan's attention, and love, shifted to his baby daughter. I'd never seen a father so enraptured with a child as your father was with you, Mara. Anyway, Margaret sought attention elsewhere. She was not very discreet either." Deirdre gave her niece a knowing look.

"You mean that my mother was . . . unfaithful to my father?" Mara found it hard to believe.

"Unfortunately, yes. With more than one man too. And your father found out about it, of course. He tried to keep her away from one certain fellow, and that's why he took you both to Galway. Declan was trying to get Margaret to come around, to stop all her foolishness and settle down. But she had told me she was determined to leave him."

All this was quite eye-opening information. Everything

that Mara had ever known about her parents and their marriage had been wrong.

Deirdre continued her tale. "And perhaps your father might have been able to persuade her. Who knows? The night of the fire changed everything."

"I remember them quarreling that night," Mara said softly. "Their yelling woke me and I crept down the hallway to her room. I don't know what they were arguing about, but they were both very angry and I remember not liking that. My mother was crying. Then my father saw me and carried me back to bed. I didn't stay in my bed though . . ."

Now it was Deirdre's turn to remain silent as she listened to Mara tell her version of the events that night.

"I didn't like that my mother was crying and I wanted to be with her. And I smelled smoke. By the time I got to her room, the flames were all along the corridor all around her room. I was screaming for her. Mama was screaming too, because she was on fire," Mara recalled softly. "If it wasn't for Papa rescuing me, I'd have died that night as well."

Deirdre wiped away some tears with her embroidered handkerchief. "That was a terrible thing for a child to witness. It's no wonder you didn't speak for a year afterward. Do you remember that?"

Mara nodded. The sight of her mother burning to death had haunted Mara her whole life. It so traumatized her that she couldn't find the will to talk for months, and she only felt safe when she was with her father.

"Truly, Mara, I wanted to keep you with me. You reminded me so of your mother. And for a while after her death, we all believed your father was the one who set the fire to rid himself of Margaret. I didn't think he deserved to raise you at that point. But as you know, it turned out not to have been him." Deirdre continued to dab at her eyes with the handkerchief. "It was just such a shame. All of it.

Losing Margaret when she was so young, and then losing you to your new family in England."

Mara began to cry a little bit herself. Thinking back on that night now, knowing how unhappy her parents were with each other, changed her perspective of things. Yet for all that her aunt told her about her mother, none of it indicated that Margaret Ryan Reeves was mad. Selfish and foolish, yes, but not insane.

"Aunt Deirdre," Mara began with hesitation. "Was my mother . . . I mean, did my mother ever seem to be . . . unbalanced in any way?"

Deirdre looked surprised. "I'm not sure what you're asking."

"With all her seemingly poor decisions and reckless behavior, did you ever consider her to be . . . well . . . a bit mad?" There. She'd finally said the words out loud. *Her mother was mad.* Mara held her breath, waiting for her aunt's response.

Aunt Deirdre chuckled a little and waved her hand airily. "Mad? You mean daft? Or crazy? No. No, Margaret was many things, my dear, and she may have acted a bit outlandish from time to time, but she was completely sane. She always knew exactly what she was doing, whether it was considered proper or not. She knew the difference. She just didn't care if she flouted the rules that the rest of us followed."

Stunned by the revelation, Mara didn't understand. How could she have believed her mother to be suffering some sort of mental deficiency when she was not? "You mean she was not insane?"

"Good heavens, child! Of course she wasn't insane!" Deirdre looked at her with a mixture of confusion and surprise. "What on earth ever gave you that idea?"

Mara was silent for a moment as she considered that

question. Why had she believed her mother was mad?
Bits and pieces of adult conversations that she overheard
as a child flitted through her memory. References to her
mother's irrational behavior as insane by her father stuck
out in particular. Was he simply calling her actions *crazy*?
Perhaps he wasn't truly referring to Margaret at all? Maybe
he was looking upon the entire situation as *lunacy* and
Mara had misunderstood what she'd heard?

No one had ever really sat down and talked to Mara
about her mother before. Not when she was a child, nor
when she was grown. Mara had been left to surmise what
she was like on her own. But it wasn't just that a child mis-
interpreted what was going on around her or overheard
something she shouldn't have. It was that, for as long as
she could recall, Mara was experiencing those sometimes
ominous premonitions, which frightened her and caused
her to believe that she was insane, or on her way to becoming so, just like her mother supposedly was.

It was rather easy to believe.

"I'm not entirely sure, Aunt Deirdre, but I think I misunderstood something I'd overheard as a child . . . and then
there were other things."

"What things?" Deirdre looked at her with such caring
concern that Mara was disarmed.

"Things about myself."

"You?" Her aunt scoffed. "There's nothing the least bit
mad about you, Mara. Since you were a child you had the
sweetest and calmest disposition. You were an astonishingly
well-behaved and obedient little girl. Everyone remarked
on it! And look at you now! Rational. Intelligent. Agreeable. You may look just like your mother, but you have your
father's temperament. You are not at all like your mother in
that respect. Have you ever caused the slightest commotion

or any bit of trouble? Of course not. You've never given any indication of being mentally unbalanced, Mara, dear."

"But I have had . . . indications . . ." she admitted slowly. "I just haven't ever mentioned them to anyone else for fear of upsetting the family."

Deirdre was about to dismiss Mara's claim, but she suddenly paused and stared at her. "Not mentioned what?"

"I see, that is . . . I have . . . premonitions about things." Again Mara waited for her aunt to react in appalled shock.

Instead, Deirdre reached across the table and took Mara's hand in hers. "Why, Mara Kathleen, you have the sight!"

She knew! Her aunt knew what Mara was referring to. "You don't sound surprised in the least, Aunt Deirdre."

"Because I'm not that surprised, really." She looked pleased. "The gift of the sight runs in our family."

Mara's heart sank. She had been right all along. Her affliction *was* definitely hereditary! She was right not to want children, for she would surely pass it on to them.

"How long have you had it?" Deirdre asked, curious to know more.

"I've been having them for as long as I can remember. I even had a hazy premonition about the night of the fire and of my mother dying. However, I think I was too young to understand what it meant. I wanted to save her, which is why I left my bedroom the second time that night, but I couldn't save her. It was too late by the time I got to her." Mara felt a weight lift off her shoulders as she confided in her aunt.

"But why have you never mentioned this to me before?" Deirdre inquired, clearly disappointed that her niece had neglected to inform her of this.

"Because I believed it meant that something was terribly wrong with me," Mara confessed. She had also been too afraid of her aunt when she was younger and Deirdre would never have been someone whom Mara would have confided in. "I still think there is something wrong with me. I never wanted anyone to know and I didn't want to worry my father or anyone else in the family."

"That's just like you. Thinking about everyone else but yourself. Trying to please everyone and not cause trouble. You are the complete opposite of your mother in every way! But my dear Mara, the sight isn't an affliction. It's a wonderful gift." Deirdre looked at her with wonder.

Mara recalled Uncle Jeffrey saying something similar to her the night she had the premonition in front of him. He seemed to think she had a gift as well. Had she a gift and not a curse, after all? Mara didn't know what to think anymore.

"My grandmother, who would be your great-grandmother, had the sight," Deirdre explained with a note of pride in her voice. "And so did one of my aunts. It's nothing to be ashamed of."

"Isn't it?" So she wasn't going mad? After all her anxiety and worry, Mara wasn't going to lose her mind? She almost couldn't believe it was true.

"Of course not." Aunt Deirdre gave her hand a comforting squeeze and then let go of her. "It's a wonderful thing, it is. My grandmother, Eileen Ffrench, used to tell me all about her premonitions. How she would sometimes know what would happen well before it actually happened. Some people would dismiss that as simply a lucky guess or good intuition. And perhaps at times it is just that. Although I do believe being naturally intuitive is a big part of it. But my grandmother would be able to tell me things with incredible accuracy that would then come to pass. It was quite remarkable. Everything that she 'foresaw' came true. It seems you take after her, Mara."

"I've never known anyone else that this happens to." Learning that her great-grandmother had visions was quite a revelation. Mara didn't feel as isolated knowing she had a connection to her mother's family.

"Well, having the ability to see the future is unusual, to be sure. But having the sight is not unheard of either. It's actually quite common in our family."

"I never knew that either. I wish I had known. It would have made me feel better about it all," Mara admitted.

Shaking her head, Deirdre frowned. "It's my fault. I should have pressed your father to let you visit us more often. I should have shared our family history with you sooner."

"I should have asked you sooner."

"In any case, we're here together now and we both know. Just wait until I tell your Aunt Ellen! She'll be terribly sorry to have missed your visit." Deirdre rose from her seat and indicated for Mara to do the same. "Come with me, dear. I want to show you something."

Mara followed her aunt from the room and ascended the staircase to the upper floor of the house. Deirdre led Mara to her bedroom, which was quite grand and spacious, and she pointed to an oil portrait of a woman in an ornate gold-edged frame that hung over the mantel.

"That is my grandmother and your great-grandmother, Eileen Ffrench," Deirdre announced. "She had the sight, just as you do."

Mara stared at the ancestor who had passed on her gift to her. In spite of the very formal pose, the woman was quite beautiful, with flaxen hair and a serious smile. Her bluish eyes appeared mysterious, almost secretive. Wishing she could talk to her, for she had a thousand questions she wanted answers to, Mara gazed up at her great-grandmother with an awed reverence. It would have been wonderful to be able to speak with her.

"I always wished that I had the sight," Deirdre confided after a moment.

Mara turned to look at her aunt in surprise. "You did?" It was one thing to accept that she had a strange and unusual gift, it was another to wish for it. Mara certainly never would have wished to have it.

"Of course! I would have loved to know if something important was going to happen. I used to love when Grandmama would tell me about her visions." She guided Mara to a small divan and they both sat down. "Tell me about your sight, Mara."

For the first time in her life, Mara did not feel ashamed or embarrassed about her visions. As they sat before the portrait of her great-grandmother, Mara gave examples of the times she had her premonitions and how they had come to pass. Her aunt listened with rapt attention.

"Yes, you definitely have some of Grandmama Eileen in you." Deirdre smiled, and again Mara was struck by how pretty her aunt looked when she smiled.

"So I'm not going mad then?" Mara couldn't help but ask.

"No more so than the rest of us, my dear!" Deirdre laughed heartily.

Blessed relief flooded Mara.

She wasn't cursed. She wasn't afflicted with lunacy and there was nothing terrible to keep any future children from inheriting. And to think she had been rather afraid of her aunt all these years! If only she had come to see her sooner, she would have been spared so much worry. Deirdre had been nothing but kind, understanding, and supportive of her.

"Thank you so much for talking to me, Auntie. I'm so happy I've come here to visit with you today."

"I'm so glad that you did too, Mara dear. And I hope you

will come to see me more often." Deirdre squeezed her hand once more.

"I promise that I will." Mara would definitely see to that.

But for now she needed to get back to London just as soon as she could. She had to see Foster Sheridan and tell him that she would marry him after all!

will come to a sad end, I fear. Poor, degenerate Lex
hadn't such a

rupture that I will. I managed decades, to see how
much I would not, not to thank to tomorrow those

from at that rate in all, as she loved Lady Mara and
him to take some money, of the asks.

21

Recriminations

Rose Sheridan had made a terrible, terrible mistake. She never should have followed the girl to Ireland.

Now she was stuck there, in that godforsaken country, feeling too ill to travel back home. While she rested at a small hotel near the River Liffey in Dublin, she let Bailey Briggs continue to follow the girl and report back to her.

Rose was simply too tired to do more than sit by the window in her room and watch the river flowing by.

And what was she thinking, coming to Ireland? Ireland, of all places! Rose detested traveling! Hated everything about it. It exhausted her.

Even more so now. The headaches were becoming worse and worse, which frightened her. Although her London doctor had told her to expect that, it still came as a shock. It was inevitable.

With a heavy sigh, she stared at the churning river below, as the rain poured from the heavy gray clouds above.

Just why she decided she had to follow Lady Mara Reeves to Dublin, she was still not quite sure. Seeing her that afternoon in the bookshop had done something to

Rose. She'd never been a jealous person before, although Lord knew, she had every reason to be jealous of others, especially of her brother. But still. Something about the girl's youth and beauty and privilege had shaken Rose to her core.

Mara seemed to have everything Rose had never had, and it still wasn't enough for her. Now the girl had the effrontery to want Rose's husband as well.

It simply wasn't fair. The girl had everything. And if she and Foster just waited, they could eventually marry too. When she was gone.

Rose was dying. Not even thirty years old, and the doctor told her she hadn't much longer to live. The tumor in her brain was growing and there was no help for her. There was nothing to be done for her now but wait. It could be months, but definitely not more than a year. Time was quickly running out for Rose Sheridan.

Should she have told Foster about it? She'd had two chances to tell him. The first time was the very day she found out about the tumor. She had come to London to see the doctor and surprised Foster by showing up at the townhouse unannounced. She had wanted to tell him then, but he'd been so cold. Colder than usual, anyway. The second chance she had to tell him was when he'd come to Sterling Hall a few weeks later, informing her that he wanted to dissolve their marriage.

Rose could have told him then. She *should* have told him then.

But she did not want to tell her husband that she was dying.

There was a sense of control in keeping the information to herself, especially in keeping the information from her husband. She wanted him to feel bad when it was over and wonder why he hadn't known. Knowing Foster, he would blame himself and feel responsible for her death, even though there was absolutely nothing he could have done to save her. But she was his wife and it would pain him to learn that he'd no idea his wife was dying until after she was dead.

Foster would be free of her when she died, but the guilt would haunt him forever.

Rose smiled in satisfaction at the thought.

Especially since he was asking to end the marriage. *Let him go to all the trouble of an annulment!* It would all be for nothing! She would most likely be dead by the time it was final, and he would wonder why she'd fought it in the first place. He would still wonder why she never told him that all he had to do was wait for her to die and he would be free.

It served him right.

Yes, she was glad she kept the secret to herself. Besides, she didn't want his pity if he knew. Rose despised being pitied. Her parents had pitied her and it enraged her. She'd be damned if the likes of Foster Sheridan would pity her.

And she'd be damned if she would allow him to marry another woman while she was still alive!

Her entire life had been ruined by this marriage and she wasn't about to go out of this world as anyone other than the Countess of Sterling. She had earned that title with misery and tears and loneliness, and she wasn't about to give it up without a fight. She would die as the Countess of Sterling.

After seeing Mara at the bookshop and talking to her that afternoon, Rose had been struck by her sweet nature and ethereal beauty. She was like a creature from another world. She'd been fascinated by her. She even understood why Foster would want to marry such a girl. But she wondered why someone like Mara, who had everything she could possibly want and had not a care in the world, would want to take up with a married man. She wondered if her family knew . . . but Rose doubted it.

Rose delighted in the power that the knowledge of the affair gave her. She could cause a scandal of momentous proportions. The daughter of the Earl of Cashelmore was carrying on an illicit affair with the Earl of Sterling. If Rose let the cat out of the bag, the ensuing scandal would ruin Mara Reeves forever.

Again Rose smiled with great satisfaction.

For the first time in her life, she wielded some power.

She liked how it felt.

She now had power over Foster Sheridan. And she had power over the girl. Just how Rose was going to assert her power remained to be seen. For now she was waiting and watching and weighing her options.

She didn't have much time left, so she would have to make up her mind soon.

In the meantime she had Bailey Briggs watching Mara. Rose wondered what made the girl suddenly pack up and leave London and Foster. Had they quarreled? It was all quite intriguing, and being that she didn't have much left in the world that entertained her, she'd decided on a whim to follow Mara to find out what was going on. To Alice Bellwether's surprise and utter dismay, they'd traveled with Bailey Briggs to Ireland.

And now she sat in a hotel room in Dublin, too tired to do more than wait there.

Truly, what was Rose going to do? March up to the gates of Cashelmore Manor and demand to see Lady Mara Reeves? No, it was best that she stay put and let a plan come to her.

But nothing had come to her yet and she was growing impatient.

Gazing out the window, Rose watched the rain fall into the swirling torrents of the river as the current flowed toward the Irish Sea. The rain washed away everything, just like the years of her life had been washed away, speeding toward a deep and lonely nothingness.

As tears fell from her eyes, Rose sobbed for everything she had lost and for everything that might have been.

She wondered, not for the first time, what had become of Andrew Cooper. Had he prospered? Had he married and had children? Did he ever think of Rose or miss her? He'd been the only person she ever truly loved and now she wasn't even positive that he had ever really loved her in return. Had he just been using her? If he'd loved her, he would have come back for her, in spite of her father's threats. All of it had been such a waste. Such a shame. If only she hadn't lost her baby. If she hadn't been so heartbroken at the loss of her son, she might have had the strength to stand up to her father's demands. She might have run away. If her son had lived, she could not have married Foster Sheridan. Perhaps if the doctor had not ruined her, she would have attempted to have a child with Foster. There was no way of knowing now.

Oh, her sweet baby boy! He would be ten years old now. Rose had marked every single one of his birthdays. She dreamed of him at night. Dreamt of holding him and watching him grow. Dreamt of being loved unconditionally by a sweet golden-haired boy with chubby cheeks and soft skin. At least her death would bring her a reunion with her beloved son.

A knock on the door startled her from her sad musings. Hastily Rose wiped away her tears with the lace handkerchief monogrammed with her initials. She hated being caught feeling melancholy.

Alice Bellwether entered the room carrying a tray of food that she would insist that Rose eat and Rose wouldn't. Alice determinedly set the tray upon the table and then turned to face her.

"Mr. Briggs has arrived, my lady. Should I show him in?"

"Yes, of course. My lunch can wait." Rose waved away the tray. As if she could eat anything now.

"Let me fix you up a bit first," Alice suggested. With efficient movements she straightened the blanket that covered Rose's legs and adjusted the shawl that covered her shoulders and smoothed Rose's brown hair. "A lady must always look the part," she said with a cheery smile.

"Thank you, Alice," Rose said, grateful for Alice's loyal care during all these years. Alice's devotion to her had been a godsend. Rose would be lost without her.

Alice bustled out of the room and returned a few minutes later with Bailey Briggs. Once he was settled in a chair, and Alice poured him some tea, he got right down to business.

"Well, she's spent some time visiting an aunt in Galway and now she's back home at Cashelmore Manor. From what I've gathered, her parents are in London and no one at the manor is quite sure why she came or how long she is planning to stay," he informed them.

"So we still don't know why she's come here?" Rose was fascinated by every aspect of Mara's life. "Except to visit an aunt?"

"So it would seem," Briggs continued. "I've discovered that her mother died in a fire when Mara was a little girl. The aunt she was visiting was her mother's sister."

This gave Rose pause. So little Miss Perfect hadn't had a perfectly charmed life after all. Mara Reeves had lost her mother as a child. Still, Rose had lost far more than that. In fact, Rose had often wished her mother *had* died. Her life might have been happier without her.

"But I have more interesting news than that," Briggs announced with a triumphant smile.

"Well, what is it?" Rose demanded.

"Your husband has arrived, my lady."

Foster had come for Mara.

Rose was stunned. She hadn't expected that.

Briggs continued, unaware of her surprise. "Lord Sterling arrived in Dublin this morning and he is on his way to Cashelmore Manor now. I have one of my men following him, while I came here right away to let you know."

A deep hurt roiled within her. *He had come for her.* Foster followed Mara across the sea, because he couldn't be without her. For the second time that day, Rose could not stop the tears and she did not care that Alice looked aghast and Briggs looked mortified.

Foster had come after the woman he loved.

No one had ever come for Rose.

22

Explanations

The carriage that Foster Sheridan hired when he arrived in Dublin jounced along the long, white gravel driveway leading to Cashelmore Manor. The sun was just setting as he caught his first glimpse of the estate. It was quite an impressive sight. Surrounded by rolling green fields, the stately manor house was a massive limestone and granite building hosting a towering portico with arcades on either side and supporting a pair of square towers topped with carved pinnacles. The residence spread out on either side of the main entrance in graceful symmetry, with Tuscan colonnades leading to the stable courts. The Earl of Cashelmore possessed a grand and beautiful home but the estate rivaled that of Sterling Hall.

Foster's sense of urgency to see Mara had not lessened since he left London. Had Rose contacted Mara or harassed her in any way? He still didn't know where his wife was, let alone what she had been up to. But the last thing he wanted was Rose's interference, which could spook an already uneasy Mara.

Foster needed to convince her to marry him and he didn't need Rose to persuade her to do otherwise.

He needed to talk some sense into her as well. By the time he left Cashelmore Manor he vowed to have Mara agree to be his wife just as soon as he was free.

But he also had to prepare himself to meet Mara's parents, which would require some delicate rationalizing. Hopefully her father wouldn't try to kill him before he could explain the extenuating circumstances. He also didn't know how Mara would receive him. They hadn't parted on the best of terms after coming to an impasse on their future together. But all that mattered to him now was seeing Mara again, convincing her to marry him, and making certain Rose hadn't been bothering her.

After the carriage came to a stop in the main courtyard, Foster made his way to the main house. The butler, who introduced himself as Collins, ushered Foster into an elegant parlor. The interior of Cashelmore Manor was just as impressive as the exterior. Yet for such a massive structure, the home was quite warm and inviting. He could easily picture Mara growing up in this atmosphere.

Suddenly Mara came flying into the room, her pretty face awash with surprise. She halted at the doorway. Wearing a simple blue gown that accentuated the gray in her eyes, she stood staring at him in disbelief. "Foster!" she cried. "I couldn't believe it when Collins told me you were here!"

Relief flooded him at the sight of her. She was happy to see him! And she was even more beautiful than the last time he saw her. How he had missed her! He longed to wrap his arms around her, but he hesitated and stayed where he was.

"Hello, Mara."

"What on earth are you doing here, Foster? Are you staying for dinner? Of course you are! I've only just arrived from Galway by train. I shall let Collins know to set a place for you. I suppose you will be staying the night as well? I'll have them prepare one of the guest rooms."

Rather excited at his presence, Mara answered her own questions and pulled the tasseled bell cord, which rang in the servants' quarters.

Pleased that she was happy enough to see him that she wanted him to stay, Foster couldn't help but smile.

The butler arrived immediately and Mara instructed him. "Lord Sterling will be joining me for dinner, as well as staying the night, so please have his things brought to the ivory guest room."

"Yes, my lady." Collins left the parlor.

Alone in the room, they both still stood there, staring at each other.

She smiled shyly, and again she asked, "What are you doing here?"

"I came for you."

At that, Mara rushed into his arms. Foster held her close, her head resting against his chest, his arms wrapped around her. It felt so wonderful to hold her like that again. He breathed deeply of her lily-of-the-valley scent and marveled again at how perfectly right she felt in his embrace. Suddenly, he realized that Mara was shaking.

"Mara?" he asked, worried. He looked down at her. "Are you crying?"

She peered up at him, her eyes wet with tears, and withdrew from his embrace. "Yes."

"Why are you crying? I thought you were happy to see me."

"I'm overjoyed to see you," she said, wiping at her eyes with a handkerchief. "It's just that I'm stunned that you are here. You came all this way just to see me?"

"Of course I came to see you." He gave her a teasing smile. "I certainly didn't come for the scenery."

"But that's what I don't understand. Why would you

come after me, when I was so horrid to you when we last parted? I left London without telling you I was coming to Ireland. How did you even know I was here?" Her delicate brows were drawn in confusion.

Foster smiled enigmatically. "I have my ways, Lady Mara."

"Really, Foster." She smiled in spite of herself. "How did you learn I had come to Cashelmore?"

He hesitated, knowing she wouldn't like his answer. "I spoke with your cousin Phillip Sinclair . . ."

Mara's joyful expression disappeared and her face turned ashen. "You spoke to my cousin about me? About us?" She took a step back from him.

"Yes, and I'm glad I did. I don't regret it at all."

Horrified, she looked about to cry again. "Phillip knows about us now? He knows it was you, then?"

"He does at that." Foster moved toward her, reaching out his hand. She refused it. "Mara, it's for the best that he knows about us. I don't wish for us to be a secret any longer."

"What did he say?" She looked quite ill. "How did he react?"

"Please don't be upset. Everything is fine. Phillip was more understanding than I would have hoped him to be. Aside from threatening me with bodily harm from time to time, which was to be expected, he was quite supportive of . . . our . . . situation." Foster moved toward her again. This time she allowed him to put his arm around her. He guided her to the small sofa.

"Are you telling me he approves of our affair?" she asked in disbelief as she sat beside him.

"Well, *approve* is a rather strong word. I think *tolerated* is a better description," he said with a rueful smile. "However, he was sympathetic when presented with all the facts."

She relaxed for a moment before suddenly exclaiming, "Good heavens! Do my parents know about us then?"

Foster was confused. "How would I know that?"

"Well, I'm guessing Phillip would have said something to them by now. This is awful. They must know." She bit her lip.

"I'm not sure how Phillip would have told them, and wouldn't they have said something to you? In any case, Mara, I'm here with you. I would like to speak with your mother and father myself. We can talk to them together tonight at dinner."

Now it was Mara's turn to look confused. "My parents are in London."

"They're not here with you?" Foster had utterly lost sight of this conversation. "I'm quite sure that Phillip told me you came home to Cashelmore to see your parents."

"Well, yes, I did," she explained, "but they apparently were coming to London to surprise me, while I was coming here to surprise them. We completely missed each other."

"Well, that is something." Foster laughed. He was oddly let down that her parents weren't at home. He'd been anxious to have all this out in the open and to prove to them that his intentions were honest.

"I suppose it is." Mara smiled. "But you still haven't explained to me why you are here."

"I already told you." He looked into her gray-green eyes. "I wanted to see you, Mara. I feel terrible about the way we parted, not only because you were so upset, but because I didn't want to part with you at all."

She remained quiet.

"If you recall, you were the one who turned down my offer of marriage."

"Because you are not free to make such an offer," she pointed out.

"Not *yet*. But I will be free before too long. But that was not the reason you told me that you didn't wish to marry me. Was it?"

She glanced away, her eyes downcast. Foster cupped her chin, forcing her to look up. "Look at me, Mara."

She raised her eyes to his. "Yes?"

"That was the answer I was looking for when I asked you to marry me." He gazed at her. "But you didn't give it then. And you wouldn't give me a logical reason for turning me down."

Mara gave him a helpless look and a regretful smile. "Perhaps I've changed my mind."

"Do you mean it?" His heart leapt with happiness at her words. "You will marry me as soon as I'm free?"

"Yes," she whispered as she leaned closer to him. "I'll marry you, Foster."

Joy flooded him. Pulling her closer to him, Foster kissed her deeply. She had agreed to be his wife! He would be able to spend his life with this wonderful and beautiful woman at his side.

As their kiss grew more passionate, her arms found their way around his neck and she kissed him hungrily. They clung to each other after having been apart. A familiar heat grew between them, and a wonderful thought occurred to Foster. He broke from their kiss and stared at Mara.

"If your parents are in London," he asked with a wicked grin, "then you are here at Cashelmore Manor alone?"

Mara sat up and smoothed her dress. She gave him a shy look. "Aside from the servants, yes . . ."

"You know what this means?" he asked. They would have the night together. The entire night.

"I won't have to leave in the middle of the night," she whispered as she fell back into his embrace.

They kissed again.

* * *

Later that evening after supper, Foster silently made his way down the dimly lit corridor to Mara's room. They had to be careful of the servants, but the two of them were not about to pass up the unexpected opportunity to be alone together. He followed the directions she had given him, and when he counted the third door on the right, he slowly turned the doorknob.

She was waiting for him, standing before the fire dressed only in a nightgown of the finest white silk. Her soft hair hung loose around her shoulders, glistening in the firelight. He could see the outline of her lithe little body silhouetted against the light. Looking like a silvery angel, she was truly stunning. And she belonged to him, just as he belonged to her.

Closing the door behind him and turning the key in the lock, he moved with quick purpose toward her.

"I've missed you so much," she whispered as she reached for him.

"Not half as much as I have missed you." He brought his mouth down over hers in a searing kiss. Then he lifted her in his arms and carried her to the bed. He lay down beside her and they kissed each other hungrily.

To Foster it felt like forever since they had been together. His passion for her only increased during their time apart, as did his love for this enchanting woman. He didn't know if he could ever get enough of her.

As that familiar heat grew between them, he broke from their kiss and began to slide her nightgown slowly up her thighs, admiring her smooth skin as he did so. Without needing to say a word, she raised her arms over her head so he could remove the garment from her body completely. Naked before him, her beauty awed him, as did her loving heart. With a swift motion he removed the robe he'd been wearing, revealing he had nothing on underneath.

Mara squealed in delight. "You naughty man! Walking down the corridor to my room practically naked!"

"It seemed the simplest solution," he replied with a wicked smile, as he eased himself over her body and settled himself between her legs.

Her excitement at his nakedness aroused him even more, and when Mara wrapped her legs around his waist, he couldn't wait any longer. This would not be a leisurely lovemaking session. There would be time for that later. No, this would be a fervent and fast coupling to ease both their needs. They both wanted each other too much. With a strangled groan he thrust himself inside her. She welcomed him, eagerly matching his thrusts with her hips.

He lost himself in her, moving faster and harder, wanting more and more of her. He loved her so completely that he could no longer imagine his life without her. They belonged together and nothing would keep them apart now. Absolutely nothing. He would get the annulment and Mara would be his wife. They would have a life together.

He felt the tension mount within her body and knew she was close. The thought of giving her pleasure excited him further, as it always did. Mara called out his name in a breathless gasp as pleasure washed over her. That pushed him over the edge and he found his release as well.

Afterward, Foster held her in his arms, where she belonged. He sighed with contentment. This woman brought him peace and happiness like he'd never known existed. The extent of his love for her astonished him. They lay in her bed, in the dimly lit room, wrapped in each other's embrace.

Placing a loving kiss on the top of her head, he asked, "So will you please tell me now? Why did you come to Ireland, Mara? What was the true reason?"

She snuggled closer to him. "It's a bit complicated, but I came because I wanted to sort through some things. I needed to learn more about my mother."

"Your mother?" Foster asked, confused. He knew her mother had died when Mara was a child.

"Yes. It's a tangle, but it's part of the reason I said I couldn't marry you."

"What on earth do you mean?" he asked.

"Throughout my childhood, I was under the impression that my mother was . . . insane," Mara whispered into the darkness. "I feared, due to my visions, that I was going to go insane as well."

Foster didn't know how to respond to her, mostly because he wasn't entirely sure what all of it meant, but he clearly knew she was troubled by it. "You didn't wish to marry me because you believed you would eventually become unbalanced, as your mother was?"

Mara nodded against his chest. "Yes. I didn't want to put you through the heartbreak of eventually watching me go insane and becoming a terrible burden to you. It's the reason I always knew I could never marry anyone."

"But you were worrying about something that might never happen," he said. It was quite illogical to him. "There is no way to know for certain that you would become afflicted."

"I was led to believe otherwise." She sighed heavily. "Believing that my mother was mad, and the fact that I have been having premonitions my whole life, added up to the irrefutable truth that I too was mad. Or at least I was exhibiting the symptoms of becoming completely insane. It was to be my fate as well."

"And so that is why you don't want children," Foster said as it all became clear to him. Mara had been afraid and had kept the burden of this worrisome secret to herself all these years. It confounded him.

"The thought of passing on my affliction to my children was the worst outcome I could possibly imagine. So there was no question of my ever having children of my own. I could never take that chance," she said softly.

"Oh, Mara." Foster hugged her closer. He couldn't imagine loving her more than he did in that moment. Her self-sacrifice was astounding. This lovely woman would have spent her life alone in order to spare others.

"Do you understand now why I said I couldn't marry you?" she asked.

"Yes, but now I'm not sure why you changed your mind and said you would."

She paused. "Do you still want to marry me, knowing that I could lose my mind?"

"Yes." He answered without a moment's hesitation. "Of course."

Mara sat up and stared at him through the flickering candlelight. "You would willingly marry me, knowing I might become insane one day? Why on earth would you do such a thing?"

"Because, Mara Reeves, I love you." Foster felt as if he would burst with love for her. "And I will thankfully take any amount of time I can have with you, rather than have none at all."

"Oh, Foster. I love you so much." She kissed him. "I'm touched that you would do that for me. But you don't have to worry about my going insane after all."

"I don't?"

"You don't. It seems I was mistaken. My mother was not mad. Not at all. She was a rather reckless and a most definitely selfish wife and mother, but there is no madness in my family."

"Well, I must admit, that is a relief. And the premonitions?" he asked.

"Apparently the premonitions *do* run in my family. I

went to visit my mother's older sister. She told me that my great-grandmother had the gift of sight. It seems I take after her." She gave him a rueful smile.

"I think it's magnificent."

"You won't mind being married to a woman who gets occasional glimpses of future events?" Her voice held a note of apprehension.

"Not at all. In fact, I think your skill could come in very handy sometimes." He gave her a smile.

She gave a little sigh of relief and kissed him again. "I love you, Foster Sheridan."

"And I love you." He held her tighter. "Now are you willing to have lots of beautiful children with me?"

"Nothing would make me happier."

They kissed for some time as her naked body entwined with his.

"Mara?" he asked finally. "What about that other premonition you had? The one you had the night we met and the night you were with me? The one with the fire?"

"I'm not sure what that means. I've had that vision four times now, and I'm no closer to knowing what it signifies. I don't know how or when the fire happens. Something terrible happens to someone, but I don't know whom. The only part of the premonition that gives me peace is knowing that you and I are safe and together at the end of it."

"I'm not certain what your visions mean either. But I'm here with you now and I will make sure you are safe and loved." He kissed her again. Thinking of Mara's safety, he was prompted to ask, "Mara, has my wife contacted you?"

She gave him quite a surprised look. "Lady Sterling? Of course not! Why ever would she wish to speak to me?"

"I'm not sure, but I have good reason to suspect that she found out that it's you that I've been seeing. I had a feeling she might try to contact you in some way." Foster supposed he'd been wrong about Rose coming to Ireland. Perhaps she'd regained her senses and changed her mind. He only had his hysterical housemaid's word that Rose was heading to Ireland in the first place. Now he relaxed, knowing that she hadn't troubled Mara.

"Good heavens, I can't imagine why your wife would wish to speak to me any more than I would wish to speak to her!" She shivered. "But what happens now, Foster?"

"What do you mean?"

"With us? What happens now?" she asked.

"As soon as my marriage to Rose is annulled, we will get married. I thought we were clear on that," he said with a laugh.

"Yes, I know that, but . . ." Mara grew serious. "We have to tell my parents. If Phillip already knows about us, I cannot keep this from my family any longer. And I must return to London tomorrow. They are expecting me home."

"Then I shall go with you and we will speak to your parents together. I actually thought they would be here when I arrived. I was looking forward to meeting them and explaining my situation," he said.

"Thank you," she said. "You're wonderful."

"There's no reason to thank me. I love you and I'm going to become a part of your family. Because they are important to you, they are important to me. There is no reason you should face them alone. I'm well aware of the scandalous position you are in because of me." There was nothing he wouldn't do for Mara to make her life easier or more perfect.

"Then we shall both sail together tomorrow?" she asked.

"I wouldn't have it any other way."

Mara settled back into his arms with a contented sigh. "This is so nice. I love that I don't have to get dressed and go home. I'm already home."

"I love that too. Before too long we will be able to share the same house and the same bed, every single day and night. But for now, I will simply return to my room before dawn. We can't have the servants gossiping about you."

Mara giggled and wrapped her arms around him. "What if I don't let you go?"

"Then your maid shall find a blissfully happy naked man in your bed come morning." He kissed the tip of her pert little nose.

"Poor Brighton! She would faint straightaway! I couldn't do that to her."

"Then I will have to sneak out of here before she does." Foster eased Mara over and positioned himself on top of her. "But in the meantime, there are still hours to go before dawn . . ."

23

Conflagrations

The following afternoon Foster and Mara left Cashel-more Manor in separate carriages, as planned, to make the journey back to London. However, the ferry to Liverpool was unexpectedly delayed, forcing them to wait until next morning. Instead of traveling all the way back to Cashelmore, they decided to spend the night in Dublin and checked into an elegant little hotel called the Dublin House.

Mara had her own room on the second floor overlooking the River Liffey, and Brighton was in a small room downstairs. And of course, Foster was in a room on the floor below her. Appearances had to be maintained.

Mara had never been so joyful, and she hoped her parents would be happy for her too. Bringing home a married man would not make them especially proud of her, but Mara believed that once they knew all the circumstances they would not be averse to her marrying Foster. At least she hoped so.

After having supper in her hotel room, Mara settled down to read a book about the gift of sight, which Foster had bought for her. It seemed to her somewhat incredible that for a girl who spent her life in a bookshop, she had never read one book on the subject! Perhaps she had been too afraid of what she might find out. Foster had suggested that the more she knew about the subject, the less frightened of it she would be. He had a good point. She had avoided it for too long.

Speaking to her aunt Deirdre had helped immeasurably as well. Deirdre had enabled her to see that her visions were nothing to fear, and were, in fact, a point of pride in their family. Mara recalled that Uncle Jeffrey had proposed that she meet with someone who was well versed in the field of visions, to learn more about them. Perhaps she would take him up on his offer.

These visions had baffled her for her entire life. Why did she have them? Why did they occur at random moments? Why did she not always know what they meant? Why was she suddenly having reoccurring premonitions? Or rather, one premonition in particular.

The vision of the fire haunted her. What did it mean? When would it come to pass? The only element of that vision of which she was certain was Foster. From the moment she first had that premonition, there was no doubt in her mind that she and Foster were destined to be together. That fact had only been reinforced last night when Foster arrived at Cashelmore Manor.

Oh, how she loved him! And now she would be able to be his wife! They had a true future together. They could have a family and—

A soft knock on the door caught her attention and she set down the book, her heart skipping a beat. It had to be Foster! Even though they both knew he shouldn't take such a risk as to come visit her while they were staying at a hotel, Mara would gladly welcome him into her room anyway. She simply could not resist him. Before she went to the door, she grabbed her shawl and wrapped it around her shoulders to cover her nightgown.

To her surprise, a woman stood before her. A woman she had definitely seen once before.

"Can I help you?" Mara asked, feeling somewhat confused as she tried to reconcile what this strange person was doing outside her hotel room.

The woman stared at her quite intently. "Do you recognize me?" she asked.

Mara nodded. "Yes, I believe we met each other at Hamilton's Book Shoppe in London."

No, she had not forgotten the odd lady who wandered into the shop that afternoon. The woman had given Mara the impression that she was ill. Then she had appeared in Mara's premonition later that day. What on earth was this woman doing in Dublin, at the same inn where Mara was staying? It was very peculiar and more than a coincidence that they should be there at the same time. She suddenly had a very bad feeling. Mara's first instinct was to close the door to shut her out, but the woman stopped her with what she said next.

"I learned your name, Lady Mara Reeves, that day at the bookshop. But I don't believe I gave you my name. It was most ill-mannered of me." She paused dramatically before stating in an imperious tone, "I am Rose Sheridan, the Countess of Sterling."

Mara gasped and her heart almost stopped completely. Good heavens! She was Foster's wife! *This woman was Foster's wife!* No wonder she had looked at Mara so fixedly. Mara fervently wished the floor would somehow open up and swallow her whole. She'd never felt so mortified in her entire life.

"May I come in and speak to you for a moment, Lady Mara?" Rose Sheridan asked.

Unable to form a coherent sentence, Mara nodded obediently and opened the door a little wider to let the woman into her room. Rose stepped slowly inside and Mara closed the door behind them. Taking a shaky breath, she turned to face Foster's wife.

"I have a feeling that you're wondering why I am here . . ." Rose said.

Mara remained silent. She knew exactly why Rose was there: to confront the *other woman*. Mara's face burned with shame knowing that *she* was the other woman. She stared at Rose Sheridan with a mixture of dread and fascination.

Foster's wife was rail thin and her cold blue eyes glittered with anger. She too was wearing only her nightclothes, a white cotton gown and a richly quilted scarlet robe. Her thick brown hair fell in loose waves around shoulders, making her appear much younger than she had that afternoon in the bookshop. Idly Mara wondered how old she was. Judging from what Foster had told her, she figured the woman couldn't even be thirty years old yet. However, Rose Sheridan had appeared far older than that, the afternoon at the bookshop. Her manners and gestures made her seem like an elderly woman.

With a brittle laugh, Rose began to explain. "Actually, *I* am wondering what I'm doing here. Coming to see you seemed like a good idea a few moments ago back in my room. When I learned that you had checked into this hotel, the very hotel I was staying in myself, I thought, well, I must pay my respects to the kind bookshop lady. Why not just run down the hall and say hello to her right now? And so here I am."

Mara still had not said a word. For what could she say? She had been caught. Found out. She was having a torrid affair with this woman's husband. There was no justification for it, however Mara tried to rationalize it. It had been easier to ignore the fact that Foster was married before his wife walked into her room. But now . . . Now Mara had no

choice but to face up to the consequences of her shameful
actions. She knew what she had done.

And she was most definitely in the wrong.

"So here I am," Rose repeated. "Although now I think I
may have made a terrible mistake in coming here. Honestly,
what does one say upon confronting her husband's mistress?" Rose eyed her closely, a satisfied smile on her face.

Mara did not answer. She thought for a moment about
flinging the door open and running down the corridor and
down the stairs to Foster's room. How she wished he would
come to her right now! What was she to say to this woman?

"You see, I've never actually met one of Foster's mistresses before, so I've no practice at this. And if you consider
the number of mistresses Foster has had over the years, one
would think I would be better prepared to greet them,"
Rose went on quite amiably, as if she were chatting with a
good friend. Yet there was an ugly undertone to everything
she said.

Then Rose Sheridan paused. "Please, do come sit down
with me for a moment, won't you, Lady Mara? We shall
discuss this situation like the ladies we are." She moved
to one of the two matching chairs by the window and sat
down.

Every instinct within Mara screamed for her to flee the
room. Fighting against her desire to leave, Mara made her
way to the matching chair near Foster's wife. A small table
stood between the two chairs, where a pretty kerosene lamp
gave off a warm glow.

"There we go." Rose praised her in a condescending
tone, her mouth twisted in a scornful grimace. "It's so lovely
we can discuss this as ladies. Although it isn't very ladylike
of you to be the mistress of a married man, now is it?"

"No, it isn't," Mara finally managed to choke out. "I am
truly sorry."

"You are sorry. Somehow I doubt that." Rose shook her

head, her lips in a sneer. "I must admit you were quite a surprise when I first met you. You were not what I was picturing in the least. Why, you're so sweet and innocent-looking! You look like a fine little china doll, if you don't mind my saying so. You're not his usual type at all. Foster's tastes usually run toward actresses and dancers. You know, flashy and tawdry types." She flashed a smug grin. "Surely you didn't think you were his first mistress, did you, my dear? Or his last?"

A tight knot formed in the pit of Mara's stomach. Of course, she assumed that Foster had been with other women before he met her. Although she had never really given much thought to the type of woman he had associated with, there was something quite vindictive in the way that Rose was insinuating that Mara was just like all the others.

Was she just like all the others? Or was she worse? For Mara knew better than to take up with a married man, yet she did it anyway. In spite of all she had been taught, she flouted the conventions she had been raised with.

Rose ignored Mara's lack of response and continued on. "Of course, it seems Foster has you believing that he's going to marry you . . . You weren't foolish enough to believe it, were you, my dear? For certainly you know that he can't marry you. Not while he's still married to *me*!" Rose's brittle laughed echoed in the room as she waved her hand airily. "I am his wife. You do realize that, don't you?"

Mara nodded. Yes, she was quite aware of the fact that Foster's wife was sitting there with her. For a moment Mara tried to imagine Rose when she was younger, back when she and Foster first married. She wondered what had happened in Rose's life to make her so spiteful and unhappy, but Mara would not rise to the bait Rose was giving her. In this situation, the less Mara said, the better. But it didn't stop her from wishing frantically for Foster to arrive.

Rose grew quiet. Mara raised her eyes to look at her,

then glanced away. For what seemed like an eternity they both sat in an uncomfortable silence.

"Foster is not going to get our marriage annulled," Rose announced at last.

"Why not?" Mara couldn't help but ask, even though she knew that Rose was wrong. Of course Foster was getting the annulment! They'd discussed it. He'd already started the legal proceedings with his solicitor. She believed him.

"Because, my sweet Lady Mara, if he continues on the path of obtaining an annulment, I will go to the newspapers and give them your name as the woman who is trying to steal my husband. Imagine the lurid stories they would print! Your name would be known throughout the country. You would become notorious and be branded as a scarlet woman. Your reputation and your life would be forever ruined." She paused, leaning in toward Mara, and hissed, "I have the power to ruin you."

Oh, God, Rose Sheridan was right!

Mara felt panic rise within her. Foster's wife was right. She could swiftly and easily destroy Mara's world. It was too awful to contemplate. When she'd embarked on this affair with Foster, she'd been so certain that they were meant to be that she went against all she knew to be right and brushed aside the consequences. In essence, Mara hadn't believed she had a future. What difference would having an affair with a married man have made when she was locked away for lunacy? But now, now that she and Foster were to marry and have children, things were quite different. Mara had the future to think of.

"Now, is that what you wish for, my dear? To become a social pariah? To humiliate your family? Have you given any thought to them? Is that want you truly want?"

"No." The word bubbled out of Mara's mouth of its own volition. She hadn't thought about her family at all, and now her conscience pricked her.

"I didn't think so . . ." Rose grinned in false sympathy. "I wouldn't think you bargained on that when you began your tawdry affair with my husband." She let out a weary sigh. "It's not fair, is it? You and Foster are both committing a sin, yet it's always the woman who gets blamed, isn't it? The men don't have to worry about their reputations at all. Nothing ever happens to the men."

Mara held her breath and listened.

"But the women! Oh, the women take all the risks. In life, we carry all the burdens and all the shame and all the ridicule. We're the ones who are ruined. We are the ones who have to bear the illegitimate children. We are the ones who are left alone to shoulder all the heartbreak while the men just carry on their merry way. Their lives don't change. They don't become ostracized. They don't get branded as loose, scarlet women. No, not at all. The men become dashing scoundrels and charming rogues and are considered daring and exciting." She shook her head ruefully. "No, the women suffer all the negative consequences."

Mara wanted to nod her head in agreement, but she did not. Rose certainly had a point. She was not wrong in her thinking, but Mara would not give her the satisfaction of agreeing with her.

"Yes, it's funny, isn't it, Lady Mara . . . Men think we are these fragile, innocent little creatures who faint at the drop of a hat and are in dire need of their constant protection. Yet they willingly seduce us and then blame it on our wicked, womanly wiles. *They* become the victims then. We bewitch them and they have no recourse. Yet how can they be the victims when they are the ones who have all the power? I ask you that . . . These big, strong, manly men with all their control over us, they blame us and shun us. And we women let them . . . Because we are the stronger ones. We bear more than any man ever could."

Mara finally nodded her head in spite of herself. Women

always had to shoulder more burdens than men. Yet men insisted on referring to women as the weaker sex. It would be laughable if it weren't so serious. "You're quite right, Lady Sterling."

"Of course I'm right," Rose said rather sadly. "And that's what I am telling you. You are treading upon dangerous ground, my dear. One word to the papers from me, and your life as you know it is over." Rose sat back against the chair as if she were exhausted after running a mile.

"Why are you here? Did you follow me to Ireland?" Mara demanded, suddenly anxious to end this awkward visit. "What is it you want from me?"

"Isn't it obvious?" Rose continued in an ominous tone. "I want you to end this affair. I want you to give up Foster and convince him not to end our marriage."

"Why would I do that when I love him and he loves me?"

"Why? Because quite simply, my dear girl, I will ruin you otherwise," Rose replied calmly.

Another silence ensued.

Mara thought it over. Rose was absolutely correct in her description of what would happen if word of her affair with Lord Sterling went public. Yes, there would be a dreadful scandal. Mara would be ruined. She would be humiliated and sorry for bringing shame upon her family. But in the end, would she care? She wasn't so concerned for herself. In actuality Mara had never cared much for society and social events, so she wouldn't care if she were ostracized. Her family would forgive her. And Foster would marry her. They would be together as they belonged, and the scandal would be worth it then. As long as she was with Foster, she could withstand anything.

Mara interrupted the tense silence with her own question. "You don't love Foster, do you?"

Rose looked stunned. "Love him? It doesn't matter if I love him or not."

Mara thought it mattered a great deal. "Has Foster ever been mean or cruel to you?"

Rose scoffed in a superior tone. "When has he not?"

"How has he been cruel to you?" Mara demanded, wishing to defend Foster, whom she knew only to be unfailingly kind.

"He has not been a faithful husband to me."

"Can you blame him? Have you been a faithful wife? You've denied him everything. Have you tried to give him children? Have you given him the family that he wants and deserves to have?" Mara snapped. She was finally angry enough to accuse Foster's wife of her own share of the blame in the demise of her marriage.

Rose looked furious. "What do you know of any of that?"

"What do I know of it? Foster told me everything I need to know about your so-called marriage," Mara declared, trembling with outrage. "I know you've never lived together and that you have never even given him a chance to have a child and an heir. What kind of a wife are you?"

"How dare you!" Rose stood on shaky legs, her face turning a mottled red. "Who are you to pass judgment on my marriage? On my personal affairs?"

"I'm the woman who loves Foster and will gladly give him the family he deserves when we marry. So how dare you come in my room and threaten *me*?" Trembling, Mara rose to her feet as well. "Please leave my room at once!"

Rose looked stunned, utterly stunned by Mara's outburst. She stalked to the door. Before she left the room, she turned to Mara and cried, "You will bitterly regret crossing me. Mark my words."

The door slammed shut behind her.

Trembling, Mara sank back into the chair. That was dreadful. Completely dreadful. She wondered if she should find Foster and tell him that his wife was at the hotel and had threatened her. She was positive he didn't know that Rose was in Ireland, let alone down the hall from her.

Another soft knock on the door startled her. Her heart raced, hoping it was Foster. She hurried to the door, opening it carefully. She'd no wish to spar with Rose again if she'd returned.

"Excuse me, my lady," said Brighton, her lady's maid. "Is there anything else you'll be needing from me for the night?"

Suddenly Mara had an idea. "Yes, there is one last thing you can help me with, Brighton."

Too afraid to risk being seen going to his room or running into Rose Sheridan again, Mara penned a hasty note informing Foster of her confrontation with his wife.

"Please see that this note is delivered to Lord Sterling right away. And that will be all for tonight, Brighton. Thank you."

"Are you sure you are all right, my lady?" Brighton asked, her expression concerned. "You look a bit distressed."

"I'm fine, but I will be much better when Lord Sterling gets my note." Her trusted maid was quite aware of what was going on with her and Foster.

"Yes, my lady. I'll take care of it," she said with a nod of her head.

"Thank you, Brighton. Good night. I'll see you in the morning."

Mara then dimmed all the lamps, except one on the night table, and climbed into bed, wishing Foster could come to her. She didn't know how she would ever sleep after what had just happened. In spite of how awful Lady Sterling had acted toward her, Mara was the one who was in the wrong. Foster was a married man, and she never ought to have gotten involved with him in the first place.

His wife had every right to be angry with them. They both should have waited until his marriage was legally over.

Mara had justified her shameful behavior by telling herself that Foster didn't have a real marriage. But according to the law, Rose Sheridan was his legal wife. And no matter how she tried to rationalize it now, Mara and Foster were in the wrong. Tears filled her eyes, and she told herself that it would be over before too long and she would become Foster's wife.

It was sometime later that night that Mara heard a tremendous amount of noise. She sat up in bed, startled by loud shouts and a great deal of banging. In spite of thinking she could never sleep, she must have fallen asleep at some point. The lamp had burned out, for the room was in total darkness. Disoriented, it took her a moment to remember where she was.

Then she smelled smoke. Something was burning!
Fire.

There was a fire in the hotel. Her heart pounded and an icy fear gripped her heart. Mara willed herself to rise from the bed. Stumbling across the dark and unfamiliar room in her bare feet, she managed to make her way to the door and fling it open.

The sight left her stricken.

The end of the hallway was engulfed in shimmering flames, and the blast of heat almost knocked her over. It seemed as if the entire hotel was on fire!

Yet Mara stood transfixed in the doorway of her room, staring at the scorching blaze before her. The swirling and glittering wall of orange and gold flames mesmerized her. They always had.

Memories assaulted her. Memories of the night her mother died.

Mama! Mama! Where are you?

Mara had to help her. But she couldn't reach her. That wall of dancing flames blocked her way. Her mother screamed and screamed. Bloodcurdling screams echoed around her. Helpless to do anything, Mara could only stand there and watch the flames surround her mother.

Screams and terror and Mara cried. She didn't know where to go. Suddenly Uncle Gerald, her father's cousin, appeared in the corridor and pushed her out of the way. He was angry. You're a bad girl, Mara! A very bad girl! What are you doing here? Go back to bed!

Mara wouldn't go. She wanted her mother and she wasn't a bad girl.

"Fire! Get out! Fire!"

The frantic shouts from somewhere, along with the increasing heat, suddenly roused Mara from her reverie. This wasn't a memory! This fire was happening right at that moment. The hotel was burning and Mara had to get out.

Yet she didn't know what to do or where to go. Panic coursed through her veins. Where was the staircase again? How could she get out of this hotel?

Agonized screams pierced the smoke-clogged air. She ran forward, toward the screams for help. Thick smoke and ash swirled around her. It became difficult to see through the black smoke. It was even harder to breathe. Someone kept screaming, pitiful cries. Mara couldn't see and she'd lost her way. She didn't know where to go.

It was her premonition. Oh, God, this was it.

Except her vision had been completely wrong. Fear raced through Mara's entire body as she coughed and tried to cover her face from the searing heat and smoke. *She* was going to die in this blaze. The vision was wrong. It was Mara's own death she had foreseen. It was inevitable. She was going to burn to death, just like her mother had.

Still the piercing shrieks of terror became louder. Were they her own screams? She wasn't even certain anymore.

Completely panicked now, Mara suddenly thought of her parents and her brother, Thomas, and how sad they would be to learn that she had died. And Foster. How she loved him! Where was he? Had he gotten out of the fire safely? Or was he, too, trapped in the burning building? Had Brighton escaped? She would never see any of the people she loved again.

Suddenly she saw a figure among the burning flames. It was the figure of a woman and she was screaming for someone to help her.

It was Rose Sheridan. Foster's wife was on fire.

Instinctively Mara moved forward to help her. A rumbling crash and a roaring surge of flames caused her to step back instead, as a heavy beam crashed down from the ceiling, just missing Mara. Glowing embers and dancing sparks flew all around her.

Gasping in terror, she backed away from the scorching heat. She was unable to help Rose, who seemed to disappear into the orange and gold flames.

Mara tripped and fell to the carpet-covered floor. The smoke was less heavy there and she could breathe somewhat better. She wished she remembered where the staircase was. On her hands and knees now, she began to crawl forward, choking on the smoke. Something hard hit her head and she reeled from the pain, as stars spun around her head.

Lost in a swirling, angry sea of smoke, heat, and flames, Mara cried as she crawled in what she hoped was the direction of the staircase. Was she going to die there? Would she ever get out of this?

"Mara!"

She heard a voice calling over the roar of flames. *Had someone called her name?*

"Mara! Where are you?"

It was Foster! She dragged herself toward the sound of

his voice, ignoring the encroaching fire around her. It became more and more difficult to see. More and more difficult to breathe. She longed to call back to him, but she was so choked with smoke that she couldn't yell at all. She just kept crawling, trying to escape the flames behind her.

Suddenly Foster's hands were upon her, lifting her off the floor and into his strong arms. She looked into his deep green eyes and saw his love and worry for her reflected in them. Mara clung to him and pressed her head against his chest, grateful for his strength as he carried her down the steps away from the fire. Peace enveloped her. She was safe now. Foster had her and she need not worry. They loved each other and they belonged together. Everything would be all right as long as they were together.

The last thing she remembered before darkness overtook her was Foster saying that he loved her.

24

Reactions

"**M**ara?"
Her eyelids fluttered open briefly, then closed again.

Foster held his breath, willing Mara to waken. He thought he'd lost her in the fire last night and he himself still had not recovered from all that had happened. As he sat beside her on the edge of the bed, he watched Mara lying there, looking so small and fragile. He gently smoothed her flaxen hair away from her beautiful face, which was marred by a swollen purple bruise.

She had been so covered with ash and soot when he found her, at first he feared she was badly burned. Yet somehow she had escaped with only some minor scrapes and burns on her arms and legs, aside from the terrible knot on her forehead. The poor thing must have hit her head on something.

Last night had been an utter nightmare.

He too had been asleep when the smoke and shouts had awakened him. He raced outside with the other hotel guests but could not find Mara anywhere. A tearful and desperate

Brighton ran to him, insisting that Mara must still have been in her room.

That's when Foster went back inside, frantic to find her. When he'd finally managed to get to the second floor, Mara had been crawling toward the staircase. She collapsed in his arms so completely that she still hadn't awakened.

As dawn broke over the smoking remains of the Dublin House hotel and a light mist began to fall on the smoldering embers, the extent of the damage and the severity of the fire was clear to everyone. It was a miracle that Mara, that any of them, had survived at all.

They were now safely ensconced in another hotel. He managed to find lodging for them until she was well enough to travel to London. While Foster had dealt with other matters, Brighton had tended to Mara's wounds and cleaned her up. But she still had not awakened, and that worried him. Actually, it terrified him.

"The doctor said she needs rest and should stay in bed all day today and most likely tomorrow. But we should try to wake her. I've just been keeping a cool cloth on that bump of hers." Brighton looked worried as she appealed to Foster for help.

"Mara," he called again, as he gently tapped her cheek. "Mara, my love, wake up."

This time her eyelids fluttered open and stayed open. Mara's wide gray-green eyes stared at him in confusion. "Foster . . ." She mumbled slowly, "What happened?"

"There was a fire at the hotel, but you're fine now, love. You took quite a hit to the head, but you'll recover in no time. You're safe here with me now. You just need to rest." Foster smiled at her. His heart filled with relief that Mara had awakened.

"Brighton is safe?" she asked with a worried frown, glancing around the room.

"I'm right here, my lady. You gave us all quite a fright, you did," Brighton answered. "Can I get you anything?"

"Water, please," Mara said. Her face was pale and drawn.

Brighton brought a glass of water while Foster helped Mara sit up against the pillows so she could drink it. With a shaky hand, Mara brought the glass to her lips and drank it all down. Then, as if exhausted, she rested her head against the pillows and closed her eyes.

"Foster?" she said, reaching her hand out to him, her eyes still closed. "Please stay with me."

He took her small hand in his and gave her a comforting squeeze. "I wouldn't dream of leaving you."

Brighton gave him an understanding look and a nod of her head. She would give them their privacy for a while. "I'll go fetch more water and bring back something for her to eat. For you as well, my lord."

"Thank you, Brighton."

As the maid left them alone, Foster turned his attention back to Mara. "How are you feeling?"

"A little dizzy. My head hurts."

"I can imagine it does. You've quite a nasty bruise there," he said. His heart ached to see her like this, but he was just grateful that she was alive. "The doctor said you should rest for a few days. I sent a message to your parents that we were delayed. I didn't want them to worry about you. We should have been almost in London by now."

Foster hadn't been sure if he'd done the right thing in telegraphing Lord and Lady Cashelmore, but he believed they had a right to know about their daughter.

"Thank you," she murmured. Mara seemed too exhausted to disagree with what he'd done.

"Can I get you anything?" he asked.

She opened her eyes again and mustered a weary smile. "No. Just sit here with me, please. I like knowing you're with me."

"I wasn't planning on going anywhere." He raised her hand to his lips and kissed her.

"Rose . . . ?"

The very name caused him to shudder.

"What happened to Rose?" Mara questioned. Her eyes searched his, her brows furrowed in concern.

"She died in the fire."

Mara closed her eyes and was still.

Foster sighed. He'd been so consumed with worry over Mara last night that he'd completely forgotten about Rose. After he'd carried Mara out of the burning building, his only thought was to get her to a doctor as soon as he could. There had been so much chaos outside the hotel and so many people, he'd been grateful to have met up with Brighton again. Together they brought Mara to the new hotel. Foster sought out a doctor, while Brighton tended to Mara. Then Foster went back to the Dublin House, or rather what was left of the hotel. That's when he learned that Rose had perished in the fire.

His wife was dead.

Saying he was relieved oversimplified matters. Of course he felt relief. He'd never wanted to be married to her in the first place and now, at long last, he was finally free. Foster wasn't exactly heartbroken either, for he had no strong emotional attachment to her. Yet still, her death made him sad. It was a terrible and tragic end to the life of a sad and troubled woman. He'd never wanted Rose to suffer and he'd certainly never wished for her death.

Although last night he'd been angrier with her than he'd ever been.

When he'd received Mara's note, Foster was stunned— not only that Rose was staying in their hotel, but that she had threatened Mara with public humiliation. So he did the only thing he could have done. He marched up to Rose's room and confronted her about what she'd been up to and demanded that she leave Mara in peace.

A very volatile argument ensued. Rose accused him of being selfish and petty and said that she'd already started writing the letters telling the London newspapers of his affair with the unmarried daughter of the Earl of Cashelmore. He told her that if she did that, he would still end their marriage, but he would not be generous with her. He'd cut her off without a cent. She screamed at him, calling him vile names, and he told her to stay away from Mara and he left.

He'd been tempted to visit Mara, but thought the better of it. Instead he went to the pub across the street to cool off and have a pint or two. Rose had infuriated him. She had no right to frighten and threaten Mara with ruination. Her vindictive threats only reinforced his desire to be rid of her. When he finally went back to his room, he fell asleep and didn't wake up until the hotel was on fire.

"I saw Rose burning . . . I wanted to help her, but I couldn't . . . I'm so sorry," Mara said as a tear ran down her cheek.

Of course, Mara would want to help the woman who wished her nothing but ill will. That was his Mara. He placed a gentle kiss upon her hand again. After what she'd been through as a child with her own mother's death, and then for her to be involved in another fire and death . . . It was unthinkable.

"I know you tried, even though she was unkind to you," Foster whispered. "It's all right."

There was a knock on the door, and thinking it was Brighton returning with food for Mara, Foster called for her to come in, unwilling to let go of Mara's hand to open the door.

But it was not Brighton. To his great surprise, Alice Bellwether entered the room. Foster had known Rose's maid as long as he'd known Rose. Alice had been Rose's only companion.

"Lord Sterling," Alice began. "I heard you were here and I have some news for you. May I speak to you?"

"Yes, of course." Foster said, curious as to why she would seek him out. "This is Lady Mara Reeves. Mara, this is Alice Bellwether, Rose's maid."

"I'm sorry to bother you, my lady," Alice said. Her round face looked worried and her eyes were red-rimmed from crying. "I can see that you are injured. But there are things I need to share with his lordship and you should hear them as well."

Mara attempted to sit up straighter, pressing her hand to her temple. Foster remained seated on the bed beside her, holding her other hand. However untoward it seemed, he refused to leave Mara's side.

Alice Bellwether came closer, unsure what to do. Foster gave her a nod to indicate that she could go ahead.

"It's a dreadful thing that happened," she began, practically distraught.

"Yes," Foster agreed. "Rose's death is quite tragic."

"My lady started the fire!" Alice blurted out, her expression horrified.

"What do you mean?" Foster cried in disbelief. "Why would she do such a terrible thing?"

"I'm not certain, but I have an idea. I loved her ladyship and always thought the best of her, I did. Truly, I did. I never thought she could have done something this awful. But last night . . ." Alice began to cry.

Foster and Mara exchanged looks. He finally released Mara's hand, and he rose from the bed, making his way to Alice. He helped the poor woman to sit in a chair and handed her a handkerchief.

"What happened last night, Alice?" he asked softly.

She dabbed at her eyes with a handkerchief and sniffled. "It was as if she lost her mind after you left, my lord. Begging your pardon, but I was in the adjoining room and I heard everything that happened between you."

Foster cringed. He had not known that his argument with Rose was overheard by anyone. Still, would that have tempered any of the things he had said to her? More than likely not. He was not especially proud of what he had said, but he had meant every word. And it had needed to be said.

"I apologize, Alice. I did not know you were listening."

"But you were right, my lord." Alice's tears streamed down her face. "I've kept my peace all these years because I was devoted to Lady Sterling. I knew her before she married you, and what happened to her was terrible, there's no doubt. But I always felt she had wronged you when you had done nothing to deserve it. You'd only been kind to her, and that was more than most husbands would have done in your place. You left her in peace, which was all she wanted after what she'd been through. You were a true gentleman, my lord. But she wasn't fair to you. When I heard you last night, I understood everything."

Foster stared at the woman, with her red hair and round face and her tearful hazel eyes. "You understood what, Alice?"

"That you were being punished for something that wasn't of your own doing. Lady Sterling cheated you and you never knew."

"She cheated me?"

Alice nodded emphatically. "Yes, she cheated you out of having a family and heirs. You were right to want an annulment because she was never a true wife to you in that sense. I know the truth of it. She confessed to me from the start that the two of you had never . . . you know"—Alice blushed—"but the thing is, even if you had, she couldn't have ever given you children."

Confused, Foster asked, "What do you mean by that?"

"I have never told this to a soul before." Alice actually glanced around the room nervously as if someone were to overhear her. "My lady gave birth to a child just weeks before you married her. It was such a dangerous delivery that she almost died. The doctor said she was ruined and couldn't have any more children. Lady Sterling was barren."

A baby! Stunned by this revelation, Foster's mind suddenly spun with a dozen questions. "Rose had a baby before we married? Whose child was it?"

Alice dabbed her tear-streaked round cheeks. "She'd fallen in love with one of the footmen at Brookwood Manor the summer before you married her. He was young and handsome and loved her too. They wanted to marry. But when her parents found out, her father had him shipped off to America. Oh, Mr. Davenport could be quite cruel to his daughter and he was furious with her, let me tell you. He arranged your marriage knowing full well that Rose had been with the footman but before they were aware of the pregnancy. Then they postponed the wedding to your lordship until after her baby was born."

So Rose had known of their impending marriage months before Foster did. His father had waited until the night before the wedding to tell Foster about it. Foster shook his head in disbelief at the entire situation. There had been so much he'd been unaware of ten years ago. "Where is the child now?"

"The poor baby boy was born dead." Alice heaved a great sob.

"Dear God." Foster didn't know what to think anymore.

With a heavy heart, Foster recalled his wedding day and the first time he laid eyes on Rose Davenport. There had been something tragic about her even then. She was quite cold and devoid of emotion. Yet there was all the crying the first weeks of their marriage. He'd simply thought she feared the marriage bed. Now he knew why. She was mourning the loss of her child, her lover, and the life she had wanted to have. No wonder she seemed inconsolable. The girl had been heartbroken.

And Foster hadn't had a clue about any of it.

And Rose's parents! They married their only daughter off to a stranger, knowing she had just borne another man's child and that she was unable to bear more children in the future. Both Rose's parents and his own parents had arranged a union that devastated all those involved, and for what? Joining some property and gaining a title and money? All four of them had since passed away, unable to see the havoc their selfishness had wrought.

"But she wasn't fair to you all these years, Lord Sterling," Alice said. "And when I overheard you last night, I knew the things you said to her were true. She didn't ever want you. She didn't ever love you. Why did she care that you wanted to annul the marriage or divorce her? It was never a true marriage. Why did it bother her that you wanted to marry the lady here and have a real marriage?"

"She was being spiteful," Foster said, with a regretful sigh.

Rose didn't want anyone to be happy if she couldn't be happy, and he had said as much to her last night. However, at the time he'd no idea just how unhappy his wife was with her own life. Would it have made a difference if he had known her past? Perhaps. Maybe at the very start of their marriage, if he had been aware of what she'd just endured, if she had confided in him, he would have had more sympathy and understanding for her instead of being completely baffled by her.

But it was too late now for any of that.

"She was more than being spiteful," Alice added. "She

was being deliberately cruel, for she didn't tell you what
was happening to her."

"Go on," Foster encouraged her, although he didn't think
he could stand listening to any more of Rose's sad life.

"Lady Sterling was dying."

Dying? Foster was speechless, but Mara wasn't. With
a knowing look on her face, she asked, "She was ill,
wasn't she?"

Alice nodded sadly. "Yes, last month the doctor in
London confirmed what her doctor in York had already told
her. There was some kind of tumor in her head. She only
had a few months left to live. The London doctor said she
couldn't expect to live past the spring."

After a stunned silence, Foster said, "That explains her
unexpected trip to London. I'd wondered about that. It
never occurred to me that she was in town to visit a doctor!
But why on earth didn't she simply tell me that she was
ill? I would have held off on the legal proceedings, if I'd
known. I'd have waited until . . ."

The unsaid words hung in the air over the three of them.
Yes, he would have had the decency to wait until Rose
passed away before marrying Mara. He could not have
annulled the marriage knowing that Rose was on her
deathbed. He was not that cruel or unfeeling.

"She was quite determined that you not know anything
about it," Alice explained. "She didn't want your pity. But
more than that, she wanted you to feel guilty about her
death afterward because you didn't know about it. She
wanted to punish you for I know not what . . ."

Foster shook his head. "She wanted to punish me for
being happy, when she could never be. But I wanted her to
be happy. I told her it wasn't too late for her to find happiness for herself. I even suggested she go abroad, maybe to
Italy, and enjoy herself. She laughed at me." Foster recalled
his last words to Rose with distaste.

"That she did," Alice confirmed. "She was outraged that you had found your young lady here and wanted to marry her." She turned and focused her attention on Mara. "She was jealous of your youth and beauty and that you would most certainly be able to give him the family he'd always wanted. But she was fascinated by you at the same time. After we saw you in the bookshop that afternoon, she insisted on following you here to Ireland, although I tried to talk her out of it. She wanted to know everything about you."

Foster glanced sharply at Mara. "Rose came to see you at the bookshop? Why didn't you tell me this?"

"Because I had no idea who she was that day," Mara explained. "I simply took her for another customer. But I had noticed that she seemed frail and ill. It wasn't until she came to my room last night, that I discovered who she really was."

"She came back from that visit last night in fine form, let me tell you," Alice exclaimed with a knowing look. "I didn't learn that she'd been to see you until afterward, Lady Mara. I thought she was in bed for the night, and I'd gone downstairs to get myself a little something from the pub, even though I know she doesn't like when I do that. When I came back to check on her, she was not just angry. She was quite livid. So much so that she threw some china figurines on the floor and shattered them to pieces. And that was when you came in, Lord Sterling."

"I can imagine," Foster said. Yes, he'd seen Rose in one of her rages before. It was not a pretty sight.

"After you left, my lord, I gave her a piece of my mind," Alice explained. "She'd turned up her nose at a perfectly wonderful husband and could have attempted to be happy in her life. But she chose to be angry and bitter, dwelling on a past that she could not change. I told her it was wrong of her to blame you for being happy and it was wrong to publicly ruin Lady Mara, who had done nothing to deserve being treated so heartlessly. We got into a terrible row.

But just before she ordered me from the room, she said she wanted to kill herself and solve everyone's problems."

"That's a little extreme, don't you think? Even for Rose?" Foster asked.

"Yes, but she was quite overwrought. I think the journey to Dublin was more exhausting for her than we realized. Anyway, she was quite upset and I wanted to stay and console her. But she wouldn't allow it. She sent me from the room and told me not to come back until morning." Alice began another bout of crying.

"If you weren't there, then how do you know that she set the fire?" Foster asked.

"Because I know. I left her sitting there at the table by the lamp, crying. Today the authorities questioned me. They said the fire began in her room. And I just know . . ." Alice sobbed, a great heaving sob. "She did it on purpose. And I think she wanted not to die alone. She wanted to take you and Lady Mara with her."

An agonized silence filled the room, broken only by Alice's sniffling.

Had Rose truly killed herself? Had she tried to kill all of them last night? Foster was beyond knowing what to believe about her anymore. He'd learned more about Rose in the last half hour than he had in their entire ten years of marriage. It was quite astonishing really.

He met Mara's eyes. She'd been quietly crying as well at the sadness of it all. The fire and Rose's horrible death. He didn't blame her for crying.

At that moment it occurred to him that Mara's premonition had come true.

25

Proclamations

The next evening, Mara was still confined to bed. Her head throbbed, not just from her injury, but from all they had learned about Rose Sheridan the day before.

The sadness in Rose's life had touched Mara's heart, especially in light of all Rose had revealed to Mara that night in her room. Rose had had no power over anything that had happened to her. Her life had been controlled by her parents and then by her husband. Rose finally took control of her own life at the end by taking it herself.

Mara was inordinately saddened by it, because it was essentially true of all women. Rose had been right. Mara had just been lucky enough to belong to a family who valued women and allowed her the freedom to make her own decisions about her life. Mara shuddered to think what would have become of her if her parents had forced her into a marriage to someone she hadn't even met. She couldn't bear the thought of it.

Mara was a very lucky girl, indeed. She couldn't wait to bring Foster home to meet her family. But she had to get well first.

She'd suffered some burns on her arms and feet, which were now covered in salve and wrapped in bandages. And then there was the pain in her head. Surviving the fire had been a miracle, indeed. Foster had saved her life and she barely recalled him carrying her out of the burning hotel.

Brighton had been hovering over her constantly, concerned that Mara was not recovering quickly enough, while Foster had been out making arrangements for Rose's burial. Mara had just dismissed Brighton for the evening, when Foster rejoined her in her room.

"Is it done then?" she asked, looking at his weary eyes.

Foster nodded sadly. "It's a sorrowful business. Three other people in the hotel died in the fire as well."

"Brighton mentioned to me earlier that others had died too." It was all heartbreaking.

"When I think how close I came to losing you, Mara . . ." Foster came and sat beside her on the bed. "I don't know what I'd do if I lost you now." He kissed her cheek softly.

"Well, you didn't lose me and you're not going to," she whispered, kissing him back.

"How are you feeling?" He eyed her ugly bruise with concern. "This looks even worse than it did yesterday."

"I'm much better." She wasn't. Her head still pounded, but she knew Foster would worry unduly if she told him.

He looked at her with skepticism. "I hope so."

"The doctor said I should be well enough to travel the day after tomorrow," she announced brightly. She longed to get out of this hotel and Dublin. She missed her parents and her brother.

"Do you want to go directly to London? Or would you rather return to Cashelmore and rest there for a bit?" Foster asked.

"Let's go straight to London," she said.

"I have another question for you." Foster hesitated.

Mara gave him a quizzical look. "What is it?"

"Well, we could wait and get married in London as we planned, or . . . We could get married here, now, before we go home."

With all her time in bed, Mara had been thinking the same things as well. Now that Foster was free, they could marry whenever they wanted to. It might be easier to face her family if she was already married to Foster. She was about to answer when the door to the room suddenly burst open.

Mara froze at the sight of her parents.

Her father and mother strode inside. They did not look happy. Mara's heart sank. This was not how she'd intended to introduce her future husband to her parents. While he was sitting beside her on a bed in a hotel room.

"Mara!" Declan Reeves called as he took in the scene before him. His eyes narrowed with indignation. "What in the hell is going on here? What are you doing with my daughter?"

Startled, Foster instantly rose to his feet. "Excuse me, Lord Cashelmore, let me introduce myself. I'm Foster Sheridan, the Earl of Sterling. And you must be Lady Cashelmore."

Her mother remained speechless, which was most unusual for Paulette, while her father stared mutely at Foster, as if debating whether to hit him or not.

"Papa, please, don't be upset," Mara said hurriedly. "Please be calm. I can explain everything."

"Good God! You've been hurt!" he cried, brushing past Foster and hurrying to her bedside. "What happened, Mara? When I heard there was a fire, I thought I'd lose my mind with worry. Are you all right, darlin'?"

Paulette too came rushing to the other side of her bed. "Oh, my God! Look at her!"

"I'm fine, Papa." Mara glanced between the two of them and attempted a smile. "Truly. Please don't worry."

"I'm not to worry that my only daughter fled to Ireland

without my knowledge? When your mother and I arrived in London to surprise you, you weren't there! But then your cousin reluctantly informed us that you've been involved with a married man"—he gave a scathing glance to Foster—"who followed you to Ireland. Just as we were about to return to Cashelmore we received a telegram from you, saying you would be returning to London. So we waited for you to come home. Then we received another telegram from a gentleman we've never met, telling us that there had been a fire and that you'd been delayed. Can you imagine how sick with worry we have been?"

"We raced here as soon as we received Lord Sterling's message, Mara. We were frantic." Paulette's expression was anxious as she took a seat on the side of the bed and touched a gentle hand to Mara's face. "We didn't know what to expect."

"I'm very sorry," Mara cried, looking at the concerned faces of her loving parents. "And I want to explain everything to you, truly I do. Papa, please, sit and listen to me."

Wordlessly, Foster moved two chairs over to Mara's father. They each took one, although her father eyed Foster skeptically. Paulette remained seated beside her on the bed and Mara was grateful for her mother's quiet support.

"First of all, why did you not tell us you were coming to Ireland?" Her father looked at her sternly.

"When I made up my mind to come home, there wasn't time to tell you and I thought it would be fun to surprise you all. Obviously, I didn't know you were returning to London to surprise me at the same time." Mara attempted a weak smile.

"Well, we did want to surprise you," Paulette said. "But we really returned early because Jeffrey said he was worried about you."

"Uncle Jeffrey?" Mara recalled their conversation in the

schoolroom. He must have written to her parents about it. "What did he say?"

"His letter was more cryptic, but I've since spoken with him. He was concerned about an episode you had with him," Paulette said softly, giving Mara an understanding look.

Mara paused. "Yes, I did have an episode while I was talking with Jeffrey. I also had one with Foster"—she indicated the man she loved—"and I've always had these visions. They were the reason I came back to Ireland. To learn more about them. And myself." Mara looked to her father. "I went to visit Aunt Deirdre."

"Deirdre?" Her father appeared stunned. "Why?"

"I needed to learned more about my mother," she said softly.

Paulette and her father exchanged glances. Then he said, "You could have asked me anything about her, darlin,' you know that."

"I know that, Papa," Mara answered. "But you've always seemed reticent to talk about her. And I thought talking to her older sister might give me more insight about her in ways that you couldn't, Papa. You see . . . over the years . . . I was somehow under the impression that my mother was mad."

"I don't understand." Declan ran his hand over his face. "I don't know how such a thing could have happened. Your mother wasn't mad. Perhaps you'd overheard things you shouldn't have. And I shouldn't have avoided talking about your mother with you, Mara. I was afraid to upset you, so I never brought her up." He looked truly remorseful.

Mara looked at his loving face and thought of all the care and affection he had lavished upon her over the years. "Don't blame yourself, Papa. I suppose it's something I did to myself. You couldn't have known what I was thinking. Because I love you so much, I was always afraid of worrying you and Mother, which is why I didn't tell either of you of my visions. I didn't tell anyone because I thought I was going mad, like Mama."

Her father was distraught. "Oh, God, Mara . . ."

"Oh, sweetheart, you could have told us." Paulette took Mara's hand and squeezed it.

"I should have, yes. I see that now," Mara said. "But I was afraid."

"And the premonitions?" Declan asked.

"I only told Uncle Jeffrey because I had a premonition when I was with him. The premonitions make me dizzy, so they can be difficult to hide. He was very understanding. And I told Foster, again only because I experienced one while I was with him. This one premonition in particular was worrying me. So I went to see Aunt Deirdre . . ."

"And what did Deirdre have to say?" her father asked, with a look of disbelief on his face. Declan and Deirdre never did get along well.

"She was quite kind, actually. She made me understand that Mama wasn't mad at all, that I was mistaken in thinking so. And she let me know that I have a special gift. Apparently the sight runs in Mama's family."

"It does?" Declan was flabbergasted. "I never knew anything about that!"

"Well, I didn't either, but now knowing that my great-grandmother had visions also makes me feel less frightened by it all."

"I wish you'd told me, Mara," Declan said, his voice full of regret.

"I wish I had too." Mara could have saved herself years of agony if she had.

"But that's neither here nor there," her father said. "I still don't know what's going on with this fellow." He pointed an accusatory finger toward Foster.

"That"—Mara couldn't help but smile—"is the man I'm going to marry, Papa."

"But isn't he already married, my dear?" Paulette asked, her brows drawn in concern. All eyes turned to Lord Sterling.

"Yes." Foster spoke up. "Yes, I was married."

Declan's eyes widened. "Was?"

"My wife died in a fire two days ago," Foster announced solemnly.

Declan buried his face in his hands.

"What happened?" Paulette cried in dismay. "I don't understand any of this. Why are you involved with a married man or why he is in Ireland with you . . ."

"Well," Mara began, "I had a vision about Foster and the fire before we were to leave for Ireland. I had just met him at Uncle Jeffrey's birthday party. I couldn't leave London until I knew what it meant."

"That's why you wanted to stay in London?" Declan asked in a tone that bordered on disgust. *"For him?"*

"Yes, for him." Mara confirmed her words with a nod. "I knew in my heart that Foster was the man I was meant to be with, and I didn't care that he was married."

"Oh, Mara," Paulette whispered, looking aghast, but she still held Mara's hand.

"I love your daughter, Lord Cashelmore." Foster lifted his head. "So much so that I was planning to annul my façade of a marriage, which was arranged for me ten years ago. It was a marriage in name only. She and I lived apart the entire time and we had no children."

"Then why now?" Declan demanded, his expression grim. "If your marriage was not a true marriage and you were both so unhappy, why have you waited ten years to end it? Why didn't you annul it years ago and get on with your life?"

Foster looked directly at Declan, hiding nothing. "I've asked myself that very question many times over the years. To be honest, I never believed I deserved any better than what I had. I suppose I didn't care enough to change things and I reconciled myself to an empty life. But everything changed the night I met your daughter, Lord Cashelmore. I fell in love with her and she gave me hope that I could change my life . . . that we could have a life together. I wanted a true marriage with her."

Declan grew quiet at Foster's words. Paulette glanced nervously between the two men.

Feeling a bit embarrassed, Mara added, "Papa, I know Foster and I were wrong to . . . to begin an affair, but—"

"Stop!" Declan cried out hoarsely. "Please, I can't hear this. Spare me those details. I haven't the strength."

Foster rose to his feet. He cleared his throat and gave Mara's father a steady look. "Lord Cashelmore, I have wanted to marry your daughter from the very first moment I met her. I love her and she loves me. It's true that we were wrong to do what we did, and I take full responsibility for it. But it's happened and we can't change it. However, due to the recent circumstances, I am free to marry her now. As soon as the doctor says that Mara is well enough to travel, we will wed. And we would like your blessings."

Mara's heart swelled with pride and love as Foster spoke. "It's the truth, Papa. We were sitting here discussing how soon we could marry when you arrived."

The room grew quiet. Mara watched her parents exchange another one of those wordless glances that spoke volumes. It pleased her that she and Foster were able to communicate that way now. They knew what the other was thinking. Mara had always wanted a relationship like her parents, and now she had one.

"If it makes you feel any better, Papa, Foster saved my life. He rescued me from the fire at the hotel. I'd have died if he hadn't come for me."

Declan stared at Foster with a look of appreciation. "The same fire in which your wife died?"

"Yes, and it seems my wife was the one who set the fire," Foster confessed.

"Oh, my God." Paulette covered her mouth with her hand.

Mara began to explain what happened the night of the fire. She told how Rose Sheridan had followed her to Ireland, how they discovered she was dying and probably set the fire, and how Foster had returned to the burning hotel to rescue her. Her parents listened with stunned expressions.

"Heavens, Mara, you could have been killed," Paulette murmured softly. "We could have lost you."

Her father's eyes filled with worry. "You were in another fire, Mara."

"Yes, it was my premonition coming to pass. They always do."

She held out her hand to her father. He took it, holding on tight. Her mother held one hand, her father the other. She loved the two of them so much. Her relief at finally sharing with them all that had happened to her buoyed her spirits. She felt lighter and happier than she could ever recall feeling.

"And I'm fine, so please don't worry. Either of you." Mara looked pointedly at her father. "But I am no longer a little girl, Papa. I'm not going to lose my voice again. I'm a grown woman and I know what I want. I know my own heart. I want to be Foster's wife because I love him."

An expectant silence ensued as her parents exchanged those wordless glances once more. Mara gazed at Foster, whose face was alight with hope.

"Well, I suppose I can't deny you anything, Mara," Declan said at last, suddenly looking resigned to the state of affairs. "Although I'm not at all comfortable with these circumstances, I can't deny that I would have done the same in his position. Your mother and I love you and only want your happiness. We give you our blessing to marry this man."

"Oh, Papa! Mother! Thank you both!" Mara cried. "You've made me so happy!"

Paulette hugged her and whispered so only Mara could hear, "One day I shall tell you all about how your father and I met. I understand more than you know." She placed a kiss on Mara's cheek.

Mara stared at her stepmother in surprise. She loved how Paulette always understood her.

Reluctantly, Declan rose from his place near the bed and turned to shake Foster's hand. "You promise you will take good care of my daughter?"

"Thank you, sir. I will spend my life doing so, I promise," Foster said as they shook hands. "She is all I ever wanted."

"Then I suppose we need to get you two married," Declan responded.

Foster looked to Mara. "Nothing would make me happier."

Mara raised her eyes to the man she loved and smiled.

26

Conclusions

"I told you Mara stayed in London because of a man," Yvette Hamilton Eddington remarked a bit smugly.

Holding a flute of champagne in her hand, Colette Hamilton Sinclair laughed lightly. "Well, yes, I suppose you were right about that after all."

"What's this?" asked Juliette Hamilton Fleming, as she joined three of her sisters in the grand drawing room of Devon House.

"Yvette was just reminding us that she was right about something," Colette explained.

"When isn't Yvette right?" Juliette laughed. She and her husband, Captain Harrison Fleming, had just arrived from New York the evening before, along with their daughter and son-in-law.

"I suspected from the start there was a romance brewing," Yvette added. "Mara is a girl after my own heart, and a bit of a dark horse, if you ask me."

"I must say it was quite a shock to return and discover that Mara had married."

"It was quite a shock to all of us, and we were here," Lisette Hamilton Roxbury said.

"It wasn't a shock to me at all." Yvette grinned in satisfaction.

"Has there been much talk or gossip about them?" Juliette asked, sipping her champagne.

"There has been some," Colette answered pragmatically. "It's unavoidable with him remarrying so soon after his wife's death, but the first Lady Sterling was not well-known in town, so I suppose it will fade away rather quickly."

"So what do we think of *him*?" Juliette asked, indicating Foster Sheridan with a slight nod of her head.

"He seems quite nice, judging from what little time I've spent with him," Lisette responded happily. "And he's absolutely besotted with her. Look at the two of them together."

The sisters glanced fondly at Mara and Foster, who were chatting with Sara and her husband. Foster indeed had a look of adoration upon his face as he gazed at Mara.

The entire Hamilton family was gathered at Devon House to celebrate the marriage of Lady Mara Reeves and the Earl of Sterling. The pair had married in Ireland at Cashelmore Manor with Mara's parents' blessing before they returned to London. The sudden wedding had surprised the family, but they had immediately rallied around the newlyweds.

Paulette Hamilton Reeves walked over to where her four sisters had gathered in a corner of the large drawing room. "So I now have a son-in-law."

"Welcome to the club." Juliette smiled and hugged her sister.

"Thank you," Paulette said. "I'm so happy you have arrived, Juliette. It was a wonderful surprise to return from Ireland to find you and Harrison here. And of course, Mara was thrilled to have Sara back." She gave her sisters a knowing look and lowered her voice. "And when things have calmed down a bit, I'll fill you in on all that happened while we were in Ireland. It's quite a story. But for now, I'm simply grateful that Mara is so happy."

Colette agreed. "It's true. I've never seen Mara like this. She's positively radiating happiness."

"She is . . . I just wish we could have given her a grand wedding," Paulette explained with a note of sadness in her voice. "Declan desperately wanted to make a fuss over her, but Mara and Foster didn't want to wait. They thought a small and private ceremony would be wiser after his wife's death."

"It was probably for the best, but I would have loved to have seen Mara dressed as a bride," Colette added with a sigh. "She would look like an angel."

"I suppose one of your boys will be the next to marry," Yvette said to Colette with a hopeful smile.

"Yes, they should be," Colette said with a little sigh. "But Phillip doesn't seem to be in any hurry to settle down just yet. Neither does Simon."

Lisette remarked, "The time will come soon enough, I've no doubt. In the meantime, let's toast to Mara's happiness and how lucky we are to have the whole family together again."

The five Hamilton sisters raised their champagne glasses and smiled.

"Honestly, Mara, how could you have possibly gotten married without telling me anything at all about it?" Sara Fleming Townsend, the Countess of Bridgeton, demanded in a teasing tone.

Christopher Townsend, the Earl of Bridgeton, nodded in agreement with his new bride. "She's been quite crushed at missing your wedding, Mara."

"May I remind you both that you were away on your

honeymoon? But I did wish many times that you had been there with me." Mara then glanced lovingly at her new husband. "Besides, it all happened far too quickly to tell anyone about it."

"You could have sent me a telegram." Sara gave a bit of a pout, but her blue eyes flashed with merriment as she teased her cousin. "But honestly, Christopher and I are thrilled that you're settled, Mara. It was a lovely surprise to come home and see you married and looking so happy."

"Thank you." Mara couldn't help but grin. She was fairly bursting with joy. "We are quite happy."

With a sharp eye, Sara looked Foster Sheridan up and down. "How do I know if you're good enough for my dearest and most treasured cousin, Lord Sterling?"

"Please, call me Foster, and I assure you, Lady Bridgeton, that no one is good enough for Mara, but I shall try my best to deserve her," he responded with a good-natured smile.

Sara's face lit up with approval at his words. "Well, I like you already, Foster. And you must call me Sara and call my husband Christopher. Now that you're in the family, we are all cousins."

"Are you talking about me again?" asked Phillip Sinclair, as he joined the group. He flashed them a charming smile.

"Yes," Sara said with a mischievous gleam in her eyes. "We were just saying that you must be next."

"Next?" He looked confused. "Next for what?"

Mara spoke up. "Well, since Sara and I are both proper wedded ladies now, it only stands to reason that you will be the next Hamilton cousin to get married, Phillip."

"Oh, no!" he cried with a shake of his head. "Don't tell me I must get shackled so soon just because you two did! I'm still a free man." He grinned wickedly and raised his eyebrows up and down. "A fact I enjoy immensely."

Both Foster and Christopher laughed.

"It's not so bad," Foster attempted to explain. "Marriage to the right woman definitely has its advantages."

"I can't get married. It wouldn't be fair to all the lovely ladies I know to choose just one to be my wife," Phillip said. "Think of all the broken hearts!"

Sara rolled her eyes and laughed. "Really, Phillip!"

"You just haven't met the right woman yet," Mara said.

"Perhaps you should come visit us in New York," Sara suggested with a sardonic look. "There are lots of beautiful girls there who haven't had the privilege of meeting you yet, Phillip."

"That's a very good point," Phillip replied gamely. "I may just do that! I could leave a trail of broken hearts on two continents . . ."

Mara and Sara immediately began to protest their cousin's vanity.

"Leave the poor boy alone," declared Jeffrey Eddington, the Duke of Rathmore, as he joined their conversation.

"Thank you for defending me, Uncle Jeffrey," Phillip said, looking quite satisfied. "You see, he's a man who knows how it is."

Jeffrey Eddington gave a roguish grin. "Beware of American women, Phillip. They won't fall for your charms as easily as you think." Laughter ensued as Jeffrey continued, "But I actually came over to congratulate the beautiful bride."

"Thank you, Uncle Jeffrey," Mara said as he hugged her. Then she subtly pulled him aside so she could speak to him privately. "I would also like to thank you for being so understanding of everything."

"There's no need to thank me, Mara." Jeffrey's expression grew earnest. "We've had our discussion and you know I am always at your service. I hope you forgive me for writing to your parents about our conversation. I only had your best interests at heart."

"Yes, I realize that, and I appreciate your concern. Of course I forgive you. I more than likely would have done the same thing in your position," Mara admitted.

"Thank you. And I am quite thrilled to see that you are so happy with your new husband. He seems a good man," Jeffrey said. "I trust that he knows about your visions?"

"He does and he still loves me in spite of it." Mara laughed a little.

"I'm glad to hear it. Ah, here is the groom now." Jeffrey turned his attention to Foster, who came to stand beside Mara. "Take good care of our girl."

"I intend to." Foster gave a knowing look. "Her father and her brother have already made clear what will happen to me if I don't."

Foster took Mara's hand in his as her uncle rejoined the cousins.

"Are you completely overwhelmed by my family?" she whispered to him. The day had been a blur of introductions for her new husband. She had watched all afternoon as he greeted each of her aunts and uncles, and gamely and candidly answered all their questions.

"I admit that I don't quite have all the names down yet, especially of the youngest cousins. All those names that begin with the letter V! And your aunts look remarkably alike, and that will take some doing, but it seems a very small price to pay to be your husband." He squeezed her hand lovingly.

"I still can't believe that we're really married!" Mara said.

The last week had been a whirlwind of events that culminated in their wedding in the Cashelmore chapel with only her parents present. It was a lovely ceremony and Mara had never felt so much love in her heart. Then they returned to London to share the news with her family, who had received word of Mara's surprise marriage with unfailingly good grace and candor.

"Well, we are married, my sweet Mara. After the last ten years, I never knew being married could make me so happy. Thank you for bringing love into my life and becoming my beautiful wife. I love you more than I can possibly say, but I intend to spend my life showing you just how much I do love you." Foster leaned over and, in spite of a drawing room full of her relatives, kissed her on the lips.

"I love you," she whispered back, looking into her husband's beautiful green eyes. It was his eyes that had mesmerized her from the start. "From that first night we saw each other, I knew you were the one for me. I saw it in my premonition."

"And what a wonderful premonition it was."

Epilogue

A few months later, the Earl of Sterling stood with his wife at the grand opening of the new Hamilton's bookshop in London. The name of the new store had been quite a surprise for him and his wife.

Mara's Book Shoppe was an enchanting little store.

The interior was something special to behold, indeed. It sseemed like it was torn from the pages of a storybook. Warm and inviting, it was the perfect place for a child to feel at home and wish to read a book. There were little reading nooks, small tables and chairs, colorful pillows and area rugs, and shelves and shelves of children's books edging the upper gallery.

Mara had been so stunned, and deeply touched, that her aunt Colette had named the shop after her that it brought tears to her eyes.

"But I thought we had agreed"—Mara wiped at her eyes—"that it was to be called Hamilton's Book Shoppe for Children."

"That name sounds as dull as paste to a child! Besides, the entire endeavor was your idea, darling Mara! How could we not name the store after you?" Colette beamed with pride at her niece. "Your mother and I wanted to surprise you on the opening day as a way to thank you, as well."

Mara looked to Paulette. "You knew about this, Mother?"

"Yes, and I couldn't agree more." Paulette hugged her daughter tightly, becoming a little teary-eyed also. "You've worked so very hard on this shop, as well as the others, and you deserve some recognition."

"Thank you so much," Mara said. "I'm very honored."

Foster also knew how many long hours Mara had worked to make her idea of the shop a reality, and he was quite proud of her. In fact, he was proud to be a part of the Hamilton family. During the last six months he had gotten to know them quite well, and he was even more impressed with the Hamilton sisters than he had been at the start.

Mara's parents, brother, aunts, uncles, and cousins had readily accepted him as one of the family. They loved Mara, so they loved him too. It was quite remarkable really. After all he had been through in his life, to suddenly have such an extended family was a wonderful and welcome change. And now he and Mara were adding to that family. As if his happiness couldn't become any greater, only yesterday the doctor confirmed that Mara was expecting a baby.

"You look like you could do with a bit of a rest," he said to Mara. "Come with me."

"Yes, Mara, you're looking a little pale," Paulette agreed, eyeing her daughter carefully. "Make sure she sits for a little while, Foster. We'll take care of all this."

In spite of protesting that she was fine, Mara allowed Foster to guide her to the private office in the back of the bookshop that was named for her.

"Now, my beautiful wife," he said as he ushered her to a comfortable leather armchair, "you shall just have to get used to not working so much and resting more often for the next six months or so. Can I get you something to drink?"

Suddenly his heart raced as he stared at Mara. With one hand she gripped the arm of the chair and the other hand was pressed against her temple. Her eyes were shut tight and she could not hear him when he called her name.

She was having one of her premonitions!

Mara hadn't had one since before the fire. During the six months that they had been married, the two of them had spent many an hour having long discussions about the sight and her visions and what it all meant. Mara was definitely not afraid of them or worried that she was going mad any longer. She now considered the fact that she had the sight as simply a quirk of her personality.

It didn't matter to Foster either way, as long as Mara was comfortable with it. He just wanted her to be safe and healthy. Especially now.

Foster waited patiently until Mara was lucid again.

After a moment her eyes fluttered open and she sank back against the chair with a sigh. A slow smile spread across her pretty face and her wide gray-green eyes sparkled with joy.

"Are you all right?" Foster asked, as he sat on the ottoman at her feet. He took her small hand in his. She didn't look worried in the least and that made him relax a little bit. It didn't seem as if she'd seen anything foreboding.

"I am more than all right," she murmured slowly.

"It was a premonition, wasn't it?"

She nodded happily, still smiling. "Yes. It was the most wonderful vision I've ever had."

"That sounds promising. Was it about the baby?"

"Yes." Her cheeks turned pink as she blushed. "I had a vision about our babies . . ."

"Babies?" Foster's heart began to race. How far into the future had she seen? "You mean to say that we're having more than one child eventually . . . ?"

"No." She shook her head slowly, but the stunned smile

did not leave her face. Her hand covered her belly. "We're having more than one child right now."

"What?" He could not reconcile what she was saying to him.

"Twins," she murmured breathlessly. "We're having twins. A boy and a girl."

"Twins!" he cried in wonder. His wife was giving him the family he had always wanted. He couldn't imagine being happier. "Oh, Mara, that is the most wonderful news!"

"It is, isn't it?" She rose to her feet as he held her hands. "And my premonitions always come true."

Foster wrapped his arms around the woman he loved. "Your premonitions have come true, my love, but so have my dreams."

And then he kissed her.